T0209523

They Call Me
Tess

DARLENE J GAGE

WESTBOW
PRESS®
A DIVISION OF THOMAS NELSON
& ZONDERVAN

WestBow Press books may be ordered through booksellers or by contacting:

WestBow Press
A Division of Thomas Nelson & Zondervan
1663 Liberty Drive
Bloomington, IN 47403
www.westbowpress.com
844-714-3454

ISBN: 978-1-6642-6185-3 (sc)
ISBN: 978-1-6642-6186-0 (hc)
ISBN: 978-1-6642-6184-6 (e)

Library of Congress Control Number: 2022905620

Print information available on the last page.

WestBow Press rev. date: 5/7/2022

This dedication is to my husband Raymond.
He has been there for me, from the beginning to the end.
Much love.

Chapter 1

Sara turned her head and peered at the clock by the bed. She was surprised to see it was almost six thirty. Her sleep had been long and deep, not the usual tossing and turning.

As the fog of sleep faded, a sense of anticipation took its place. This day would somehow be special. She couldn't recall the last time she'd been excited about a new day.

Her mother had died six months earlier. While she was still able to talk, she'd told Sara that she had been adopted. The shock had settled into the core of Sara's soul. For years, she'd felt something was not quite right.

Sara knew she didn't look like either of her parents, but it was explained that she resembled a relative from generations ago. How her adopted parents could keep this secret from her was mind-numbing. Did this have something to do with her feeling alone and abandoned?

Enough of this! I've got to focus on the present, not the past. I need to move on.

She went into the master bathroom to get ready. The mirror she stood in front of reflected an image of an attractive woman. It amazed her she would soon be forty. *Where have the years gone?* she thought as she brushed her thick, wavy hair. The blue eyes staring back brightened as she thought about the day.

"Enough daydreaming!" she shouted, hurrying down the stairs.

Once downstairs, she put the coffee on and waited for its tantalizing aroma. For years, her day had started with the sweet elixir. She smiled, thinking about her father and how he called it the nectar of the gods.

With the first sip completed, she took her coffee into the living room. She grabbed the newspaper from the day before and opened it, not surprised to see the usual bad news splashed across the front page.

The feeling from that morning came rushing back, almost making her spill her coffee. It was as if someone was telling her to stop with the morning routine and get on with the day. *I must be losing it*, she thought as she tried to get interested in the newspaper.

Suddenly, the thought from earlier crowded its way into her mind again. This time, she didn't fight it but got up and walked over to the living room window. Looking out over the front lawn, she saw something lying on the grass, not more than six feet from the front porch. Slowly she moved to the side window next to the front door and peered out. It was a body! She rubbed her eyes to erase the image, but when she looked again, it was still there. She hadn't imagined it!

She stood frozen. *I must be hallucinating. What should I do?* she thought, then opened the front door and tiptoed outside. Walking hesitantly, she moved closer to the body.

That area of the lawn was still shaded, making it difficult to see, but light enough to make out the form of an old woman dressed in worn and dirty clothes. Her white, straggly hair was spread around her head, hiding her face. Sara slowly moved closer to the body, wondering whether the woman was dead or alive.

When she stretched out her shaking hand to touch the body, it suddenly moved! She jumped backward, almost falling. It was as if the devil himself had reached out to grab her. *Well, that answers one question. She's alive!*

Chapter 2

Sara's mind raced with conflicting thoughts, making it hard to approach the woman again. But she did. The temperature had been in the low forties the night before, and she knew it was a miracle the poor old soul hadn't died of hypothermia.

She imagined the headlines splashed across the next day's paper: "Woman Found Dead on the Front Lawn of the Lutheran Church's Manse." *Not something our members would like to see.* She wrapped her arms around the woman's body, half walking and half dragging her up the porch steps toward the front door. By now, the woman was somewhat alert and resisting Sara. She was obviously weak, but it didn't stop her from trying to get away. *Poor thing. She doesn't know where she is or what's happening to her,* Sara thought as she continued dragging the poor woman.

"Please don't be frightened," Sara said in her most pleasant voice.

She got the woman inside and stumbled toward the living room couch, planning to lay her down on it. Her back was hurting from the weight of the woman's body. She was almost to the couch but lost her balance, and they both fell, Sara landing on top of the old woman. The old lady let out a bloodcurdling scream, loud enough to bring back the dead.

Well, there's nothing wrong with her lungs, Sara mused as she struggled to get off the woman. After more pulling and dragging, she half lifted, half pushed the woman onto the couch. Then, out of breath, she collapsed on the floor.

"What in the world am I going to do with this woman?" Sara was talking aloud now. "Kevin would know. He approaches every situation with logic. But I can't ask him; he's at a ministers' retreat. I have to handle this myself."

Looking down at the stranger lying on her couch, Sara offered a quick prayer, asking God for guidance. If ever there was a time for a quick response, it was now.

Within seconds, an answer came. God was telling her to follow her heart and wait for the stranger to tell her story. This was not what she expected, but lately she'd been working hard to listen to God's messages.

While the woman rested quietly on the couch, Sara ran upstairs and got a blanket to warm the poor woman who looked pitiful in her worn, dirty clothes.

When she returned, the old woman was sitting up and looking around. Sara approached her and gently put the soft, warm blanket around her fragile shoulders. Taking the blanket with her chapped, dirty hands, the old woman pulled it tightly around her, trying to stop her shivering.

Their eyes met, and Sara saw the old woman's beautiful blue eyes. The woman stared at Sara with warmth, not fear. Sara stared back, surprised to see warmth in the woman's eyes.

Finally, the old woman spoke. "Where am I, and who are you?" She spoke in a tone that suggested she was accustomed to getting answers without delays.

"My name is Sara Richardson, and you're safe in my home. I found you lying on my front lawn, half frozen to death. I brought you in out of the cold."

"Why in the world would you be naive enough to bring a total stranger into your house? Especially one who looks like me?"

"That's the way I am. My husband tells me all the time to think before I act, but I couldn't leave you out there. I've already prayed about what I'm to do with you. God answered my prayer—rather quickly too. I just hope I get it right this time."

The old woman laughed. "Well, what was God's answer?"

Sara stared at her to see if she was making fun of her. Instead of a smirk, the old woman was smiling, transforming her worn, creased face into a picture of genteel beauty and youthfulness.

She must have been exceptionally beautiful in her youth, Sara thought, *but something in her past was cruel to her, taking its toll on her beauty along with her spirit.* "You have to understand that sometimes when I pray, I'm not sure if the answer I get back is really what God wants from me. However, I'm pretty sure this time I got it right—the answer, I mean."

"What was different about his answer this time?" the old woman asked, looking at Sara with disdain. Obviously, she found the whole idea of prayer amusing.

"The reason I know it's the right answer is because it sounded strange to me. God said that I was to follow my heart and wait for you to tell me your story. That was the exact message. I wouldn't have had that thought, so it has to be the right answer."

Then Sara asked, "Are you a Christian?"

"You have got to be kidding! Christians are busybodies, sticking their noses in other people's business while trying to force us to change our ways. They judge others to make themselves appear better. No, I'm not a Christian, thank you!"

This woman is going to be a major pain in the rump. Sara knew God's instructions needed to be followed, so she forced herself not to respond to the woman's anger with a nasty remark. Actually, she had thought the same way about Christians a few times herself. *Maybe she and I have something in common.*

They sat quietly together, each in their own thoughts, until Sara decided it was a good time to change the subject. "I'm going to the kitchen to put some fresh coffee on. Would you like something to eat? I could fix you some bacon and eggs. I'm sure you must be hungry. You can rest here on the couch."

As Sara headed toward the kitchen, she heard the old woman mumbling something and assumed she was agreeing with her suggestion.

"You know, dear, out of all the front lawns those disgusting people could have dumped me on, I'm sure glad it was yours. I feel like I'm in a bed-and-breakfast, and I'm hoping the next luxury, after food, will be a hot bath and a soft, warm bed to lie down on."

Sara stopped and looked at the old lady. She wondered whether she was being sarcastic or sincere. The old woman's impish smile said it all; she was grateful and glad to be safe and warm for a change.

Sara went into the kitchen to get the old woman something to eat. Her mind raced with thoughts about what to do with her.

As she filled the coffeepot with water, she spilled some of it because her hands were shaking. *Stop it!* she told herself. *You have got to get hold of yourself. For crying out loud, she's an old lady who somehow landed on our lawn. Why couldn't this kind of stuff happen when Kevin was home? He's the rational one, always in control and … why is God giving this to me? I'm not the rational one! Yes, I said I was sure of God's answer to my prayer, but maybe I was wrong. Maybe it wasn't the right answer. Stop it right now, Sara Richardson, and get back to doing what God told you to do.* She turned back to preparing food for the old woman.

The sound and smoky aroma of sizzling bacon filled the kitchen. Sara realized she was hungry, too, and decided to join her guest. "Breakfast is just about ready," she yelled.

Not getting a response, she called out again. Still no answer, so she walked into the living room to see why.

Sara found the disheveled woman with her hands covering her face, sobbing her heart out. Without thinking, Sara knelt down beside her and embraced her. At first, the old woman tried to pull away, but then she allowed Sara to comfort her. While the old woman cried, Sara made her mind up she would get to the bottom of what had happened to this poor old soul and how she got dumped on her lawn.

What a picture they must have made there in the living room of the manse. The old woman, dirty, untidy, and smelling like she hadn't had a bath in weeks, and Sara, a well-groomed, proper, middle-aged minister's wife.

She held on to the woman as if she were a special gift from God.

They sat that way for some time before Sara gently pushed her back against the couch.

Just as quickly as the dam of emotions had erupted, the old woman plugged them up. She wiped her eyes and composed herself, then looked into Sara's eyes. Through her own tears, Sara saw the old woman's face looking younger and more relaxed. Maybe letting go of her pent-up tension helped her, or having another human gently touching her made the difference. Whatever the reason, she looked years younger, even serene.

"Tell you what. Let me show you where the bathroom is so you can wash up before we eat. I'm sure you'll feel better after freshening up a bit." Sara helped her up off the couch and walked her to the downstairs bathroom. She noticed the old woman was still shaky on her feet.

"It's been a while since I've had the pleasure of a home. I miss having a bathroom with privacy." The old woman leaned on Sara's arm. "I'll only be a minute. The smell of that bacon is making me hungry."

Sara showed her where the towels and washcloths were kept, then quietly closed the bathroom door. Walking back toward the kitchen, she felt less stressed about what to do, as if a little bit of sunshine had filtered through her cloudy thoughts and she could finally see clearly.

Whatever happened from then on, she knew she had to allow God to lead her, and she couldn't let other things interfere.

She heard the bathroom door open. The old woman, still weak from her ordeal, shuffled toward the kitchen.

"What a lovely home you have, Sara," the old woman said as she gazed around the kitchen. Sara saw longing in her sad eyes.

"Thank you. I've worked hard to get this manse up to standard. Some of the houses Kevin and I've lived in have been in bad shape."

"Well, you've done a wonderful job. It feels nice and cozy in here."

"Just what I was trying to do," Sara said, smiling. "Better sit down and eat your breakfast before it gets cold."

"Wouldn't be the first time I've eaten cold food, especially food that was supposed to be hot when you eat it. It's a pleasure to even have food to eat for breakfast. Sometimes I've gone days without anything but garbage scraps. It's not bad once you get over the idea of eating other people's half-eaten food."

The thought of eating food from a garbage can took Sara's appetite away, but she sat down anyway, trying to make the old woman feel comfortable.

"Aren't you hungry?" the old woman asked.

"No, I had plenty to eat this morning," she lied.

While the old woman ate her eggs and bacon, Sara tried to figure out how she was going to get some answers from this woman—like who she was and how she got onto their lawn. She couldn't go much longer without answers. She didn't know whether to call Kevin first or the local police.

Casually, Sara said to the old woman, "In all the confusion, I haven't even asked what your name is."

The old woman stopped, her fork midway between her plate and her mouth. "I knew you'd get around to that eventually." She put down her fork and turned to face Sara. "I'm deciding whether to give you the name I've been using while living on the streets or my birth name."

Her eyes peered intently into Sara's. She paused, trying to figure out where this was going to go before turning back to her plate. She scooped up another forkful of food, raised it to her mouth, then stopped long enough to say, "They call me Tess."

Chapter 3

"Tess ..." Sara said, pouring another cup of coffee. She looked at the woman, wondering whether it was the truth or a lie.

After breakfast, Sara convinced Tess she needed to get some rest before anything else was decided. She wasn't sure she wanted to, but she was exhausted. The thought of a real bed won her over.

Sara helped her upstairs to the back bedroom. Tess crawled into bed fully dressed and quickly fell asleep. Sara stood in the doorway, listening to the rhythm of her steady breathing, then quietly closed the door and went downstairs.

As she settled down in the overstuffed chair by the fireplace, she thought about how right Kevin was about her being gullible. He said she would believe anything anyone told her. Maybe he was right, but she was determined to figure this one out for herself.

Suddenly, the phone rang. She jumped up to answer it before it woke up Tess.

"Hello," she answered a bit too quietly.

"Sara, is that you?" She could barely hear Kevin's voice over the background noise.

"Yes, it's me. Why do you sound so surprised?"

"You sound strange. Are you all right?" Kevin shouted.

"I'm fine—just a bit concerned about what I should do with a situation that's come up this morning."

"What situation? Are you sure you're all right?" Kevin asked, concerned.

Sara quickly shared the events of the past few hours and waited for the usual lecture. Seconds ticked by before she heard the familiar frustration in his voice.

"Now let me get this straight. You have a total stranger sleeping upstairs in one of our bedrooms, and you haven't called the police?"

"Yes, that's right."

"Sara, how many times have I told you to think before you do things? Do you realize how gullible you're being?"

Kevin was speaking in his ministerial voice. "I'm on my way home. I should be there in about an hour. In the meantime, you need to call the sheriff's office and have someone deal with this situation now."

"Kevin, I don't want the police involved just yet. Tess is so fragile right now, and I know God is leading me to take care of her."

"Honey, you are a loving and caring person, but you've got to use your smarts and call the sheriff and let him take care of this. What did you say her name is?"

"Tess … at least I think it's Tess. She said she wasn't sure whether to tell me her real name or her street name, but I think she told me the truth."

Kevin's voice rose a full octave as he tried to control his anger. "Oh, good grief! I'm on my way!" Then the line went dead.

Why does he do that to me? I didn't get a chance to tell him about my prayer and how God told me to follow my heart. Kevin treats me like a child, and it hurts. I'm not calling the sheriff … at least not yet.

While she waited for Kevin, she jotted down some questions she could ask Tess. Even if she wouldn't give correct answers, they might be able to get clues from whatever information she revealed.

Lulled by the warmth of the fire, Sara slipped into a troubled sleep. The sound of a slammed car door and hurried footsteps startled her awake. The front door opened and slammed shut as Kevin rushed in, bringing cold air with him.

"All right, where is this woman you've given free rein to our home?" Kevin asked before greeting her with a kiss or hug.

"Kevin, would you please keep your voice down? If Tess hears that tone and the anger in your voice, you're sure not going to get anywhere with her—or for that matter, with me."

He looked at her and realized he was behaving poorly. "I'm sorry. You're only trying to do what you think is best." He walked over and took her in his arms, kissing and holding her close. "I missed you while I was away," he whispered as he nuzzled her neck.

"I missed you too," Sara responded. She began to relax as he continued to hold her close. She felt safe and secure in his arms, and the tension from the stress of the morning left her.

Gently Kevin stepped away and looked into her eyes, which revealed the mixed emotions she had been feeling. Taking her hands, he gently led her to the couch. After they sat down, he wrapped her in his arms, neither speaking, lost in thought.

Sara knew Kevin was trying hard to be patient with her, but she also knew he didn't think she was trying hard enough to figure out what to do about Tess, at least not in the way he thought she should. He wanted her to call the sheriff, while she wanted to wait until tomorrow.

"Hello. You must be Sara's husband." Tess stood in the hallway.

They both jumped at the sound of Tess's voice. Sara got up and rushed over to Tess, introducing her to Kevin before he had time to start asking questions. "Tess, I'd like you to meet my husband, Kevin." Sara's voice was strained and high-pitched.

"It's a pleasure to meet you, Tess," Kevin replied in his most formal voice. She blushed at being treated with such courtesy.

Extending her hand toward Kevin, Tess gently nodded her head and greeted him in a manner that surprised them both. There were not many homeless people who had such grace and presence.

Kevin, visibly humbled by Tess, took her hand and greeted her warmly. Her face lit up as they both stood, smiling at each other. Amazed, Sara lifted her eyes upward and said a quick prayer, thanking God for a great beginning with Kevin and Tess.

Kevin asked Tess if he could help her over to the big, cozy chair near the fireplace. Her demeanor changed when he gently took her by the arm. She sat down, got herself settled, then smiled at Kevin and Sara like a queen sitting on her throne.

Sara blinked twice to make sure she wasn't dreaming, but there she was—Tess, in all her glory. She found it hard to believe this was the same woman who, only hours earlier, had been lying on her front lawn. Now, here she was sitting in Kevin's overstuffed chair, warming herself by the fire.

Kevin talked to Tess like she was a true guest in their home. Instead of asking questions about who she was and where she came from, he talked to her like she was a long-lost family member. They chatted about the weather, his recent trip, and how pleasant it had been.

"Uh, Kevin, could I see you in the kitchen for a minute?" Sara asked, interrupting their conversation. "We'll only be a minute. Please sit there and enjoy the fire."

As they walked toward the kitchen, Sara blurted out, "Kevin, what is the matter with you?"

"What do you mean? You wanted me to be nice to her and not pressure her about where she came from or who she really is. Why are you acting so upset?" He looked toward the living room to make sure Tess hadn't overheard them.

"I wanted you to be kind—not act as if she belongs here," Sara said.

"We just have to stay calm—and for Pete's sake, let me handle everything."

"Fine. You handle everything, but make sure you let me know before you start asking her questions, so I can work with you. OK?"

"All right, I will."

Sara took a deep breath, then started toward the living room, when Kevin grabbed her arm and pulled her back to the kitchen.

"What's the matter now?" she asked, agitated.

"We have to build her confidence before we start asking questions. So, we'll go in there, share some casual conversation about our lives, and hope she feels she can offer something about herself to us." He grinned, feeling proud of his logic.

Sara couldn't believe she was hearing this, but it sounded better than going in and acting like the FBI. "Fine, let's go." She followed him into the living room.

As they returned, Tess turned her head and gave them her best smile. Sara was beginning to think she really was a con artist. She knew exactly how to use her charm.

Clearing his voice, Kevin used his own charm to disarm the visitor. "Tess, Sara and I have decided—if it's all right with you—we'd like to have you stay with us for a few days, at least until you can make other arrangements. We can't let you go back out on the streets. We've got to come up with a plan for how you'll be taken care of."

As soon as the words were out of Kevin's mouth, Sara's mouth dropped open in disbelief. What happened to the deal they had made earlier, about clueing in each other before taking action?

Tess looked over at Sara to see her reaction. Sara quickly closed her mouth and smiled reassuringly at Tess.

"Yes, I think Kevin's right. We have plenty of room in this big old house. You can stay with us as long as it takes to get arrangements made for your safety."

Sara's heart warmed to Tess when she saw the emotion on her face. Their words of kindness had gone straight to her heart. *This poor old lady is trying not to let her guard down, but our kindness is making her vulnerable.*

Tess recovered quickly. Returning to her street-wise voice, she responded, "I can take care of myself quite well, but it would be nice to have a few days out of the cold. The thought of a warm place to sleep sounds pretty good to me. But I'm not a charity case, so you better come up with some chores for me to do."

Kevin and Sara tried not to smile. Although she was not a young woman by any means, her will was strong and durable. They knew they could find a few chores for her.

Sara said, "I think the first thing we should do is get you settled in one of the bedrooms upstairs. You can have your own space to feel comfortable. Stay here with Kevin by the fire, and I'll get things ready before lunch."

Heading for the stairs, Sara looked back at Kevin and Tess, chatting like old friends. Kevin looked up and caught Sara's eye. She smiled, letting him know how much she loved him.

Chapter 4

Sara hoped Kevin understood what he was getting himself into by allowing Tess to stay with them. She knew there would be consequences, but did he? Pushing the thought out of her mind, she walked into the largest of the three bedrooms at the back of the house and decided it would be perfect for Tess.

The first thing on the agenda was to find clothes for Tess. Sara couldn't let Tess wear those disgusting old pants and flannel shirt she found her in. At the local thrift store, they found slacks and a nice sweater, then purchased toiletries at the local drugstore.

Sara still needed to do some errands before dinner and asked Tess if she wanted to go back to the manse or tag along with her. *Maybe I can get information about where she's been living before she got dumped here in Jonesboro.*

Tess said she'd like to stay with Sara, especially after Sara told her they could stop at the local coffee shop after the errands.

They spent the next few hours doing errands, and then they stopped at the coffee shop. After sitting down, Tess gently asked Sara a question.

"Sara, if you don't mind my asking, do you and Kevin have any kids?

"No—no, we don't."

"How come?" Right after she asked, she regretted it. The sadness she saw in Sara's eyes said it all. Something bad must have happened to match that look. "Hey, you don't need to answer that. It's none of my business really," Tess said, looking down at her hands awkwardly.

"I don't mind, Tess. It's just you startled me, that's all. I haven't talked about this for a long time. Maybe I need to."

"Now don't do it because I asked, but if it would make you feel better, then go ahead. You know, even though it's been such a short time knowing you, I've sensed you haven't been feeling yourself lately. It's none of my business why, but I'm a pretty good listener."

"After Kevin and I married, we decided to wait a few years to start a family. He had his loan to pay off for graduate school, and I wanted to continue teaching interior design at the local college. After a few years, we felt we were ready to have a child."

"Sounds like that was a good decision. Kids bring a lot of good and bad in a marriage. I know firsthand about that, but that's a story I'm not ready to tell," Tess said. Sara was lost in thought and didn't pick up on her remark.

"We figured I would get pregnant within a few months, but by the time six months had gone by and I wasn't, we decided to see a doctor to make sure we both were all right."

"What did the doctor say?" Tess was leaning in toward Sara to be able to catch every word.

"The doctor ran some tests on both Kevin and me, and when they came back, they found I was infertile due to my fallopian tubes being damaged. We asked about surgery but were told the tubes were so badly damaged that surgery couldn't solve the problem."

"Oh, sweetie!" Tess said, patting Sara's hand. "I feel so bad for you and Kevin. Did you all think about adopting?"

"We did, but I don't know … I just couldn't get my head around not being able to have a child of my own. I was being selfish."

"How'd Kevin feel about that—you not wanting to adopt?"

"He wanted to do whatever was best for me, even though I knew he wanted to have a family."

"That sounds like Kevin. He loves you so much, Sara, but I'm sure you know that."

"Yes, I do. Anyway, we settled into a life that revolved around the ministry and my teaching until we moved to Jonesboro. That's when I decided to take a break and just spend time helping Kevin in his ministry and working in the community."

"Do you ever think about what it would have been like to have kids?"

"Not as much as I did in the beginning, but life's good for Kevin and me. I have Kevin's nieces and nephews to love, so that helps. Now let's finish up our coffee and muffins," Sara said, squeezing Tess's hands that still held hers.

Tess was such good company and so easy to talk to. It was like being out with a dear friend instead of a stranger. Sara forgot to try to get information out of her.

Chapter 5

By the end of dinner, Kevin and Sara were exhausted from playing private detective. They decided to stop with the questioning until morning.

"Tess, I think it's time to turn in for the night. We've all had a pretty hectic day, don't you think?" Sara asked. "Come on. I'll help you get ready. You can put on one of the pairs of pajamas we got while we were at the thrift shop. They should keep you warm."

"Sara, I can't imagine what would have happened to me if I hadn't collapsed on your front lawn. I'm truly thankful. To sleep in a real bed and eat food that's warm and talk to people who are so caring—well, it's overwhelming!"

Sara saw tears in Tess's eyes, and her own eyes filled up. She quickly turned away so Tess wouldn't see them. In less than twenty-four hours, this woman was becoming a part of her life.

Kevin was getting ready for bed when she walked into their bedroom. She could tell he was tired and frustrated by the situation she'd gotten them in. She acted like nothing had happened, not wanting to get blamed for the mess she'd made, but it didn't work.

"Sara, I hope you're happy with what we have to do with Tess."

"What's that supposed to mean?" she retorted as she headed toward the bathroom.

"If you had only called the police when you saw Tess, we wouldn't be facing this mess."

At times like this, one has to make a decision to respond to a spouse's angry remark or keep one's mouth shut. Sara decided to keep her mouth shut, but she slammed the bathroom door with gusto, hoping Kevin got the message.

Slipping down among the frothy bubbles in the old-fashioned clawfoot tub, Sara felt the stress of the day beginning to disappear as she relaxed and prayed. "All right, God, I guess I messed up by not calling the police. I hate it when Kevin's right. But when I asked you what to do, I know your answer was real. Somehow, we'll get through this with your guidance. I just know it."

Sara calmed down, realizing she needed to tell Kevin how much she loved him and that she couldn't have gotten through the day without his help. He just made her so angry when he pointed out her faults. Heaven knew she was aware of her faults. She didn't need him or others reminding her.

She smiled, remembering the first time she met Kevin. They were both attending the same college, where he was a junior and she was a freshman. Julie, her roommate, was dating a ministerial student and wanted to fix her up with his best friend, who was also planning on the ministry.

She knew the life of a minister because her father, who had died a few years earlier, had been one for almost thirty years. She'd spent her childhood being uprooted because of his ministry—not the kind of life she wanted as an adult.

Julie was persistent, and she finally agreed to go out with this guy just so she would leave her alone. The night of the blind date arrived, and she was feeling nervous yet excited about meeting Kevin. Julie decided they would meet the guys at one of the local hangouts that peppered the campus.

They arrived first and found a table with a bird's-eye view of the front door, but far enough away from the entrance to give her time to get a good look at Kevin before he and Julie's boyfriend saw them.

Sara kept her eyes glued to the front door. When he finally arrived, her heart skipped a beat. Kevin was gorgeous. His six-foot-three frame with broad shoulders and slim body made her heart beat even faster. As they talked, she noticed his dark brown eyes sparkled with gentleness and caring. Back then, he had the most luscious, thick black hair she'd ever seen. It was long and curled up at the nape of his neck—quite sexy. What could she say? She was hooked.

Kevin and Sara were complete opposites in personality. They had things in common, but she was bubbly and talkative, while he was lowkey and soft-spoken. She used her hands when she talked, waving them around and gesturing. Kevin, on the other hand, stayed calm and relaxed, not showing much emotion. He was a caring and compassionate man but hard to read at times. Two of the qualities that made Sara fall in love with Kevin were his compassion and dedication to what he wanted to do in the ministry. He talked about his goals and ideas, and she liked what she heard. She'd have to rethink her future life.

Her thoughts drifted to the present. Kevin hadn't changed much since they first met. He had a few fine lines around his eyes, his thick hair had thinned a bit, and there was graying at his temples, but other than that, he looked the same.

She smiled, thinking about Kevin's smile. *Hmm. Tess has the same kind of smile. That's why Kevin likes her—she smiles like him—as if both of them are going to burst out laughing at any moment.* Sara used to call it Kevin's impish grin, but he didn't like her saying that. She supposed he thought it took away from the image people had of a pastor.

Sara's shriveled toes, sticking up through the diluted bubbles, told her it was time to get out of the tub. She needed to make amends with Kevin. *Why couldn't he, just for once, not be so logical? What am I thinking? That's Kevin—always logical!*

He was propped up in bed with his nose stuck in a book. When she came out of the bathroom, he continued reading, refusing to look at her.

"So, what are you reading that's so interesting you're ignoring me?" she asked.

"Nothing that would interest you."

This is going to be harder than I thought. Her inability to say "I'm sorry" was one of her worst qualities. She'd rather have a root canal than say those two words. "Kevin, we've got to talk about this. We promised we would never go to bed angry with each other. Let's get it over with now, so we can get a good night's sleep. Waiting until morning isn't the answer, and anyway, we both won't sleep if we don't talk."

He slowly put down the book and gave her a hurt look. "Every time we argue, I end up the heavy. For once, I'd like to be the right one in an argument. I've tried in our marriage to not get upset with you when you do things I feel are irrational. I'm not going to explain or go over everything that happened today to make my point, but walking off and slamming the bathroom door doesn't help."

"I wish you'd stop treating me like a child, Kevin!"

After saying that, Sara silently prayed to God, asking him to help her keep her temper under control. Otherwise, this discussion would turn into a full-blown argument.

"You're right, Kevin … and I was wrong." She waited for his response, but none came.

"Did you hear what I said?"

He still didn't respond.

"Kevin, what is the matter with you? I said I was wrong. What more do you want? I'm tired, and I don't want to continue this discussion." She hoped her expression and gentle smile assured him she meant what she said.

When it finally registered that she really was sorry, he jumped out of bed, took her in his arms, and swung her toward the bed, where they both fell in a heap laughing. Lying side by side, they knew their love would keep them warm and cozy for the rest of the night.

"I can't stay mad at you for long," Kevin said.

The tenderness and love in his eyes melted away her anger. He gently pushed her hair away from her face and covered it with soft, caressing kisses. When his lips reached hers, her response let him know she truly was sorry. Kevin and Sara had different personalities, but their love and passion for each other ran deep and strong.

"Kevin."

"What?" he whispered in her ear.

"You'd better get up and lock our bedroom door. Remember, we're not alone in the house tonight. We have a guest … in case you forgot."

"Oh yeah, that's right. I almost forgot about Tess." He grinned boyishly and got up to lock the door. When he returned, they picked up where they had left off until a loud and persistent knocking at their door startled them. Sara cried out in alarm, nearly falling out bed.

"Sara," Kevin growled in her ear, "this is going to be a test for our marriage. Take care of this, and please do it quickly."

She couldn't blame him.

The loud knocking continued.

"I'm coming, Tess. Just hold on."

Sara stopped and straightened her hair before unlocking the door. She didn't want Tess to know she'd caught them in an awkward situation.

"What's the matter, Tess?" Sara opened the door just enough to peek out. "Are you all right?"

"Yes, I'm fine—just feeling a bit lonely and nervous sleeping way down the hall away from you and Kevin."

Sara was surprised to hear her say that since she was used to being alone out on the streets. After shutting the bedroom door behind her, Sara joined Tess in the hallway. "I'm sorry you feel lonely, Tess, but I'd think you'd be used to that. Didn't you stay by yourself out on the streets?"

"Well, yes, but there were lots of people living out on the streets besides me. People don't realize how many homeless folks there are. Even though I slept by myself, I felt comforted knowing some of my street friends were close by—just in case I needed something."

Sara felt compassion for this old woman and couldn't imagine what it must be like to be homeless and all alone. Tenderly she asked, "How would it be if I slept in the other twin bed? It's just for tonight. I can't be doing this every night."

Tess's face lit up. "I don't want to be a bother, but if you could just for tonight, I'd sure appreciate it."

"You go back to your room, and I'll be there shortly." Sara smiled, watching Tess shuffle down the hallway. She seemed to have a knack for getting her way.

It's too late to figure this out tonight. I'll work on it in the morning. I have more important issues, like how am I going to tell Kevin we can't finish what we started.

She entered their bedroom and in her most apologetic voice said, "Kevin dear, I have a bit of bad news. Tess is feeling scared and lonely, and I told her I would sleep in the other twin bed for tonight. She really is afraid, and I know if I don't do this, she'll keep us up all night. We can finish our romantic evening another night, I promise.

She quickly left and closed the door before he could say a word. Through the closed door, she heard him moan and say, "Oh, good grief!"

She covered her mouth to stifle a giggle. She didn't want him to know she'd heard him, and she wasn't looking forward to spending the rest of the night feeling cold and lonely without him.

The bedroom they gave Tess was at the back of the house. She had decorated the room with bright, cheerful colors. The furniture consisted of garage sale finds she'd transformed into her own works of art. She loved refurbishing other people's castoffs. Maybe that was why she was so determined to help Tess. What better way to do God's work than to take one of society's castoffs and turn them into the best of God's art.

At that moment, her soul received a burst of sunshine. "Thanks, God," she prayed. "I needed to be reminded of your unconditional love, but I can't say I like having to spend the night away from Kevin."

When she got to the room, she knocked before entering. She wanted Tess to know she could have some privacy.

She thought Tess would tell her to come in, but instead the bedroom door swung open, and there stood Tess, looking tiny and frail in her pajamas. They were two sizes too big, but she didn't mind.

As Sara entered, she could tell by the look in Tess's eyes that she'd be calling the shots.

"Sara, I'm embarrassed telling you I was afraid and lonely. I thought about just slipping out of the house and finding my way back to the people I call my friends, but that wouldn't have been fair to you and Kevin after all you've done for me."

"I'm glad you didn't do that, Tess. I know there's reasons why you ended up on our front lawn, and we'll have to be patient and work this out together. Actually, I'm surprised Kevin hasn't called the police already."

As soon as the words were out of her mouth, she regretted it. There she went again, not thinking before she spoke.

"What do you mean Kevin's going to call the police about me?" There was fear and anger in her eyes. She grabbed Sara's arm, squeezing so tightly it hurt.

"Ouch! Tess, you're hurting me! Just calm down. We're not calling the police, at least not yet. I shouldn't have said aloud what I was thinking. I'm sorry to have upset you."

She took Tess's hand off her arm and gently held it. "Let's not discuss it anymore tonight. I'm tired, and I know you must be too, so let's get into bed and get some sleep. All right?"

Sara looked at Tess and was relieved to see her nod her head in agreement. She mumbled something under her breath and turned toward her bed, already rumpled from earlier in the evening.

"Let me help you into bed," Sara offered.

"I'm not an invalid, Sara. I can get into bed quite nicely by myself. Why do young people think if you're old, you're incapable of doing simple tasks? I told you I can take care of myself!"

"I'm sorry. I wasn't suggesting you couldn't take care of yourself. I'm just trying to make you feel at home, that's all. I used to tuck my grandmother in for the night when she came to visit. It was my special way of letting her know how much I loved her. I miss doing that. She's been gone for ten years now, and I really miss her. I thought if I tucked you in, you'd see that I want us to be friends."

Sara turned away before Tess saw the hurt in her eyes. Tess's curt words stung her. She was on the verge of tears. *All I wanted to do was comfort her and make her feel welcome,* Sara thought. *She sure is a crusty old lady.*

Sara fumbled with the comforter on her bed, trying to fold it down. A gentle touch on her shoulder made her turn around. Tess looked at her with regret.

"Forgive me, Sara. I guess it embarrassed me when you suggested helping me into bed. I've had to take care of myself for some time now, and I've forgotten what it feels like to have someone care for me. You learn early out on the streets to trust no one, and never, under any circumstances, allow someone to show physical affection. Life is pretty difficult out there. I'm truly sorry I hurt your feelings." Kissing Sara lightly on the cheek, she turned and shuffled over to her bed.

Sara sat down on the bed in shock, not saying a word. Tess crawled into her bed and closed her eyes quickly, letting Sara know she was finished with talking and wanted to go to sleep. Sara got into bed and reached over to turn out the light. In the darkness, she could have sworn she heard Tess whisper, "Sweet dreams, sweet Sara."

Chapter 6

When Sara woke up sometime around seven, she didn't know where she was. Recalling the events of the previous day quickly brought her back to why she was sleeping in another bedroom. Tess.

She slipped out of bed and tiptoed quietly toward the closed bedroom door, hoping to make a clean getaway from the sleeping Tess. Cracking open the door produced a squeak from the old, rusty hinges, sounding loud in the early-morning quiet. *When is Kevin going to oil these hinges like I've asked? If Tess wakes up because of this squeaky door, he's the one who's going to deal with her.*

Sara squeezed through the small opening, closed the door, and made it safely to the hallway. She pressed her ear to the closed door and listened … nothing. *I'm not ready to deal with Tess right now and the whole situation. It's too early. I need my coffee and time with Kevin,* she mused. *Then I'll deal with Tess.*

Downstairs, she put the coffee on and went to get the morning paper. Before opening the front door, she paused. *What are the chances of finding another body out on the lawn?* Smiling, she ventured out into the cold and retrieved the morning paper.

Walking back to the kitchen, she wondered if Kevin had gotten much sleep. *Poor guy. I shouldn't have left him alone like I did. I know what I'll do. I'll make breakfast for the two of us and serve it to him in bed. That way, we can have time alone before we have to get back to Tess.*

Balancing the tray laden with food, she went up the stairs to their bedroom. Before entering, she glanced down the hall to make sure Tess wasn't watching. She quietly entered, put the heavy tray down on the dresser, and approached their king-size bed.

Kevin was fast asleep. The bed covers were in a heap, as if he'd tossed and turned all night. One foot stuck out from under the covers; the other foot lay tangled in the bedding. Sara giggled softly, seeing him hugging her pillow.

She bent down and gently kissed him on his cheek. "Good morning, sleepyhead," she whispered. His eyes fluttered and opened just enough to let her know he knew she was there. She repeated, "Good morning, sleepyhead." This time, he opened his eyes wide and smiled.

"What time is it?" he asked.

"I think it's around eight," Sara said cheerfully as she opened the curtains to let the morning light fill the room.

"Boy, you're in a good mood this morning. Wish I felt that happy." He stretched his arms.

"I have a treat for you. I decided this morning I would make breakfast for us and have it here in bed. We'll be dining on eggs, bacon, cinnamon toast, and of course, steaming hot coffee."

Sara had her back to Kevin and couldn't see his reaction, but she expected a positive response.

"Kevin, did you hear what I said?" She turned and looked at him.

He stared at her as if she were a total stranger.

"What's the matter? You're looking at me as if you don't recognize me."

"I don't, at least not the you who said she fixed breakfast."

Sara laughed because he was right. She seldom fixed breakfast. Kevin usually ate cereal, and she had toast and coffee. Occasionally, she fixed a real breakfast if it was a holiday or they had company.

"All right, wipe that surprised look off your face and get your pillows fluffed up. We'd better eat fast before Tess comes knocking on our door. While you're at it, would you please fluff my pillows too? I might as well lean back and relax in bed too. Despite what you might think, I didn't sleep much last night either."

"What do you mean *either*? I slept."

"Sure you did!" Sara grinned.

Kevin grinned, too, then fluffed their pillows and motioned for Sara to climb in bed beside him. They settled back against the pillows, diving into their food before it got cold.

After finishing, they sat quietly sipping their coffee.

"Kevin."

"What?"

"Do you know much about homeless people? I know there are a lot, especially in cities, but do you think we have any around Jonesboro?"

"I hate to burst your bubble, but we do. Even small communities like ours have the homeless. They're just hidden away among the rural areas that surround Jonesboro."

Sara thought about what Kevin said and decided to do some research on the subject. Maybe the information she came up with would help her find out more about Tess's situation.

Kevin and Sara discussed their strategy on handling Tess, then decided to get dressed before she came knocking at their door again. It was nice having time together, just the two of them.

Sara headed to the bathroom to get dressed. After she'd gotten ready and Kevin had showered, she gathered up the dirty dishes, carried them downstairs, and loaded them in the dishwasher.

She cleaned up the kitchen, then went upstairs to look in on the sleeping Tess. Slowly she opened the door and peaked around to see if she was still asleep. The light from the window was enough, so Sara didn't turn on a light. To her surprise, Tess wasn't in her bed. *She must have run away last night like she said she would,* Sara thought. She ran down the hall to her bedroom. Bursting into the room, she yelled, "Kevin, come quick! Tess ran away!"

Kevin had just finished dressing. When he heard Sara, he rushed out of the bathroom.

"What do you mean 'she's gone'?" Seeing Sara's face, he knew she was scared.

"Honey, calm down. I'm sure she hasn't run away. She's probably in the bathroom, or you missed her when you went downstairs. Did you check the bathroom?"

"No, I panicked when she wasn't in her bed. I'll go see if she's in the bathroom. She told me last night she thought about sneaking out and going back to her friends, the ones she hung out with—you know—the ones who lived on the street like her. That's why I got so upset."

Sara headed to the bathroom around the corner from the guest room. The door was open, but Tess wasn't there. Forcing herself to stay calm, she went back to the guest room to check one more time. This time, she turned on the overhead light.

For some reason, she decided to check on the other side of Tess's bed. Sure enough, there was Tess, sound asleep on the hard, cold floor.

Sara couldn't believe her eyes. Why would Tess prefer to sleep on the floor than in the warm and comfortable bed?

Tess was curled up with the comforter wrapped around her like a cocoon. Under her head was the small decorative pillow from the bed. She looked so contented Sara didn't want to disturb her. She waited a minute to make sure Tess hadn't heard her, then quietly left the room.

She met Kevin coming up the stairs. He'd looked all over the house but hadn't found her.

"Kevin, come here." She grabbed his hand and led him to the guest room door.

"What is it?"

"Shh … I found her."

They entered the room and walked around to the side of the bed where Tess was lying on the floor. Kevin didn't seem surprised, which surprised Sara. They tiptoed out of the room and went to their own bedroom before saying anything.

"OK, what's the deal with you?" Sara asked in frustration.

"What do you mean?" he answered, puzzled.

"You didn't seem the least bit surprised to see Tess sleeping on the floor. For crying out loud, it's not normal to sleep on the floor when there's a nice, comfortable bed to sleep on, especially for a woman who looks to be in her seventies. Why would she do that?" Sara said.

Kevin led her to the bed and sat down beside her. "I could be wrong about this, but I think she's on the floor because she's used to sleeping on the ground. Think about it. She's homeless and most likely slept on hard surfaces like a bench or even the ground."

Sara realized that he was right. Tess probably couldn't sleep and decided to sleep the way she was accustomed to—on a hard, cold surface. She had a lot to learn about homeless people and planned to find out more. She complained about little problems when all the while there were people who had no place to sleep or food to eat.

Poor Tess. The thought of others going through the same thing brought tears to Sara's eyes. *God sure put me in a humble mood this morning,* she thought.

"Kevin, God must be trying to make a point with me."

He looked at her—his own emotions written on his face.

"Sara, I think we both have an opportunity here. Tess has been brought into our lives for a reason. You said so yourself. That reason is homelessness. This whole thing has been an eye-opener for me too. God gives us a push in a certain direction to get our attention. Then it's up to us to follow. Do you think you're up to the challenge?"

"Yes," she answered, feeling revived.

"I just hope we can do this and do it right," Sara replied. Kevin hugged her tight, kissing the top of her head. "If anyone can do this, you can."

With that said, they went downstairs to plan where to start. Before long, Tess showed up. They were so involved in discussing their next move they didn't hear her come into the kitchen.

"Good morning, you two," Tess said, stretching her arms high above her head.

"Good morning to you," Kevin and Sara said in unison, then laughed.

"Are you both always this cheerful in the mornings?" Tess asked. She looked around the kitchen to see if there was any coffee left from breakfast.

"No, not always." Sara smiled at Kevin, then jumped up to get Tess a mug of coffee.

"What's the occasion this morning?" Tess asked, taking the hot coffee from Sara and sitting down at the table.

"We made a discovery," Sara replied.

Kevin walked over to Tess and planted a kiss on her wrinkled cheek. She frowned at him, but he knew she was pleased with his show of affection. She blushed, then took a quick sip of coffee, hoping he didn't see.

"Um, do you think you could fix me some more of that good food you fixed for me yesterday, Sara?"

"You mean the bacon and eggs?"

"Yeah."

Sara gave Tess a peck on her other cheek before turning her attention to fixing another breakfast.

"Boy, you two are sure lovey-dovey types," Tess mumbled as she went down the hall to wash up.

Laughing, Kevin got up and headed toward his office at the rear of the house. After being gone a few days, he needed to attend to church business before dealing with Tess.

Sara liked him having a second office at home. It gave her comfort knowing he was around the house more often.

As she fixed Tess's breakfast, she wondered how someone like her could become homeless. The strength and power of God's love touched her heart right there and then, reminding her of her favorite scripture, "Joy comes in the morning." Now she had the joy of Tess.

While Tess ate breakfast, Sara cleaned up the dishes. Grabbing another cup of coffee, she started planning how she was going to get Tess to reveal more about herself. "Tess, how long have you been living on the streets?" Sara asked.

"A little while."

"Are you from around here or close by?"

"Nope."

"You're going to make me work hard to find out about you, aren't you?"

Tess could see Sara was frustrated and getting a bit agitated. "It's not that I don't appreciate what you and Kevin are doing, but I need time to think about what I want to say before I tell you. There are things in my past that are difficult to explain, and I don't want to involve anyone until I know I can trust them. If you and Kevin can't be patient with me, then maybe I should leave now before we all become too involved with each other."

"We can wait."

"I want you to know how wonderful it is to be off the streets and in a real home with such caring people."

Sara saw the pain in Tess's eyes. She knew she couldn't let her just walk out of their lives. She remembered what God said when she prayed about Tess in the beginning of this adventure. He said she was to follow her heart and allow Tess to tell her story. He didn't say it had to be done right away—just that it would be told in good time.

Sara walked over and took Tess's worn and wrinkled hands into her own. "We want you to stay with us, and we'll wait until you're ready to talk about your past. I know it must be hard not knowing what to do next. Maybe you're worried we'll turn you over to the police. Kevin and I have already talked this over, and we want you to stay here as long as you need to."

Sara squeezed Tess's hands, and Tess returned the gesture. Her eyes filled with tears, but Sara saw a renewed sense of purpose in them. Her sagging shoulders straightened, and she seemed to have more strength than the day before. In just a short time with Kevin and Sara, she'd built up a bit of trust and hope.

"Tess, why don't you finish getting ready while I finish up around the house?"

Tess headed toward the stairs, then turned around and gave Sara that special smile of hers. "I don't really have much faith in religion, but I must say you and Kevin are showing me there is some good in it. I see real Christian love in the two of you, and I want to thank you for giving me time to figure out what I need to do next."

Sara watched her walk up the stairs without shuffling her feet like she did the day before. It was amazing what a little tender, loving care could do in a mere twenty-four hours. The telephone rang, bringing her back to another day in the life of the ministry.

"Hello."

"Good morning, Sara. This is Martha Jewel. Is the pastor home this morning?"

"Yes, Martha, he's here. I'll get him for you."

"Thanks, dear. I hope I'm not disturbing him."

"No, of course not."

She put her hand over the receiver and called for Kevin to pick up the phone. Martha Jewel could talk a blue streak, so she didn't attempt to start a conversation with her. There was too much to do, and she didn't need to get sidetracked. When Kevin picked up the extension in his study, she hung up the phone in the kitchen.

A little later, he came into the kitchen to tell her that Martha had called to remind him to tell his secretary, Cathy, to put the information about the church's annual turkey dinner in the monthly newsletter.

"Why didn't she just call Cathy at the church and tell her instead of calling you?" Sara asked.

"You know her. For some reason, she likes talking to me. Maybe it's my good looks. When you got it, you got it." Kevin smiled, running his hand through his hair like some male model.

Sara laughed and threw the dish towel at him. "You are sure full of yourself this morning," she told him. "Is it that time of year already?" she asked, opening the refrigerator to see what was available for lunch.

"Not for another two months, but you know how she is. She starts with the information two or three months in advance. I guess that's good. You know how she loves to take charge of the whole thing."

He leaned over Sara's shoulder to see what there was to snack on.

"Is there any dessert from last night?"

"No, I think Tess ate the last bite of it before she went to bed," Sara answered, moving out of his way as he peered deeper into the vastness of the refrigerator.

"I guess with her around, we'll be competing for the leftovers," he mumbled, grabbing an apple to satisfy his midmorning hunger.

"I'm just glad she's eating. Didn't you notice how thin she is? I'll make extras on the dessert so the two of you won't fight over who gets the last bite."

He grinned and gave her a quick hug before heading back to his office. "Oh, I almost forgot to tell you. Martha needs you to be in charge of getting the pies for the turkey dinner." He tried not to laugh as he conveyed Martha's message. He knew Sara hated being in charge of committees, especially food committees.

Irritated, she muttered, "Why didn't Martha tell me herself?" But she knew why. Martha knew Kevin would convince her to head the committee.

People always assumed being the minister's wife meant you automatically headed committees. She needed to work harder at saying no and meaning it. Having Tess around was going to be enough work. *I don't need to be saddled with all that calling and asking for pies!*

There wasn't much food in the house, meaning she needed to get to the grocery store. She decided to take Tess with her.

Walking into Kevin's office, she announced, "I'm going to the grocery store and taking Tess with me." He was on the phone, and she heard him say he would be sure and tell her about the situation. Then he hung up.

"Who was that and what are you supposed to tell me?"

"That was Sheriff Adams. He said some car thieves stopped at the local gas station early yesterday morning to buy gas."

"What does that have to do with us, and how in the world did they know they were car thieves?"

A chill went down Sara's spine. She knew this had something to do with Tess.

"The employee at the station became suspicious when two women came in to use the restroom."

"What's so odd about someone using the restroom?"

"One of the women fits Tess's description. He said one woman was young, and the other was old. By his description, the older woman looked like Tess.

"Oh, come on. Are you telling me that Tess is part of some gang that goes around stealing cars? That's just silly. She wouldn't do something like that."

"Wait! Let me finish!" Kevin said, excited. "When the car pulled out of the gas station, the employee ran outside and got the license plate number. He called the police, and they checked the number. Lo and behold, the car was listed as stolen, and that's not all. They found out that a bar in the area where the car was stolen from was robbed, and the owner was killed!"

Did Tess have anything to do with these crimes? Sara thought. *Please, dear God, don't let this poor old lady be involved in something as horrible as murder.*

"I know what you're thinking—and no, I don't think Tess had anything to do with this. Sara, did you hear me?"

Looking at Kevin, she tried to focus on what he was saying.

"The gas station employee told the police that the older woman seemed real nervous and frightened. He said the younger woman looked like she had something pushed up against the older woman's back. It could have been a gun. That's what made him suspicious. Anyway, the sheriff called to warn us to make sure we keep our doors locked until these people are caught or spotted elsewhere."

"Why would he call us? We're not on the main road."

"Because the car was seen around five o'clock yesterday morning, speeding down our street, stopping briefly before taking off again, squealing its tires. I think Tess was in some kind of hostage situation, but she got herself out of it when the car stopped."

Sara's heart skipped a beat when she realized this was how Tess came to be on their lawn. Thank God they didn't hurt her or, God forbid, kill her! She bet they would have if she hadn't gotten away.

"Should we call the sheriff back and tell him about Tess?"

"Not yet," Kevin replied. "We'll have to eventually, but let's wait a little longer. We can't keep her hidden away forever, but a little more time will help us come up with a reason why she's with us. She could be a fugitive on the run, but let's wait … at least a few more days."

Kevin saw fear and concern on Sara's face. He put his arms around her. "Honey, we'll figure this out, and we'll make sure Tess is taken care of. I promise."

The phone rang again; Kevin answered. Others were getting the news about what had happened in their community, and whoever he was talking to wanted to know what Kevin knew about the situation.

She left him to deal with the problem and headed back to the kitchen. She needed to figure out how they were going to tell Tess about what the sheriff had told them. If Tess was involved, she'd react to the news.

Tess walked into the kitchen. "Sorry I took so long getting ready, Sara, but it sure felt good to soak a while in a real tub." Tess had a big grin on her freshly scrubbed face.

Noticing Sara's odd expression, she asked, "What's the matter? You look like you've seen a ghost."

"I was thinking about something Kevin and I were talking about earlier. I'm fine, really. Sometimes the ministry brings upsetting news, and I get frustrated about dealing with it. That's all."

"Well, it must have been pretty upsetting because you look pale. Maybe you need to go lie down for a while. I can find my way around the kitchen, so you don't need to be waiting on me." Tess helped herself to what was left of the morning coffee.

"Let me put some fresh coffee on, Tess."

"Don't bother. I'm used to drinking leftover coffee. I guess I've drunk it that way for so long that I prefer it old and strong—like me." She laughed that funny laugh of hers and sat down at the kitchen table.

"Tess, you're looking lovely this morning," Kevin commented as he walked into the kitchen.

"Why, thank you." She smiled, looking proud that he had noticed she had taken extra care to fix herself up before coming downstairs. Her hair was pulled back into a French twist, and her usually pale complexion glowed from a hint of blush and a bit of lipstick. She looked regal instead of poor and homeless.

"I decided to add a little color to my face this morning to celebrate being here with the two of you. I've carried this little bit of makeup around with me for years. Don't know why. There was a time I wore makeup every day."

"Well, you look very nice, Tess," Kevin said again. "We appreciate you wanting to look your best for us. Don't we, Sara?"

"Yes, of course we do," Sara agreed. Her stomach was in knots as she thought about how they were going to deal with the latest situation.

"Tess, why don't you, Sara, and I go into the family room? We need to talk about our plans while you're staying with us."

"I haven't finished my coffee yet," Tess told him, stalling.

"That's all right. You can bring it with you. We're very informal around here."

"All right, if you're sure you don't mind." She sounded like a small child.

They went into the family room, where Kevin and Sara sat on the couch and Tess got comfortable in the big, overstuffed chair by the fireplace. She really liked sitting in that chair. It seemed to make her feel special.

Kevin cleared his throat. "Tess, I received a call from the sheriff's office this morning, and I need to talk to you about it." He saw Tess's face turn pale. Then she grabbed her chest.

"Are you all right?" Kevin asked, alarmed.

Sara jumped up and ran to Tess, kneeling down in front of her. She looked at her and knew right away. Tess was the older woman the sheriff talked about. The look in her eyes said it all.

"I know what you're going to tell me, Kevin. I can explain what happened, if you'll let me."

Kevin and Sara looked at each other, feeling concern for Tess. What kind of life had she had?

"This being such a small town, I should have known. You can't keep nothing quiet. Someone was bound to find out about those hoodlums and that I was with them." Her face showed defeat as she confessed.

"What in the world were you doing with people like that in the first place, Tess?" Kevin asked.

"Well now, it's hard to explain, but I hope you both will believe me when I tell you how it all happened. There's a reason I was in that stolen car with those horrible people.

"You see, it was late on Sunday night, and I was trying to find a warm place to spend the night out of the cold, you know? There weren't any rooms left at the women's shelter house, so I started looking around for anything I could crawl in or slide in to get out of the cold.

"I was walking down State Street near the bar district around midnight when I spotted a nice-looking car parked down one of the alleys between two of the bars. Now that I think about it, I should have been suspicious about a fancy car parked in that alley. But anyways, I was tired and cold and just wanted to get warm.

"I quietly walked up to the car, felt the hood to see if the car had been used recently, and since it was as cold as the night, I figured it was all right to peek inside. There was some empty beer cans and a few packs of cigarettes on the front seat but not much else. That back seat sure looked good and comfortable, so I checked to see if it was unlocked, and sure enough, it was. I climbed in, only planning on staying long enough to get warm, but I fell asleep almost the minute I lay down."

"Tess, didn't you think the owner would be coming back before too long?" Kevin asked. "And what town were you in when this all happened?"

"Nah, not on a Sunday. It was an off night, and the kind of people who visit the bars in that area of town are mostly regular patrons who stay until the wee hours of the morning, and don't never mind where this State Street is. That's not important right now."

"OK, so what happened next?"

"Well, I heard voices like they were coming from far away. I thought I was dreaming and didn't pay much attention at first. Next thing I hear was the radio blaring country music. That sure got me awake. I heard a man's voice say, 'We'd better get out of here before the police start looking for us.' Then a woman laughed and said, 'Let's see how fast this baby will go.' Then the man backed the car out of that alley so fast I almost fell off the seat. I held on tight and tried to be quiet so they wouldn't know I was in the back seat."

Tess started shaking, remembering that night.

"Kevin, maybe we should stop for now."

"No, Sara. I want to finish telling you what happened so I can have some peace with this," Tess insisted. "It's been bothering me ever since I opened my eyes and found myself lying on your couch. Remember, Sara, what you told me about God's answer to your prayer? You said you was to listen to my story."

"She's right, Kevin. I did tell her that. Go ahead; tell us the rest of what happened."

"Well, after we got out on the street, the man told the woman they couldn't go fast because they'd be taking a chance of getting noticed by the police. He said they were going to take all the back roads around town until they got far enough away from the bar, so no one would be looking for them. I tell you what—that woman sounded out of her head. She was a yelling and whooping it up. Now the man, he was at least acting like he had some sense about him.

"It must have been about a half hour or so when the man told his lady friend to check the back seat and see if there was any beer or food in the car. That's when my heart just about stopped. I figured my days was numbered because she sure enough was going to find something, and it wasn't going to be beer.

"Well, she leaned over and looked in the back and started yelling, 'God almighty, we got us an old lady back here, Tom!' She started to laugh as if it was funny, and I was ready to pass out."

"What happened then?" Kevin asked.

"The man, whose name was Tom, slammed on the brakes, and I fell right off that seat onto the floor. He turned around, yelling profanities at me and asking what I was doing back there.

"I was real scared by then. He was really angry, and I didn't know what he was capable of doing. I told him I was just an old homeless lady trying to stay warm and had crawled into the back seat of the car to get warm.

"He glared at me, and I could see he was trying to figure out whether I was telling the truth or not."

"You must have wondered what in the world was going to happen next!" Sara said.

"I sure did! I thought for sure I was a goner.

"You know, maybe there is a God because they decided to use me as a hostage in case they got stopped by the police. That's when I found out they had not only stolen the car but had robbed the bar where they had been drinking."

"How did you find that out, Tess?" Kevin asked.

Tess slowly told him. "The couple started fighting over what had happened. The woman said they were in enough trouble, having stolen the car, but because of Tom, they now were on the run for robbing the bar owner."

"What did they say next?" Sara asked, her hands clenched in her lap.

"Well, Tom told his girlfriend to get me out of the back seat and bring me up front, so the two of them could keep an eye on me. He stopped the car long enough for her to get out, grab me out of the back seat, and force me to sit with her in the passenger's seat. Thank God we were both on the thin side, so as to fit in that seat. She kept laughing as if it was all a big joke."

"About what time of the night was this?" Kevin continued questioning.

"Oh, I don't know … maybe around one thirty or two. It's hard to tell because I didn't know how long I'd slept before they came out of the bar. They talked the situation over for about fifteen minutes, then decided to keep on driving until they could figure out what to do with me when it got light. It must have been going on five o'clock when we came into Jonesboro. That's when we saw the gas station was open."

Sara interjected, "You must have been scared to death by then!"

"I sure was. That's when I came up with the idea to tell them I had to use the john. I figured maybe I could get a message to whoever was working in there."

"That was smart thinking!" Sara exclaimed.

"I thought so too, but it didn't work the way I planned. I didn't know the girlfriend had a gun until I was told if I tried to escape or caused trouble, she would shoot me."

"Oh my goodness, Tess," Sara said, looking at Kevin to see how he was reacting to Tess's story. His face turned pale when he realized Tess could have been killed.

"Scared isn't the half of it. After I found out she had a gun, I really did need to use the john." Tess grinned.

All three laughed, relaxing a bit from the stress of her story.

"Go on. What happened next?" Kevin asked.

"Well, me and the girlfriend went into the store and asked the clerk where the ladies' room was. He looked at us sort of funny, but I couldn't do or say anything 'cause that woman had me right in front of her, with the gun pushed in my back.

"The ladies' room was down a long narrow hallway, so I walked as slow as I could, hoping to come up with some way to get away from her. She pushed me real hard and told me I'd better hurry up, and if I tried anything, she'd shoot me. I'm telling you, I think she would have.

"After we got back to the car, Tom told me to get in the back and told the girlfriend to get in beside me. She didn't want to and started yelling and swearing at him. He told her if she knew what was good for her, she'd do it or else. The clerk heard the yelling and swearing and came to the door and looked out toward the car. They were so busy yelling at each other, they never saw him."

"God was looking out for you, Tess," said Sara.

"I think you're right. Anyhow, we got back in the car, and Tom took off, squealing tires as he drove out of there."

"Is that when Tom decided to take a side street through town?" Kevin continued to encourage Tess.

"Yeah, he figured since it was still early in the morning, the local police would start their early shift through town, not looking at cars on side streets. We were coming down your street, and for some strange reason, I decided to jump out of the car. I knew if I didn't, they'd end up killing me."

"That took a lot of courage, Tess!" Kevin looked at her with admiration.

"Well, Tom slowed down at the stop sign just there at the corner of your lawn, and that's when I jumped."

"You could have seriously hurt yourself," Sara told her.

"I know, but if your life is in danger, you do some ridiculous things. Anyway, after I jumped, that girlfriend of Tom's came after me, jumping on my back and beating my head on the ground."

Kevin and Sara said in unison, "How frightening!"

"I know! Then Tom yelled for her to stop and get back in the car. She did, and they took off like a … well, you know what I mean."

"I can't believe this was happening right here on our street." Kevin was amazed.

"I was starting to feel really bad, but I did get up and walked toward your front lawn. Then I sort of blacked out. I don't remember much after that. I guess the banging on my head made me pass out. The next thing I remember was Sara dragging me into your house."

Kevin and Sara said nothing, not knowing what to say.

"Are you all OK?" Tess asked.

"Uh, yes, we're fine. We're just stunned by what you've told us."

"But you do believe me, don't you?"

"Yes, of course we do. But I've got to report this to the local sheriff," Kevin said.

"I know. I sure hope that this God you both love and follow will find it in his heart to help me out of this mess. If it'll help me, I'll try even harder to understand the ways of your God."

"God always wants to help people, Tess. It's your heart that has to want it." Sara hoped she would believe her.

Kevin got up and went into his office to call the sheriff.

"Sara, I'm so scared!"

"I know you are, sweetie. Don't worry. It will work out. Just remember, you have Kevin and me on your side. What are you worried about the most?"

Sara was not prepared for her answer, and it showed on her face.

"It's the police looking into my past that worries me the most," Tess confessed.

"Why's that?" Sara asked.

"Because I don't want to be taken back to that place."

"What place are you talking about?"

"The place I ran away from."

Tess started crying uncontrollably, and Sara worried she might have a heart attack. "Tess, try not to think about that now. Let's just deal with one thing at a time."

"Sara, that prayer you prayed for me yesterday morning, could you do another one?"

Sara looked at her, surprised. "Of course I will. Is there something special you want me to say in this prayer?"

"Could you ask God to not let them send me back to that place and let me stay here with you and Kevin? You know that first prayer did the trick. Maybe it could work again."

Sara tried not to smile at Tess's request, not wanting to hurt her feelings. "I'll pray for you, Tess, but I can't make any promises. We'll have to wait and have faith that God's will will be what's best for you. Praying isn't like asking Santa for gifts. We have to be patient and wait for results or answers. Sometimes it's an answer we like, and sometimes we're not thrilled about it."

"OK, I'll try to wait and have faith. Is there anything special I need to do to get ready for this prayer?"

"Well, some people like to close their eyes and bow their heads. Some people like to get down on their knees in reverence to God, but it doesn't matter how you do it, as long as you're sincere."

"I think for now, until I get the hang of this prayer stuff, I'll just close my eyes and bow my head. I'm ready when you are. Let's do it!"

"Let's do it together."

Sara sat down beside Tess, taking her hands into her own. Closing her eyes, she began to pray.

"Dear God, I come to you in prayer for one of your troubled children who is in need of your love and guidance."

Tess sat quietly, holding Sara's hands … both children of God.

Chapter 7

Offices of the Ad Agency Conner Williams in New York City

Jonathan Farnsworth paced back and forth in front of his oversized office desk, waiting for the phone to ring. Almost two years had passed since his mother escaped from the Central Foothill's mental health facility, and his patience was running thin.

The lawyer he hired to find her after his father's death six months ago had finally come through with information that sounded promising.

His phone rang, and he quickly answered it.

"Hello, Jonathan Farnsworth."

"Mr. Farnsworth, this is Daniel Graves from Graves and Hunter. We've completed our follow-up on information we received yesterday about a woman who could possibly be your mother. The woman in question was involved in a situation where a robbery and murder took place in Zanesville, Ohio."

"I can't believe my mother could have done something as horrible as that, Mr. Graves. Are you sure this is a real lead, or are you just covering up another mistake? I told Mr. Hunter this is the last chance for your company to come through, so this had better be good."

"I understand, Mr. Farnsworth, and I also realize we haven't come through with all our promises, but I feel this could be the lead we need. It seems a woman matching your mother's description was seen with a younger woman in a gas station in Jonesboro, Ohio. One of our investigators got a call from an informant who lives in the Jonesboro area. He's been working for us for five years."

"So, you have confidence in his work?"

"We do. His information has always been right, and I don't have any reason to think otherwise with this investigation."

"Please forgive me for not feeling the same," Jonathan replied. "I don't know whether to be delighted or upset with this latest news about my mother. First you tell me she could be involved in a robbery and a murder, and now you're telling me she's been seen in Jonesboro. Do you realize how far Jonesboro is from Zanesville? How could she have possibly gotten that far?"

"Please, Mr. Farnsworth, let me finish with the information I have, and it should clear up some of the reasons for her being in Jonesboro."

"All right, Mr. Graves. Please continue."

"Thank you. I'll be as quick as I can. Our agent has contacts with many of the sheriff departments throughout Ohio, and, like I said, a report came in yesterday about this older woman who was seen in the company of two people thought to be involved with the robbery and murder in Zanesville. If possible, I'd like to meet with you in private to discuss this new lead. Are you available this afternoon or evening?"

"Yes, I am," Jonathan replied. "I appreciate your discretion about not using the phone to discuss this information. I wouldn't want it to get in the hands of the wrong people. Also, I apologize for my curtness. I've been frustrated with the slowness of this issue, and it's caused me to sound gruff. Could you meet me at my club in town around six o'clock? We could have dinner and discuss your findings."

"That's fine, Mr. Farnsworth. I'm free after five. What's the name of the club?"

"It's the Union 21 Club, next to the National Bank on Forty-Eighth Street."

"Yes, I know where that is. I'll see you at six."

Jonathan hung up and sat down in the plush wing-back chair, contemplating the latest update. *Well, Mother, it seems your luck has run out, and I'll finally get what's coming to me. And so will you.*

Smiling, he reached for a cigarette, his hand shaking. He supposed all the excitement about his mother was making him nervous, but after taking a deep draw on his cigarette, he instantly relaxed.

I need to calm down and get control of my emotions. This last year and a half of that old bat eluding me has affected my health. Last week, the doctor told me if I don't stop smoking and get more rest, I'm headed for a heart attack, just like my father. I'll work on that after I get her back where she belongs.

Jonathan took another drag on his cigarette and reached for the phone. The other line was answered after the first ring.

"Delilah, it's Jonathan. I have good news. The agency thinks they've found my mother."

"Oh my goodness! You must be beside yourself with joy! Where is she?"

"I was told she's in a small town in northern Ohio called Jonesboro, near Toledo. I can't tell you the details yet, but I had to let you know. Can we meet at our regular place around nine this evening?"

"Anything for you. I'll tell David I have a late meeting with a client. He never questions my schedule. I can't wait to see you and hear all about your good news."

"It sounds as if we'll finally be able to get on with our plans to be together. I can't tell you how much I want to have you all to myself."

"Keep that thought until I see you this evening. Love you."

"Love you too."

Jonathan arrived at the club early. He needed to swim to relax. His muscles were tight from stress. He could only imagine how this whole thing would work out for him. If the information Daniel Graves had was not correct, he didn't know if he could handle more disappointment about his mother.

After forty-five minutes of swimming, he felt relaxed, and his mood had improved. He climbed out of the pool and headed for the showers.

Jonathan Farnsworth kept his six-foot-four body in shape, working out four times a week at the gym conveniently located in his private club. Now in his midforties, he maintained his muscular body. He inherited his father's good looks and his mother's thick, wavy hair. The gray around his temples added to his good looks. He carried himself as a man who knew what he wanted and how to get it. Now if he could just get this issue with his mother back on track, the world was at his fingertips—and so was a life with Delilah.

Chapter 8

Before dialing the sheriff's office, Kevin took a few minutes to think about what he was going to say about Tess. He didn't want to say too much, but he knew he had to move ahead before the situation with Tess went any further. He was shocked to think he and Sara could be arrested for harboring a fugitive who was involved in a murder, robbery, and God knew what else.

"OK, I can do this," he muttered under his breath.

He reached for the phone and dialed the local sheriff's office. While he waited, he said a quick prayer, hoping it would help calm his nerves.

"Hello. Sheriff's department. This is Deputy Harris. How can I help you?"

Kevin's mouth was dry, and he couldn't say anything. Deputy Harris asked again.

"Sorry, I'm a bit nervous, and I couldn't speak for a moment. Uh, my name is Reverend Kevin Richardson, and I'm calling about a situation my wife and I have found ourselves in. I really need to speak to Sheriff Adams about this. Is he available?"

"Can you briefly explain the situation, so I can tell Sheriff Adams? It may be something I can help you with," Deputy Harris asked.

"I'd rather not. I need to speak personally with Sheriff Adams, if you don't mind."

"Of course, Pastor Richardson."

"Thank you."

When Sheriff Adams answered, Kevin began again. "Sheriff, this is Kevin Richardson, pastor at Trinity Lutheran Church. I have a situation that I need to speak to you about, but I'd rather it not be over the phone."

"This sounds serious if you can't talk about it over the phone."

"It's about those people at the gas station yesterday morning. You know—the ones who had an older woman with them, and she looked to be in trouble. Well, I have information about her and the couple she was with, but I can't tell you on the phone. Could you to come to the manse so we can talk in private?" Kevin's voice continued to shake as he shared the information.

"I can come this afternoon around two, if that works for you."

"Yes, that's fine, Sheriff. I will see you then."

"No problem."

Sheriff Adams hung up, wondering what this was all about. He knew Pastor Kevin was a well-liked man, but he also knew he had made a few enemies this past year. It seemed his work with the local citizens group against corrupt politicians hadn't sat well with some of his parishioners. *Mixing church and state was not a good idea, especially in this small town*, he thought as he popped another Tums. *Mental note: make a doctor's appointment for next week.*

⁓

Kevin entered the front room where Sara and Tess sat on the love seat. They both looked at him with fear in their eyes. He knew this was going to be hard, especially for Tess. He didn't want anything bad to happen to her, but the longer they kept this whole situation a secret, the worse it was going to get.

"Well," Sara said, "what did Sheriff Adams say?"

"I didn't tell him what it was about, only that it was a serious situation and we needed him to come to the manse."

"Did he seem surprised or curious or what?" Sarah asked, her voice louder than usual.

"He seemed curious but calm. He will stop by around two o'clock this afternoon. That gives us some time to work on our stories, making sure we all sound credible."

Suddenly, Tess jumped up and ran toward the stairs, startling Kevin and Sara. She was halfway up the stairs by the time they reached her.

"Stop, Tess!" Kevin yelled. "Don't move another step. Do you hear me?"

Hearing the tone of his voice, she knew he meant business. Slowly she turned around and sat down on the steps. "All right, Kevin, I'm listening." Her voice was strong, but her heart was beating a mile a minute.

"Come back down these stairs and help us figure out what we're going to tell Sheriff Adams. You can at least give Sara and me the courtesy of working with us, not against us. I'm sorry to sound so harsh, but we're putting our own lives in jeopardy to help you. Now come help us."

Tess stood up, straightened her shoulders, proudly returned to the front room, and sat regally on the love seat.

"You're right. You and Sara are just doing your best to make better choices than I've made. If it weren't for the two of you, I could be dead … or even worse, back at that place I ran away from."

Kevin and Sara wanted to ask about the place Tess kept mentioning, but they knew it would have to wait. Sheriff Adams's visit was top priority for now.

"I feel Sheriff Adams is a reasonable and honest man and will help your situation, not hinder it." Kevin looked at Sara and then Tess to see their reaction.

"I have to agree with Kevin, Tess. This is a small town, and everyone knows each other. You really can't hide much from them. If we tell Sheriff Adams the truth, I believe he will help us figure out what to do next. Eventually people are going to start talking and questioning what is going on with us and who you are."

"Tess, say something, will you?" Sara said, hoping the something would be helpful and not another roadblock.

Tess cleared her voice and looked at Sara, then at Kevin. "I agree with the two of you. Honesty seems to be the best solution for the mess I've made of my life, and now I've gotten the two of you involved. I've spent too much time running away from the past."

"That's wonderful!" Kevin said, relieved.

"But," Tess added, "I will only tell Sheriff Adams what I've already told the two of you, nothing more. I am not ready yet to tell you or anyone else about my past before I crawled into the back seat of that stolen car. If you can't accept my decision, then I'll leave now!"

Kevin and Sara looked at each other, trying to decide whether to do as she asked or tell her no. They both knew if they said no, she would be out of there—and out of their lives.

Sara started crying. Kevin looked at Tess with frustration. He knew how much Sara was starting to care about her. He hated to admit it, but he was growing fond of her too. This last demand, however, was almost too much to ask of either of them.

Kevin was the first to speak. "All right, Tess, we'll not pry into your past for now, but eventually we will. Can you accept that?"

"Yes, I can. All I ask is for the two of you to give me some time.

"All right then. I will tell you what you need to hear later. Now let's focus on what we're going to tell Sheriff Adams about this mess. I am wondering though … could we eat something first? I'm so hungry I could eat the rear end of an old horse."

Kevin and Sara laughed as the three of them headed for the kitchen.

Chapter 9

Daniel Graves entered the foyer of the exclusive Union 21 Club and walked directly to the large desk near the entrance.

"May I help you?" the beautiful receptionist asked.

"Yes. My name is Daniel Graves, and I'm here to see Jonathan Farnsworth. We have an appointment for dinner."

"Let me just check the dinner guest list, Mr. Graves. Yes, I see your name. If you'll follow me, please, I'll take you to the dining area."

The interior of the club had a definite masculine look. Lining the oak-paneled walls were large oil portraits of the many leaders since 1932. *So*, thought Daniel, *this is what you get when you're vice president of one of the largest ad agencies in Manhattan.*

"Here we are, Mr. Graves. Mr. Baird will escort you to Mr. Farnsworth's table. I do hope you enjoy your dinner."

"I'm sure I will," Daniel responded, then followed the waiter.

They approached the table where Jonathan Farnsworth sat. His back was facing away from the entrance, giving Daniel time for a quick assessment of the man.

"Mr. Farnsworth, this is Mr. Graves, your dinner guest."

"Thank you, Charles." Jonathan stood up and shook Daniel's hand warmly. "Please have a seat."

"Thank you." Daniel took the seat directly across from Jonathan. He wanted to be able to see his reaction when he shared his findings about his mother.

"Before we get into the information about my mother, I need a drink, and I hope you will join me."

"I would like that, and please call me Daniel."

"And you may call me Jonathan."

After the men ordered their drinks, Jonathan got down to business.

"Tell me, Daniel, how long have you worked with Timothy Hunter?"

"We've had our agency for almost ten years. He and I went to law school together and stayed friends afterwards. We started out as interns with prestigious law firms, but both of us became bored with corporate. That's when we came up with the idea of starting an investigative agency."

"I see," said Jonathan.

"We both enjoy a good mystery, especially the who and why of a situation. So here we are, nearly ten years later."

"How's that worked out?" Jonathan asked casually.

"Quite well. Tim has a knack for organization, and I have the people skills. We make a good team."

"Good to hear that. I do hope the information you have about my mother helps me find her and quickly. I don't know if you know this, but I think the stress of her escaping from the mental health facility caused my father to have his fatal heart attack. He felt responsible when she put herself in that place. She said it was necessary for her mental health. Anyway, it'll be a relief to have this all behind me so I can get Mother the help she needs."

"Here's a copy of the information we acquired from our informant. We trust him fully. In the report is the description the gas station attendant gave the local sheriff."

Jonathan glanced quickly at the information Daniel gave him.

"I'm still trying to find out what happened to her after she left the gas station," Daniel continued. "An APB was put out on the stolen car by the Zanesville police, but nothing so far from the Jonesboro sheriff's office."

"Is there a lot of farmland around Jonesboro?" Jonathan asked.

"I'm assuming there is. Why do you ask?"

"It makes it harder to track them. Trust me, I know. I grew up in a farming community. A person can get lost and not be found for days." Jonathan was obviously frustrated.

"Hopefully your mother isn't in any immediate danger."

"My mother can take care of herself."

"If they get desperate, they could use her as collateral. Let's hope not. Anyway, I think you'll find this information helpful."

Jonathan took the folder and quickly scanned through it. Days had passed since the clerk reported the two women. The likelihood of them still being in the area of Jonesboro was slim, and he wasn't even sure this woman was his mother.

"Daniel, this report shows you're not any closer to finding my mother than you were."

"If you'll notice, we've obtained permission from the owner of the gas station to view their surveillance tapes from that day. We have compared the picture you gave us with the image of the older woman from the gas station tape. The quality of the tape is poor, but one of our technicians was able to clear it up a bit, and here's what we saw."

Daniel removed the last page from the report in Jonathan's hand and showed him the copy of the image caught on the surveillance tape. The images of the woman on the surveillance tape and his mother were similar, but the one from the gas station showed a woman looking much older. For one thing, the color and length of her hair were different. The picture showed a woman who had long white hair, unkempt and pulled back into a ponytail. His mother's hair had always been short and well kept. The color was a soft light brown, and she wore it pulled away from her face, making her appear younger than her age. Jonathan studied the picture from the tape, but he wasn't convinced it was his mother.

"I just don't know what to think, Daniel. I can see some resemblance to my mother from this photo, but this woman looks much older … very thin and fragile."

"You have to understand, Jonathan, your mother has been on the run for almost two years. She most likely has been homeless for much of that time. Think about what it would be like not to have access to a bathroom and showers and the right kinds of food. She's not going to look like the woman who was well taken care of. I would like for you to sit down with me and view the actual tape. Maybe seeing the way this woman moves and her mannerisms will give you more confidence that this is your mother."

"You're right. If I can see the way the woman moves, it might help me decide if it's my mother."

"I could stop by your office sometime Friday morning, if that's good for you," Jonathan offered.

"How about ten? I'll make sure our technician is there to help clear up the video even more. I know it must be difficult for you right now, Jonathan. You were hoping the information I've found to be right on the nose, and it's not what you were expecting. You have to trust my instincts when I say I'm ninety-nine percent sure this is your mother. Go home and get some rest, and Friday we can work together to find her." Daniel hoped he sounded convincing.

"You're right. I did expect the information you found to be correct. It's just been so frustrating these past few weeks, hoping that this mess would finally be over. A good night's rest and another round of drinks will help me feel better, so let's order our dinner and just enjoy the evening."

"Sounds good to me," Daniel agreed.

"Charles, would you bring Mr. Graves and me another round of drinks? And we're ready to order."

"Of course, Mr. Farnsworth."

When the drinks arrived, Jonathan offered a toast for the success of the search for his mother. Daniel agreed, and the two of them turned to more pleasant topics while they waited for their dinner.

Chapter 10

New York City—Law Offices of O'Donnell, Young, and Murphy

"Good morning, Mr. Keith," Jennifer said as she walked into Brandon's office.

"Good morning, Ms. Spencer." Brandon smiled, revealing a perfect set of teeth. "What brings you to my office? Too much stress with O'Donnell?"

Jennifer smiled, taking the top file off the stack of files in her arms and dropping it on Brandon's desk.

"So, to whom do I owe this added work? As you can see, I'm up to my chin already with files to work on."

Jennifer looked at his desk. All she saw were three thin files. Everything else was a desk accessory, but she offered a sympathetic smile anyway.

"Mr. O'Donnell thought you might be able to finish up this missing person's case before the statute of limitations runs out. It looks like there are only three months left. Ross has been working on it for the past few months, but Mr. O'Donnell needs him on another case." Brandon smiled sardonically, then picked up the bulky dog-eared file.

"Thanks, Jennifer. You owe me."

"Hey, don't take it out on me; I'm just the messenger!"

"You're right. I'm sorry."

"Apology accepted." She smiled and headed back down the long corridor to her office.

Brandon had been with the firm less than two years. His father, also a lawyer, had helped him get this job. He knew it was good for his future to be willing to work on the less attractive cases, but he wanted to get his hands on a case that had some pizzazz, not the boring ones he'd been given so far.

He opened the file and looked at the information about the case. He was puzzled why a law firm would work on this kind of case. He'd ask Ross about it. They had been friends for years. Ross had worked for the law firm for almost eight years now and was experienced in many kinds of cases.

He figured he would see if Ross was available for dinner that night and ask him about the case. Jennifer said he had worked on it for three months, so he should have quite a bit of information.

Being the youngest member of the firm had its pros and cons. So far, he was treated fairly by the other members. Some would have said it was because of his father's influence, but he felt his hard work, no matter what the case, was the real reason.

Brandon was good-looking. His blond hair, blue eyes, and muscular body turned many heads. Even though he knew he was attractive, he never used it for personal gain. Instead, he was shy about his looks.

Brandon had been raised in a Christian home. His parents taught him that being a Christian was more than just attending church. It was being compassionate, loving, and committed to living the faith. It wasn't easy living those beliefs, especially when he was a teenager. Back then, he wanted to be like the popular kids.

He was deep in thought when his phone rang. "Good afternoon. This is Brandon Keith."

"Brandon, this is Chet O'Donnell. Did Ms. Spencer deliver the missing person's file to you?"

"Yes, sir, she did. I have it right in front of me and was just starting to go over the information. I was thinking of seeing if Ross would be available to discuss the case with me."

"Actually, I'd like to be the one to explain why our firm is handling a missing person's case. You see, I have a personal investment in it. Could you meet me this evening for dinner?"

"Uh, sure, Mr. O'Donnell, I can meet you this evening. Do you want to meet at the country club? I can let them know I'll be using our family's table."

"Why, thank you, Brandon. That's a wonderful idea. Would seven o'clock work?"

"That's fine with me. If you arrive before I do, Mr. O'Donnell, just let them know the reservation is for Keith."

"I will, and, Brandon, I look forward to talking to you this evening. It will give us an opportunity to catch up on how things are going for you at the firm. See you this evening at the club."

After hanging up, Brandon decided he'd better finish reading the file. He wanted Mr. O'Donnell to see he had done his homework with the case. It appeared this woman came from old money and had control over the inherited wealth. She had committed herself to a mental health facility nearly two years ago, feeling her mental health was fragile and she needed a rest.

Knowing her husband and son were planning to commit her, she decided she'd do it herself, before they did, hoping it would give her more control over her life. Then, six months later, she escaped and hadn't been found or heard from since. The police investigated the case for about six months, but without strong leads, they turned it over to the cold case department. After another six months, it was turned over to O'Donnell's law firm, where it had remained for some time. The file contained details about the investigation in the early months after she escaped. Her doctor was questioned on whose authority she was committed to Central Foothills Mental Health Facility in the first place, and he said she committed herself. Everything had been done legally. It appeared she'd signed the papers with no outward signs of pressure from her husband.

Her doctor said she told him she needed a place to rest and heal after difficulties in her personal life. When questioned six months later, he said he felt her husband was behind the committal. He also said he couldn't prove it, but after talking to her that first week, he was sure it hadn't been her idea. He even wondered if she thought her life was in danger if she didn't consent to the confinement.

Brandon was curious why this woman's name was blacked out in the file. Besides her name, the name of the family members and her physician were also blacked out, as if some kind of conspiracy was going on. He hoped he'd find the missing information when he had dinner with O'Donnell that evening.

Brandon decided to call Ross to see if they could meet for a drink that evening at the country club. Ross and his family were members too. He figured he could meet Ross around five thirty, quiz him about the case before having dinner with O'Donnell. He picked up the phone and dialed Ross's extension.

Ross answered, sounding preoccupied.

"Ross, it's Brandon."

"Hi, Brandon! How are you?"

"Great! Hey, I was wondering if you had time for a quick drink after work."

"This wouldn't have anything to do with the missing woman's file, would it?"

Brandon laughed. "How did you guess? You know me too well."

"I heard old man O'Donnell was going to give you that case and put me onto something more recent." Ross checked his calendar to see if he was free that evening.

"Brandon, you're in luck. I have free time until eight. Then I have another commitment."

"That's great—so drinks around five thirty?" Brandon said.

Ross wrote the time on his calendar. "Where did you say you wanted to meet?"

"I thought the club would be good, if that's all right with you?"

"Yeah, that's fine. See you at five thirty at the club."

"Sure thing, and thanks. I appreciate this. If O'Donnell sees I've done my homework on this case, he may consider giving me some real cases sooner than later."

"No problem," Ross said. "See you this evening."

Chapter 11

Kevin, Sara, and Tess jumped when the doorbell rang. They had just finished lunch and were sitting in the family room, going over what they were going to tell Sheriff Adams. They wanted to make sure it all sounded credible.

"Now Tess, let me and Sara do most of the talking in the beginning. We want Sheriff Adams to feel confident about our stories before he starts asking you questions. When he does ask what happened, make sure you have direct eye contact and keep your voice firm and confident."

"Give me some credit, Kevin. I wasn't born yesterday, you know. You have no idea what I've been through in my life. I know how to conduct myself in front of the law! Now, go answer the door."

Kevin went to answer the door, followed by Sara and Tess. When he opened the door, Sheriff Adams spoke first. "Kevin, nice to see you."

"It's nice to see you too, Sheriff. Please come in. You know Sara, and this is Tess, our—uh—our guest." Sheriff Adams noticed Kevin's nervousness.

"Sara, nice to see you again."

Sara smiled and shook his hand. He knew Sara from her work with the local Boys and Girls Club of America.

Next, Sheriff Adams looked at Tess, smiled, and extended his hand. Tess took it and smiled back.

"Tess, it's a pleasure to meet you. I don't think we've met before, but you do look familiar."

"No, Sheriff, we haven't met. I would have remembered."

She smiled and looked him straight in the eyes. Her piercing blue eyes cut right through him. He knew his work was cut out for him.

Sara led Sheriff Adams into the family room, with Tess and Kevin following. She offered him the chair directly across from the love seat where Kevin and Tess sat down. She took the chair near the fireplace. Tension among the three was obvious to the sheriff.

Kevin cleared his throat, hoping to calm his nerves. He began to explain why they wanted to speak to him there at the manse instead of over the phone.

"Sheriff Adams, Sara and I have found ourselves in a delicate situation with our guest, Tess. You see, she became our guest by— uh—showing up on our front lawn this past Monday. I wasn't home at the time, but Sara …

"Sara, maybe you should tell what happened." Kevin was so nervous his voice climbed an octave.

Sara glared at Kevin until his face turned red. Sheriff Adams saw his response, making Kevin even more embarrassed. Kevin offered Sara a helpful smile, but she wasn't having any of it.

"I suppose telling the truth is the best way to plow through this mess we seem to have found ourselves in," Sara said. "I just seem to get myself in situations all the time, and it appears I've done it again."

Sara's eyed teared up. Dean Adams noticed but tried not to let it show. What he knew about her, as well as Kevin, was that they both were good, caring folks who had done a lot for the community. He wanted to make everyone feel relaxed, but he also wanted them to understand he had a job to do. He needed to get to the bottom of the problem, which seemed to be the older woman sitting next to Kevin.

"Sara, it appears you and Kevin are having a tough time explaining what happened over the past few days. I want you to relax and tell me what this is all about. I promise I'll listen and not judge until I've heard all the facts. Then we can move on from there." He hoped he had made himself clear.

Sara took a deep breath and started again to tell what had happened on Monday.

"I had just gotten my coffee and sat down to look at the paper. Oh, before I go any further, when I got up that morning, I had a strange feeling that something unusual or strange was going to happen to me that day. I've been feeling a bit depressed lately and thought maybe that was all it was, but the feeling became even stronger after I got downstairs."

Sara glanced over at Kevin after she'd shared about being depressed. The look on his face told her he was shocked. She hadn't meant to reveal her depression—at least not this way—but it just came out.

"Anyway, I sat down with the paper, when suddenly, a strange premonition came over me. I almost spilled my coffee! I got up and walked over to the window by the front door. When I looked out, I saw a body lying on our front lawn!"

"I'm assuming this body was Tess. Is that right?" Sheriff Adams asked.

"Yes. The body was Tess," Sara replied.

"What did you do next?"

Sara told Sheriff Adams what happened after she found Tess and she tried to get Tess into the house.

"Did she respond to your offer of help?"

"Not at first."

Tess interrupted. "Sheriff Adams, let me just say that what Sara did and what Kevin and she have tried to do is help me get back on my feet. They're a sweet and caring young couple, and their only motive is to help me in any way they can. I do hope you are not going to interrogate them like some hardened criminals."

"That's not my intention," Sheriff Adams told Tess.

Tess continued. "I've tried to make them see it would have been better for them if I'd just left after that first night, but they were very firm about my staying on. Even after I told them how I came to be on their front lawn, they still were determined to help me with what we are calling my *situation.*

"Now, you've established how I came to be in their home. I would appreciate it if you let me tell the rest of this story. All I ask is you leave Kevin and Sara out of the interrogation for now."

Tess sat back on the love seat, folded her hands, and looked straight at Sheriff Adams. Her body language and the firmness in her voice said it all—she was not budging on her request.

"I see this is getting complicated. Tess, I'm not trying to interrogate Sara, as you said. I'm trying to establish a time frame and a reason for me to be here. I need all of you to tell me what is going on. That's it! That's all I'm out to do!"

Turning to Sara, the sheriff asked, "Do you want to continue with your story, or do you want Tess to step up to bat for now?"

He wanted to get either one or the other to get to the point of this mystery. He knew there was cause for concern, but at this point, he was not quite sure what that cause was.

"Sheriff," Sara said, "I'll let Tess tell her side of the story for now, but just let me finish up one more detail. After I got her in the house, she did come around and seemed to be aware of what was going on. Tess, I'm turning it over to you for now, but if I think you're not telling the story the way I saw it, I will let Sheriff Adams know. Is that all right, Sheriff?"

He looked at Sara, then Tess. He knew this older woman was sharp and seemed to handle herself quite well around authority, so he agreed to allow Tess to finish the story.

"All right, Tess, tell me what happened in your words … after Sara gets you on the couch."

Tess began to tell what happened, all the way up to the point where Kevin told her and Sara he had to call the sheriff's office, knowing they couldn't continue to keep her without contacting the authorities. Throughout Tess's story, Sara at times intervened with her point of view. When it came to the part of being logical about what to do with their situation, Kevin stepped in with his point of view.

With the story completed up to the present, Sheriff Adams now knew why he thought he'd seen Tess. He had seen her on the surveillance tapes that he and his deputy had viewed after being called by the gas station clerk.

The sheriff shared what he saw on the tapes and then waited for what seemed an eternity before he cleared his throat and began to tell all of them what he heard from their stories. "Kevin, I'm glad you called this morning. Sara, I do wish you had called the minute you found Tess. If you had, we could be further down the road on finding the couple who held Tess hostage. By waiting until now, these people are long gone out of the area."

The sheriff's stinging words hurt Sara, but she tried not to show it.

"What I need from you, Tess, is more detailed information about this Tom and his partner. We've already put out an APB on the vehicle and a description of the woman from the surveillance tape. The clerk couldn't see the man, so I need you to describe him for me. Can you do that, Tess?"

"Yes, I can. It's etched in my memory."

"I know this is disturbing to all of you, but the faster we act, the sooner we find those hoodlums. I'm angry about what happened to you, Tess. This shouldn't have happened in my town. I promised to keep the citizens of Jonesboro safe, and I plan on keeping that promise."

Tess looked at the sheriff. "It's not your fault, Sheriff. They probably didn't even know the name of this town when they drove through. Don't take it personally. You'll get them. I know you will!"

He saw sympathy in her eyes. Now, along with his officers, plus Tess, Sara, and Kevin, he could move forward, finding and apprehending the suspects.

"Sheriff, it would be an honor to give you a description of Tom and any other information you need to get those disgusting people off the streets. I'd be happy to come down to the station so your sketch artist can draw a picture of Tom from my description. I've watched cop shows, so I know how this works, though I never thought I'd be involved in one. It's been really stressful for me—and Kevin and Sara, too, but it's also brought some purpose back into my life. So, just say the word, and I'm with you all the way!"

"Tell you what. Let me make a couple of calls, and then we can set a time for you to come down to the station. Is that OK with you?"

"You just say when. I just want to put this all behind me and move on. Thank you for not asking me who I really am, at least for now. I promise, I'll tell all of you my story as soon as we get those disgusting people!"

"Thanks, Tess. I appreciate that."

Sheriff Adams stood up and walked with Kevin to the door. He told Kevin he would contact him later that day or first thing in the morning. A sense of relief flooded over Kevin as he returned to the family room.

"Well, I don't know about you," he said, "but I feel such a sense of relief." Sara and Tess agreed.

Tess made Sara and Kevin happy when she said, "You both have given me a lot to think about with this love and faith you have in God. I've started trusting the both of you, so I suppose I could put some trust in your God. That's the least I can do!"

"Let's celebrate!" Sara said, heading to the kitchen. "Who wants ice cream and cake?" Kevin and Tess followed her, both feeling as if a weight had been lifted off their shoulders.

Sheriff Adams went back to his office to make some calls about Tess and to find out when the sketch artist was available. He didn't want to put out the APB until he had a description of Tom. They found a name for the woman by matching her face from the surveillance tape with their list of felons. She already had a long rap sheet, showing petty crimes but nothing more serious. Being involved in a murder was a whole new ballgame. Most likely, she didn't pull the trigger, but she still could be considered an accessory to the crime.

The sheriff picked up the phone to call Travis Chandler, the department's sketch artist. He hoped Travis could meet with Tess that afternoon. He knew the chances of finding the two suspects were slim, since days had gone by. Tom had a gun, so he and his girlfriend were considered armed and dangerous. If Sara had called when she found Tess, he could have moved faster. It frustrated him that Sara's kindness most likely helped a murderer and his accomplice get away—at least out of Ohio.

The phone rang. Sheriff Adams answered quickly.

"Travis, this is Dean Adams. I need you to help with a case. Are you available later today?"

"Let me check. Yes, I could be at your office around five o'clock if that works."

"Great! I appreciate it. The person I want you to work with is an older lady. She's pretty feisty for her age and could be difficult, but you're one of the best with handling people. I feel confident you can get a likeness of the guy we're looking for. I'll get back to you about the time, if that's all right."

"Sure thing. No rush."

"Thanks, Travis."

Next, he dialed Kevin's office at the church. He wanted to talk to him without the ladies overhearing their conversation.

Kevin's secretary put him on hold, and choir music filled his ear. He hadn't been to church for a long time. This reconnecting could be God's way of getting through to him. He smiled as he imagined what God would say to him right now. "Dean, don't you think it's time for you to put me back in your life? It wasn't me who severed the relationship; it was you. I've never left you; I don't do that to my children. I know you still feel the pain of losing Josh. Losing a son is not easy. I know. I lost my only son too."

"Sheriff Adams. I didn't expect to hear from you so soon."

It took a few seconds for Dean Adams to respond to Kevin. A year ago, his son, Josh, was killed in a car accident. They say time heals the pain of loss, but to him, it felt like it happened yesterday.

"It doesn't always work out this fast, Kevin, but our sketch artist is available around five this afternoon if Tess feels up to it."

"I'll give Sara a call to see. We don't usually eat dinner until six thirty, so the time sounds good. How come you didn't just call the manse?"

"I wanted to talk about Tess without her knowing it was me on the phone. She seems very alert and curious, so I didn't want to risk her overhearing our conversation."

Kevin laughed. "Yes, she definitely is. Sara and I discovered that within hours of getting to know her."

"I imagine it's been a bit of a ride, working with her and knowing eventually you would have to contact us. I know Sara is feeling upset that I came down a little hard on her for not calling sooner. I'm sure you understand the situation we're in. The longer we wait for correct details about the couple Tess was with, the less likely that we'll find them, but you know that. Let's hope Tess can come through with describing Tom, so I can get that APB out this evening."

"I agree. Tess will give a thorough description of Tom. I'll call you back as soon as I can. Sara probably will come with her. They've become close in such a short time, but you saw that right away."

"Yes, I did. I think Sara's made a good impression on Tess too. It's obvious Tess doesn't trust people easily, probably because of what she's been through. We'll get to that eventually. For now, catching Tom and Sharon is our top priority. Call me as soon as you can if five works."

Dean hung up the phone and sat quietly, thinking about church. He used to be involved, but after Josh died, all he could think about was his anger at God. How could God have allowed this tragedy to happen? His wife, Joyce, and their daughter, Heather, continued to attend services. They tried to get him to go, but he asked them to not pressure him. He told them in time he would go back, but his anger continued to keep him away. After a while, they gave up trying. While they went to church, he stayed home puttering around the house. He had to admit, he still felt guilty for not attending church. *Maybe I'll talk to Kevin about my anger toward God*, he thought. *He seemed to be an understanding person. Anyway, I think it's time I got on with my life by accepting Josh's death. If Tess had the guts to come forward and help find the couple who could have killed her, then I ought to be able to face my anger.* The phone rang, and he automatically answered.

"Sheriff, it's Sara Richardson."

"Can Tess come in today at five to work with our sketch artist?"

"Yes, she's excited about it. She's like a kid going on a new adventure. I think she's enjoying all the attention."

"Well, it's probably been a while since anyone's given her much attention. It shouldn't take long. She's pretty sharp and appears to have a good memory."

"I agree. We'll be there around four forty-five, if that works."

"That's great. I'll make sure I leave my schedule open so I can show Tess around the precinct. I bet she'll enjoy that."

"I'm sure she will. We'll see you soon."

"Thanks, Sara."

Dean hung up the phone and turned his attention to the pile of paperwork on his desk. For the first time in months, he truly felt positive. His mood was lighter, and his heart less burdened. It puzzled him why, but he had to admit it felt good.

Sara called up the stairs to Tess. When she didn't get a response, she called again.

"I hear ya, Sara. I'll be there in a minute. I've got to get my new shoes on, and they're not cooperating. These new shoes are going to make my feet hurt all day."

Tess finally got them on, found the purse Sara bought her that held the twenty dollars Kevin had given her, and grabbed the blue sweater from the thrift shop. As she took one last glance at herself in the mirror, she was amazed to see how nice she looked. Her hair was all done up, she had on a touch of blush and lipstick, and the light gray dress Sara had chosen for her made her thin body look svelte. She might have been in her seventies, but she thought she looked exceptional!

"Sara, I'm on my way down," Tess yelled from the upstairs hallway. "Is there anything you need?"

"No, I'm fine. All I need is you."

Sara smiled, thinking how quickly this older woman had made

her life feel complete. *Complete* was the only word she could think of to describe how she'd felt since Tess showed up.

"I sure hope I look decent enough for those people down at the precinct," Tess said as she came down the stairs. "I hope they don't think I'm a criminal or something. When I was living out on the street, I was told I had shifty eyes—whatever that means. I suppose when I size someone up, I do glare a bit at them. I had to stay safe, you know. Some of those characters out there would just as soon steal you blind as help you out."

Sara was surprised and pleased to see Tess looking quite attractive in her new clothes. When Tess got to the bottom of the stairs, Sara took her arm and gave it a gentle squeeze. "What was that for?" Tess asked.

"Oh, I just wanted you to know how beautiful you look all dressed up and your hair in a French twist. No one would ever know that a few days ago you looked like the devil. Now look at you! You look sophisticated and lovely. I'm delighted to accompany you to our sheriff's office. Your carriage awaits, my lady."

Sara escorted Tess to the car, opened the door for her, and helped her get her seat belt buckled. She tried not to laugh when Tess, holding her head higher than usual, looked around the neighborhood like a queen surveying her kingdom. Maybe she and Kevin needed to pull back a little on showering Tess with so much attention. It could go to her head. *No, Sara thought, I could never see Tess doing that. She's just feeling special right now. She knows this most likely won't last.* Sara figured once the sheriff caught the couple who held Tess hostage, she would have to start telling them her story, and the jig would be up.

Sara found a parking spot near the front door of the precinct. On the way, Tess told her she was afraid they would keep her there and not let her go back to the manse. Sara assured her Sheriff Adams would never do that. He was a kind and caring person, looking out for her well-being. All he wanted her to do right now was describe this man named Tom.

"I suppose you're right. I just had a moment of panic. It never is a good thing if a homeless person ends up at a police station. The do-gooders try to find places for the homeless to stay and then try to get them help with local agencies, but sadly, most of us homeless just want to be left alone. Maybe a night in a homeless shelter is nice, and a hot meal helps too, but we just want to be on our own."

Sara looked at Tess with sad eyes. *It must be hard on her right now,* she thought, *coming down here and facing the law. She probably feels trapped, but at least she's willing to do this, knowing she risks opening herself up to questions that could lead to her real identity.* Sara needed to convince Tess that she and Kevin—and even Sheriff Adams—were there for her.

She held the door to the precinct open for Tess. Tess paused slightly, then walked in with shoulders straight and eyes forward. Her attention was focused on the officer standing behind the front desk. Sara followed Tess as they approached the officer. "Yes, ma'am, how can I help you?" the young officer asked.

"I'm here to see Sheriff Adams. If you would please let him know Tess is here as requested. I believe our appointment was for five o'clock, and I expect Sheriff Adams to be on time."

The young officer looked at Tess in surprise, then smiled. "I will do that right now, ma'am, and may I say, it's an honor to meet you. We here at the sheriff's department have heard of you and your bravery getting away from the people who held you hostage. The story goes you jumped out of the car when they stopped at a stop sign. I sure hope that's true because it's an amazing story. I'm not sure I would have had the courage to do that, considering the guy had a gun."

"Why, thank you. Yes, it's true. I did jump out of the back seat of the car. I was just lucky they didn't shoot me. Oh, this is Sara Richardson, Mr. ... I'm sorry, dear; I didn't get your name."

"I'm Deputy Harris, ma'am. Nice to meet you, Mrs. Richardson. I'll let Sheriff Adams know you folks are here. Just have a seat over there, and I'll be back in a jiffy."

"What a nice young man," Tess commented. "It appears his mother taught him some manners. Can't say that about a lot of young people today. They treat us older folks with distaste. Well, someday they will be old like me. I hope they get what's comin' to them in their older years!"

"Tess, that's not nice."

Sheriff Adams greeted the women. "Tess, Sara, glad you could make it this quickly. If we can get a good description of the two suspects, we can put out an APB this evening and hopefully get some leads on their whereabouts."

"Sheriff Adams, I'm glad to help you get those people! Who knows what they've done since they left Jonesboro. I have confidence in you and your officers to catch them. Now, where's this young man who's supposed to help by drawing a picture from my description? Times a-wasting!"

Sheriff Adams smiled, then picked up the phone. "Travis, I have Ms. Tess with me here in my office. Do you want me to bring her to your office or will you come here?"

"I'll come there, Sheriff. I'll be right there."

"Thanks, Travis."

"Travis is coming to my office, Tess. That way, Sara and I will be here to give you support. Describing a person for law enforcement can be a bit intimidating. I want to do everything I can to make you comfortable."

"Sheriff, I do appreciate your concern, but I'm fine. If there's one thing I'm good at, it's remembering people's faces. But it'll be a comfort to have the both of you here."

Before Sheriff Adams could say more, there was a knock on his office door. The sheriff told him to come on in.

Travis Chandler opened the door and entered. He was tall and lanky, with curly hair in need of a cut. He wore black-rim glasses, making him look older than he most likely was. He had an infectious smile revealing beautiful white teeth.

"Travis, this is Sara Richardson and her house guest, Tess. Where would you like to sit to do your work?"

"It's a pleasure to meet you, Tess, and you too, Sara." Travis extended his hand in greeting.

"If you don't mind, Sheriff, I would like to sit at your desk, so I can have a place to draw comfortably. It also helps to see Tess better."

"That's fine. I'll sit here next to Sara. Tess, just relax and tell Travis everything you remember about Tom. He'll prompt you with questions to help him draw the face. Sometimes it helps if the witness closes their eyes to get a clearer picture. If you need to stop for any reason, just tell us."

"I will if I need to, but I won't. I can see his face clearly whether my eyes are closed or open. I don't think I'll ever forget that face."

"All right, Tess, whenever you're ready," Travis said. "It usually helps to start with questions I think are easy, like what was the shape of his face? Was it round? Square? Oval? Was his jaw line distinctive—wide or angled?"

"His face was square and broad," Tess said. "His jaw was firm, and he had a cleft in his chin. I couldn't see much of his teeth 'cause he didn't smile or nothing. But I saw his face enough from the rearview mirror, so I could tell he had a wide mouth with a small upper lip and a fuller bottom lip. His nose was straight and had a bump in the middle. It looked like it may have been broken once. It leaned to one side, if that makes much sense?"

"Yes, it does." Travis smiled and told her she was doing great. "Now, what about his complexion? Was he fair, or dark, or was his complexion ruddy?"

"His skin was pale and pockmarked, as if he suffered acne in his teens. He had a large mole underneath his right eye. He didn't have much facial hair, but he had a three- or four-day-old beard—light brown. His eyes were large and round and close together. His eyebrows were dark and bushy but straight across at the top and angled down toward his nose. The color of his eyes was dark brown. They were so dark you couldn't see his pupils. They also were cold and mean-looking, especially when he looked at me. I can't say how tall he was because he never left the car while I was with them. He sat tall in the seat and had the seat pushed back, so I would say he was at least six feet or taller. His hair was long and stringy; the color reminded me of mud! Anyway, that's as much as I can say to give you a picture of him."

"Tess, that was fantastic!" Travis said. "Give me a few minutes to smooth out the details, and I'll let you see if what I've drawn looks like this man named Tom."

Sheriff Adams got up and asked if he could get the ladies something to drink.

"A good shot of whiskey would do the trick for me," Tess said, grinning. She knew that wasn't going to happen, but she said it anyway.

Sheriff Adams laughed. "Tess, you are such an amazing woman. You just described a man who nearly killed you, and here you are making jokes."

"Did you think I was kidding, Sheriff? I'm serious about that drink. But if I can't have whiskey, I'll take a root beer, if you have it."

Dean Adams laughed again, shaking his head. After getting everyone's drink orders, he headed down the hall to the break room.

"Glad I could make the sheriff happy." Tess grinned from ear to ear. "I guess this place doesn't give people much to laugh about. I'll just have to come by for a visit now and then to keep the sheriff happy."

"Tess, I've finished the drawing. What do you think? Does this look like Tom?"

"That's him! That's him, Travis! You got that picture from what I told you? I can't believe it!"

As Tess gazed at the drawing, a chill ran down her back. The fear she had when she was discovered in the back seat of the stolen car came rushing back as if she were living the experience all over again.

"Sara, can we go now? I'm not feeling too good. I'd like to go back to the house and lie down, if you don't mind."

"Of course, Tess. We can leave as soon as Sheriff Adams comes back. Thinking about this man has upset you. I should have told the sheriff we would do this drawing thing tomorrow. You're just too tired from what you've been through these past few days."

"I think you're right, Sara. I have to admit I'm feeling mighty tired right now. A rest will do me good."

Sheriff Adams came back with the drinks. The moment he saw the look on Tess's face, he knew something had happened. "Here's your root beer, Tess. Are you all right? Travis, what happened?"

"She was fine until I showed her this drawing."

"Is that true, Tess?"

"Well, at first I was excited because Travis got the picture right on the nose. Then, all of a sudden, I felt cold and frightened to death, as if Tom was sitting right across from me. That's how good Travis's drawing is. I never thought about how this whole thing has scared me."

"I'm sorry. I've pushed you too hard. It's my fault, Tess," Sheriff Adams told Tess.

"Now, Sheriff, don't you go making yourself feel bad. It's not your fault. I was in the wrong place at the wrong time. Now that I've told you what just happened, I feel much better."

"Do you still want to leave, Tess?" Sara asked.

"I suppose I could stay long enough to drink that icy root beer. I wouldn't want it to go to waste now, would I?"

They laughed at Tess.

While she drank her root beer and talked to Travis, Sheriff Adams motioned for Sara to follow him out into the hallway.

"I think Tess needs to pull back a little on thinking about what's she's been through. Maybe you and Kevin can find something for her to do that will take her mind off all this. I know it's been hard on you."

"You're right. I do think she needs a break. I'll talk to Kevin after dinner tonight and see what we can do to give her either a change of scenery or just an activity that will relax her."

Sheriff Adams and Sara came back into the office just in time to hear the end of a joke Tess had told Travis. They were laughing so hard they didn't notice them come into the room. When they did, they both looked a little sheepish.

"What's so funny, you two?" Dean asked.

"Oh, Tess was telling me a joke she heard from a homeless guy she knows."

"Tess, why don't you share it with me and Sheriff Adams?" Sara suggested.

"Uh, I don't think that would be a good idea," Travis said, smiling uncomfortably.

"Why not?"

Tess looked at Sara. "Sara, you're such a sweet and pure young lady. I don't think this kind of joke would be proper for you. So, if you don't mind, I'd rather not."

Sara looked at Tess, then back to Travis, who was still smiling and holding back a snicker. She said, "I know you think I haven't heard any off-color jokes before, but I have. For the sake of keeping this visit respectable, I will not push the issue. On that note, it's time to leave, don't you think, Sheriff?"

Dean smiled, agreeing. He looked at Tess and could see she was a little uncomfortable, but she agreed.

"Tess, thanks again for coming down and helping us out. We have enough information now to put out an APB and check to see if this Tom might have a record already. He most likely does, but until we find that out, this picture is all we have. If you think of any other relevant information, please let me know."

"I sure will, Sheriff, and thanks for the root beer. You and I will have to go out for a real beer sometime. You, too, Travis, but we'll leave Kevin and Sara at home. We wouldn't want them to get in trouble with their church folks, would we?"

Travis and Sheriff Adams laughed but stopped when they saw the look on Sara's face. They could tell she wasn't too happy with Tess right then.

"Thank you, Sheriff, for your hospitality. Travis, thank you for helping Tess with her description of Tom. Now, if you will excuse us, Sheriff?" With that, Sara and Tess got up quickly and headed for the door.

Tess knew she was in trouble for saying what she did to Travis and the sheriff. Sometimes her mouth got her in trouble.

Sara helped her get in the car and buckle up. Then she slid into the driver's seat and started the car. She slowly pulled out into traffic, all without saying a word.

Tess broke the silence. "I know you're upset with me for what I said back there at the precinct. It was unacceptable, and I'm truly sorry. Sometimes I don't know what gets into me with my mouth. I suppose I was just glad to get that mess with describing Tom out of the way, and I just let loose by flapping my lips. Would you please accept my apology?"

Sara was upset, but after Tess tried so hard to make amends, she couldn't stay angry. To be honest, Tess was right about the church members being upset if they found Kevin and her in a bar having a cold one.

"I forgive you for what you said. It did embarrass me, but most of it was true—what you said about our church members. There are times when I get weary over worrying what the church members think about what Kevin and I do in public. Having you say it makes it all too true. But next time, please think before you speak."

"I will! I'm glad you have such a forgiving heart! You are truly a good example of what you Christians call a witness for your God. Thank you kindly for your forgiveness!"

"You are welcome. Since you think highly of the Christian way of forgiving, you'll have an opportunity this Sunday to worship with others who share my belief of forgiveness. Services start at eleven o'clock sharp, and you and I will be sitting in the third row from the front of the church. Now, let's stop by the bakery and take home a nice apple pie."

Chapter 12

Jonathan stayed in bed longer than normal, thinking about the information from the meeting he had with Daniel and his technician the day before. His impatience was growing to find his mother. If he wanted to get control of her wealth, he needed to move forward—and quickly. He wanted to put the old bat back in the mental health facility so he could keep an eye on her … or maybe have her disappear for good. Since she ran away and most likely became homeless, it should be a breeze to have her declared incompetent. The doctor who signed her in died recently. With him out of the way, and for the right price, he'd find another doctor who would make sure his mother was certified incompetent!

Jonathan sat up and stretched his arms. He rotated each shoulder back and forth before standing up. He felt good for a change, but he had been waking up stiff and sore in his neck and shoulders. He supposed it wouldn't hurt to go see his doctor. He had always been healthy. Working out as often as he did kept him lean and agile. He supposed being in his late forties brought on a few changes, but he was up to the challenge.

The phone next to his bed rang; he reached and answered it. "Sweetheart, it's me."

"Delilah, what a pleasant surprise! I thought I wouldn't hear from you for a few weeks. Didn't you say you were going with David to his convention in Vegas?"

"Yes, I did, but he decided he didn't want me to go. I'm sure the reason is his gambling. If he thinks I don't know about his gambling debts, he's wrong. But enough about David. How are you?"

"I'm in a bad mood this morning. I woke up thinking about whether the woman I saw on the surveillance tape was really my mother. I must confess, it's possible. The woman on the video looked older and very thin, but the way she walked and held her head is exactly like my mother. Mother always did think highly of herself. You would think being homeless and who knows what else she's gone through would bring her down a few notches. Anyway, I've got to move on this information as quickly as possible. I'll talk to you later today. Hopefully, I'll have more to tell you when we meet this evening."

"Can't wait to see you," Delilah purred into the phone before hanging up.

After talking to Delilah, he looked for the number for the sheriff's office in Wood County. He knew from the information Daniel had given him, the surveillance tape from the gas station was in the hands of the Wood County Sheriff's Department.

It seemed the case was being investigated by Sheriff Dean Adams. Sheriff Adams had been in the department for over twenty years and sheriff for ten. He was well liked and had a good track record for solving the local petty crimes typical of small towns everywhere.

Jonathan dialed the number.

"Sheriff's office. Deputy Harris."

"Good morning, Deputy Harris. I would like to speak to the person in charge of the case involving an older woman who was involved in a possible hostage situation. I heard through a friend of mine that the woman in question is hiding her identity. I'm calling on behalf of a client who thinks he can help clear up who this woman really is."

"What did you say your name was, sir?"

"I didn't. I'm keeping my identity unknown for now. My client doesn't want to get involved any further if the woman in question is not who he thinks she is."

"Excuse me. I'm putting you on hold while I see if Sheriff Adams can speak to you."

"Thank you," Jonathan replied. He could imagine this small-town law officer trying to figure out how to handle the situation. *This is fun*, Jonathan thought as he waited for the sheriff.

"This is Sheriff Adams. My deputy tells me you may have some information about the woman who may have been involved in a hostage situation. Is that correct?"

"Yes, Sheriff Adams, that's correct. I have a client who wishes to remain anonymous for the time being, but he thinks this woman might be his mother. He wants to make sure before he reveals who he is."

"And my deputy tells me you wish to stay anonymous also. I'm assuming it's for the same reason. Is that true?"

"Yes, that's correct. If that's a problem, then I'll have to find out the identity of the woman in a different way."

Sheriff Adams became angry and said, "First of all, I don't appreciate the way you're trying to get information about the woman, but I have to admit, we'd like to know her identity. I've not pushed the issue so far about who she really is. She's been through a lot lately. Let me think about this and get back to you. How can I contact you?"

"I'll contact you, Sheriff. Just let me know when."

"All right. Give me until Monday; I'm off tomorrow. Hopefully we can work this out. I'm as interested as you and your client are as to her identity. Just so you know, we may be a small town and a small sheriff's department, but we're not backwoods either. So, I'm putting you on alert. Do we understand each other?"

"Yes, Sheriff, we do. I'll be talking to you again." Jonathan hung up the phone and smiled, knowing he had the sheriff at a disadvantage. The old saying, curiosity killed the cat, seemed to be true of Sheriff Adams. All Jonathan had to do was wait. *Mother*, he thought, *this better be you! If not, when I do find you, I'm putting you away for the rest of your life!*

Chapter 13

Brandon arrived at the country club before Ross and found a seat near the club entrance. He enjoyed watching people. The way they walked, talked, and dressed and their facial expressions said something about them. He was thinking about that when Ross arrived.

"How long you been here, buddy?"

"About thirty minutes," Brandon replied.

"What's the matter with you?" Ross asked.

"Sorry. I guess I'm just frustrated about this cold case O'Donnell put on me. I feel more like a detective than a lawyer."

"Let's get a drink, Detective Keith." Ross laughed. "It sounds like you need it more than me."

"You're right about that. I've read all the information so far on this missing woman, whatever her name is. O'Donnell said you've had it for a few months."

"Yeah, that's right."

"Why so much interest in an old lady escaping from a mental health facility?" Brandon asked.

"I know," Ross agreed. "I thought the same thing when O'Donnell gave it to me."

Brandon was acting as if this was a cloak-and-dagger case. Ross only saw it as an old lady smart enough to get out of the loony bin and live her life the way she wanted.

"I think there's more to this case than meets the eye," Brandon replied.

"There is," Ross agreed. "Yesterday afternoon, I overheard O'Donnell telling someone on the phone that this woman's father and his grandfather had been close friends during their childhood. It seems her family's money is the main reason she entered the mental health facility. That information was missing from the police report."

"Did he say anything else?" Brandon asked.

"Yeah, things like her marriage was a mess, and her son wanted her in a mental health facility. He thought it would be good for her. He also knew she had recently found out about an affair his father had with the wife of a prominent pillar of the community, sending her into a deep depression. Some of this is in the file."

"Wow!" said Brandon. "That's a lot to take in."

"Do you think her son would do anything to hurt her?" Brandon asked.

"People do terrible things for money," Ross replied. "She could be in danger."

"That must be why O'Donnell is so interested in finding her—to protect her," Brandon said. "Poor old lady."

"She must have thought her son was trying to get control of her money. This case is turning out to be better than we thought, and you're in charge. What do you think?"

Brandon laughed. "I'm pumped!" he said.

Ross laughed at his enthusiasm. "So, your theory of a cloak-and-dagger case is valid. Just don't let O'Donnell know I overheard his conversation yesterday."

"I promise, I won't," Brandon reassured his friend.

"I'll tell you one thing; I'd sure like to know who he was talking to." Ross said. "You've always been a guy who likes intriguing cases. Anyway, have a nice dinner with dear old Chet, and act surprised when he tells you everything I just told you."

Chapter 14

Tess sat on the edge of her bed, thinking about what was ahead of her in less than an hour. *Today is Sunday morning, and I must go through with attending church. It isn't a choice; it is a commitment,* she mused. Many years had passed since she'd been inside a church. The last time was to attend her father's funeral.

He and her mother had been members of a Methodist church in Zanesville, but in their later years, they only attended for special occasions, such as Christmas and Easter. Now here she was being pressured to go. There was a knock on her door. It was Sara.

"Come in," Tess said, trying to control the fear in her voice.

"Are you about ready?"

"I suppose I'm as ready as I'll ever be," Tess replied. "I have to tell you I'm really nervous."

"Why on earth would you be nervous? These are just people like you and me. There may be a few who are pains in the butt, but most are caring, loving folks."

"But my life hasn't been lived the way you and Kevin have lived yours. I'm not sure God wants me to be there, considering how selfish I've been. When I was younger, I put my own needs above everyone else. From your generation's lingo, I suppose you could say I was a diva."

"I don't see you as a diva, Tess."

"Well, I was. After I got older and my life turned sour, I saw how I'd wasted my life. I didn't show love, and at times I was even cruel to others. I tell you, these past two years have made me realize I'm not worth the ground I stand on!"

"Oh, Tess!" Sara hugged her tight. "God doesn't punish us by keeping us away from him. He does the opposite; he draws us to him. We're the ones who make our relationship with him difficult. Just let God take you by the hand and lead you back to him. Don't fight it! Just go in with a heart in need of healing."

When she let go of Tess, she saw tears streaming down her wrinkled cheeks, dropping quietly onto her new dress. Sara, deeply touched, saw Tess for a change, not cocky and controlling. She knew she'd have to be extra gentle to help her through this unsettling journey.

"Let's pray a very quick prayer for both of us. Is that all right with you?"

"I would appreciate a prayer right now. These prayers have been doing fine so far, so I think another fix would help me."

Taking Tess's hands, Sara smiled and began to pray. "Dear Father, I ask that you help Tess conquer her fear of rejection by you and the folks she'll meet this morning. Allow me to be the one who has the honor of leading her back to you. May her heart become healed from the pain and loneliness she's lived these many years, and may she continue to take a step closer to you each day. In Christ Jesus's name, amen."

Tess looked at Sara, and for the first time in more years than she could think about, she felt peace coming from inside her heart. The loneliness and anguish she'd lived with for so long seemed to have left. She didn't know what had happened, but whatever it was, it made her happy.

Sara hugged her once more and then stood up. "Now, finish getting ready, and meet me downstairs in about five minutes."

"Will do."

Tess heard Sara singing softly as she headed downstairs.

"OK. God, the show is about to start, and I'm ready if you are. Just help me keep this feeling through the whole service. After that, well, I'll leave that up to you. Until then, I'm going to saddle up; it could be a bumpy ride!"

Tess left her room, smiling from ear to ear. She, too, started singing on her way downstairs, but her song most likely couldn't be sung in church. That made her smile even more.

∞

Sara and Tess entered the church through a side door. Sara knew it was difficult enough for Tess to attend her first church service in years. *Why make it harder by entering through the front door?* she reasoned.

The majority of church attenders were arriving, and Sara knew she'd have to introduce Tess. She could imagine Tess turning on her heels and walking or running for the nearest exit.

"Sara, I don't think I can do this. I really don't think I can!"

"Yes, you can! Take a deep breath and follow me. Don't look anywhere except at my back. OK?"

"OK."

They entered the sanctuary and headed to the third row from the front, where Sara usually sat. She made her way into the pew first; Tess sat next to the aisle. After they were seated, the organ prelude began. Sara reached over and took Tess's hand and gave it a squeeze. After a few minutes, she looked at Tess out of the corner of her eye and was surprised to see her smiling.

It appeared Tess enjoyed organ music. Who would have thought she even remembered hearing an organ? That's when she realized Tess's past must have included some cultural experiences.

After the prelude, Kevin came to the lectern to welcome everyone. He knew he had to make a reference to Tess, or he would be confronted by members about their visitor. "Good morning, everyone!"

"Good morning, Pastor Kevin," the congregation responded.

"I'm sure most of you are wondering about the lovely lady sitting with Sara this morning. Sara and I are thrilled and pleased to have Tess as a house guest for the next few months. Tess needed a place to stay, due to a family situation, so Sara and I jumped at the opportunity to offer her a temporary home. I hope you will greet her warmly after church, allowing her to keep her journey personal. Please let her know she is welcome to our church family."

You could have heard a pin drop after Kevin explained Tess's situation. He looked at Sara for support, and she responded quickly, jumping to her feet, turning to the congregation, and, in her best and sweetest voice saying, "I'm so glad Kevin was honest about our guest. If there's one positive thing I can say about our church family here at Trinity, it's the love and support you give to Kevin and me and to each other. God sent Tess to us for a reason, and for that I am thankful."

Sara sat down.

"Let us now draw our hearts together in prayer."

While Kevin gave the pastoral prayer, Sara took a quick look at Tess to see how she was holding up. She looked so fragile sitting there with her head bowed and her eyes closed. Sara was renewed again, knowing God had brought Tess into their lives for a reason. She hoped in time the reason would be revealed.

Chapter 15

Dean didn't sleep well Saturday night. He kept thinking about the man who called and wouldn't identify himself. The caller hadn't stayed on the line long enough for a trace … most likely using a burner phone.

He slept better Sunday night, but the weekend hadn't given him an answer as to what to do about Tess. Before talking to the stranger, he wanted to talk to her.

He dialed the manse, hoping to see Tess that morning. Earlier, he'd called the office and told Officer Harris if the man from Saturday called back, he was out on police business and would be back around noon. This would give him a few hours to figure out what he was going to say.

"Good morning!"

"Kevin, good morning. This is Sheriff Adams. Sorry to call so early, but I need to speak to Tess as soon as possible. A situation came up, and it involves the possibility of revealing Tess's true identify. I need you and Sara to convince Tess to give me more information about who she is. If she stalls, I'm not sure I can protect her."

"This is not what I wanted to hear first thing on a Monday," Kevin responded. "What's the situation?"

"A man called me on Saturday, saying he represents a client who thinks he may know who Tess is. He wouldn't give me his name or the name of his client. I stalled him until today, but I have to tell him something."

"This doesn't sound good. What do you want us to do?"

"I need you and Sara to tell Tess I'm on the way over, and she needs to help me find a way to give enough information to this man to get him off her trail. If she doesn't cooperate, she could be headed back to whatever it was that made her homeless."

"I'll talk to Sara right now, and the two of us will confront Tess about this. Can you be here in an hour?"

"Yes, I can do that. I'm willing to keep Tess safe, but the law doesn't allow me to lie. She needs to know that. Be sure and tell her, so she'll see how serious this is. If this man identifies her as his relative, then she is most likely his mother."

"If true, I'll move forward by digging into the missing persons files from two years ago. Isn't that about how long Tess has been on the streets?"

"Yes, that's what she told Sara."

"All right then. I'll be there around nine o'clock."

"We'll be ready, but I don't know about Tess. This is going to frighten her."

"I know, but it's the only way I can help her."

"I understand. See you in an hour."

Dean hung up, realizing he couldn't do this by himself. For the first time in over a year, he needed to pray. Prayer hadn't helped in his grief over losing Josh, but he was willing to give it another chance. His wife had left for work, and his daughter was in school, so he was alone in the house. Without hesitation, he got on his knees and started to pray. "God, I'm sorry I haven't spoken to you in a while. If it's true you know my heart and my thoughts, then I don't have to share my concern for Tess with you. I just need to ask you to give me strength and wisdom to do what's best for her. I'm willing to stretch the law as far as I can, but to protect her and myself, I have to be careful. Please be with me. I pray this in the name Jesus Christ. Amen."

He got up feeling calmer. Right then, he knew God was going to help him handle Tess's situation—and work on his faith. He decided the time had come to go back to church. Kevin and Sara had made a huge impact on his understanding of Christian love in such a short time. Hopefully, Joyce and Heather would be willing to change churches. But whatever they decided, he was sticking with his decision.

Dean whistled as he made himself breakfast. He admitted it felt good to reconnect with God. Life was starting to change and in a positive way.

✑

Kevin, still holding the phone, tried to understand the conversation he'd just had with Dean about Tess. How in the world would he and Sara be able to convince her to tell them who she really was?

There were two ways it could go. One, she would share her story. Two, she would run away again. Either way, it was going to be intense. He went to find Sara to tell her that Sheriff Adams was coming by in less than an hour.

He found her in the kitchen, cleaning up from breakfast. He came up behind her, put his arms around her waist, and kissed the back of her neck. Smiling, she turned, put her arms around his neck, and kissed him warmly. They stood wrapped in each other's arms, almost making him forget what he had to tell her.

"Kevin, what's gotten into you this morning?" Sara laughed. "You're being quite affectionate. Don't get me wrong—I like it, but are you trying to distract me?"

When she saw the look on his face, she knew she was right. Something was going on. "What's the matter? You have that look you get when someone's hurt or upset. What is it?"

He let go of her and stepped back. "Sheriff Adams called. He's coming here in less than an hour to talk to Tess."

"Why today and why so early?" Sara asked. "Oh, no! Something has happened! What is it? Is it about the people Tess was with before she got away?"

"No, it's not about them; it's about Tess and the surveillance tape. Sheriff Adams got a call from a man saying he represented a client who thinks he knows who Tess is. The man refused to name his client. He wouldn't even tell the sheriff his name. This happened on Saturday, but Sheriff Adams stalled him until today. He has to tell him something soon."

"Well, what does he expect us to do? We don't have any information about Tess. I thought he wasn't going to push the issue until after this whole thing with the kidnappers was over. Now you're saying we have to get Tess to fess up on who she really is—today?"

"That's what he wants. He's asked us to tell her what she has to do before he gets here. He didn't say what will happen if she decides not to tell him, but I'm sure it could involve legal stuff or even jail. I just don't know the law enough."

"What are we going to do? You know she most likely will leave at the first opportunity. If she does, that means this man who's asking about her will find her on his own, and who knows what he'll do to her."

"I know, but Tess is smart, and we've won her trust. Let's just go ahead and tell her. Then we'll hope for the best."

Kevin went to the stairway and called up to Tess. She came and stood at the top, looking down. "What do you want?"

"Tess, we need to talk to you. Can you come down please?"

"Sure, I'll be right down." She paused, then looked at Kevin. "Is something wrong? You have that preacher look."

"No, I'm fine. But we have a situation that only you can solve, so come down as quickly as you can."

"Let me just finish dressing, and I'll be down in five minutes."

Kevin and Sara knew they had their work cut out for them. They decided to sit at the kitchen table in a nonthreatening environment.

Knowing how much Tess loved her coffee, Sara put on a fresh pot while they waited.

After what seemed an eternity, Tess came into the kitchen, looking happy and relaxed. Going to church and having so many people welcome her had apparently made a positive impression on her.

"All righty, you two, what's up? Kevin, you sounded pretty worked up over something, so go ahead come out with it."

Kevin cleared his voice. "Sara, would you bring me and Tess a cup of coffee please?"

"Of course. I'd be happy to."

"Do we still have coffee cake left from yesterday?" he asked. "I'd love to have a slice. How about you, Tess?"

"Oh, that sure was good cake! I'd like a piece, but you come sit down, Sara, and I'll get it for us. Both of you need to let me do some things around here. You're doing too much for me."

"It's all right, Tess. I can get it. It won't take but a minute. I'll even put it in the microwave and heat it up a little. You can put some butter or jam on it."

"Boy that sounds good." Tess already was licking her lips, thinking about the warm coffee cake slathered with butter and jam.

Kevin and Sara were doing everything they could to get her happy before lowering the boom on their news.

Sara brought over three big pieces of coffee cake to the table. She got the butter and strawberry jam from the refrigerator and sat down. Her stomach was in knots.

"Tess, Sheriff Adams is coming over in a few minutes to talk to you. He told me what the visit was about. He asked that Sara and I tell you why he's coming before he gets here."

"I think I know what this is about," Tess said, her voice shaking. "I knew it was going to happen sooner or later, but I hoped later. Does this have anything to do with that surveillance tape?"

"Yes, it does, but the sheriff wants to talk to you about it."

"I understand."

"In the meantime, is there anything we can do before he gets here? And just for the record, you are like family. Please remember that."

Leaving her coffee cake untouched, Tess got up and said, "If you don't mind, I need some time to figure out what I'm going to say. I'd like to go to my room and think about it." Tess saw the concern on both Kevin's and Sara's faces. "Now don't you both look at me that way! I'm not about to leave! Think about it, you two. There's no back stairway to get out of this place, and I'm not about to climb out the window … not that I didn't think about it when you told me the sheriff was coming by. I'll get through this, Lord willing. It's nice to know I have him and the two of you on my side, so relax. Call me when the sheriff gets here."

"We will, and we'll get through this," Kevin added.

They watched Tess climb the stairs. She moved slowly, showing her age for the first time in days. They wished she didn't have to go through this, but then again, they wanted to know who she really was. Sara remembered again what God told her when she first saw Tess. That time had come, and like Tess said, Lord willing, they'd get through it.

Chapter 16

Dean was almost out the door to go see Tess when the phone rang. He thought about letting it go to voice mail but changed his mind.

"Sheriff Adams."

"We got some news about those people who kidnapped Tess!" Deputy Harris was so excited he was gasping for breath. "You got to come in right now! Time is key!"

"Calm down, Richard. You're talking so fast I can hardly understand you."

Deputy Harris took a deep breath. When he spoke again, his voice was calmer. "Sheriff, the Indiana Highway Patrol just called and said they have our suspects, Tom Applebee and Sharon Brown, in custody.

"They were picked up about two hours ago, hitchhiking along Route 24 near the Indiana and Illinois border. It seems they ditched the first stolen car and stole a van outside Woodburn, just over the Ohio-Indiana border. They haven't found the first car yet, but they think the two pushed it into the Maumee River. Anyhow, the van broke down near Kenland, Indiana, so they decided to hitchhike. Guess who gave them a ride?"

"The Highway Patrol!" Dean laughed.

"You are so right!" Deputy Harris said, laughing too. "Are you coming in?"

"Not right now. I'm on my way to see Tess. I have to tell her about the caller from Saturday. She's going to have to tell me who she is if I'm going to protect her. This new development might give me the leverage I need, at least for now. Who's in charge of the case with the kidnappers?"

"Hmm, let's see." Deputy Harris checked his notes for the name of the arresting officer. "It's Sergeant Sikes. I'll give you his number. He said he'd be at the patrol station until around ten. Then he'd be on the road."

"Thanks, Richard. Keep this information quiet for a few hours if you can. I'll call the officer from here and see if we can make a case against these two suspects. I hope it will give me the authority to keep Tess's identity secret, at least for the time being. This case is now technically a burglary, murder, and kidnapping.

"As far as we know, Tess is the only witness to the knowledge of these crimes. She may not have seen them kill the owner of the bar, but she heard Tom admit he pulled the trigger."

"I'll take care of it on this end, Sheriff. Let me know how it goes with Tess."

"Thanks, Richard. I will."

Dean called the number Deputy Harris had given him. "This is Sheriff Dean Adams of the Jonesboro, Ohio, Sheriff's Department. I'm calling about two suspects who were picked up this morning around seven on Route 24 near Kenland. Is there someone I can talk to who knows about this?"

"Yes, sir. That would be Sergeant Sikes, and he's standing right here." Dean could hear the trooper tell Sikes who was calling and what it was about.

"Sheriff Adams, Sergeant Sikes is going to his office so he can speak to you in private. I'm transferring you now."

When Sergeant Sikes answered, Dean explained his interest. "The two suspects you picked up this morning are possibly involved in a burglary, murder, and kidnapping incident that happened a week ago. The woman who was kidnapped escaped and has been in a safe place here in Jonesboro. The woman was homeless and got caught in the middle of the burglary and the murder by being in the wrong place at the wrong time. She had crawled into the back seat of a car parked near the bar where the crimes took place."

"Was she aware that a crime had just happened?" Sergeant Sikes asked.

"No, she just saw an opportunity to get out of the cold, and the car was unlocked. She said she fell asleep right away and didn't wake up until the car started moving. She heard the man and woman talking about something that happened in the bar, but she was groggy and didn't pay much attention at the time. The two suspects had no idea anyone was in the back seat."

"What happened next?"

"When they discovered her, they decided to keep her as collateral in case they got caught. They took country roads, trying to avoid the police, and ended up in Jonesboro."

"About what time was that?" the sergeant asked.

"It was around six this past Monday morning. The woman said when the car stopped at a four-way stop sign, she saw a chance to get away and jumped out of the back seat. The other woman jumped out to get her, and they wrestled on the ground. The suspect banged the homeless woman's head on the ground."

"Sounds like a tough old bird." Sikes laughed.

"Trust me, she is," Dean said.

"The man who was driving was afraid someone would see them, so he yelled for the woman to get back in the car, and they took off. The rest of the story is even more interesting, but I don't want to take up your time, so if you can confirm that you have these two suspects in custody, I would appreciate that."

"I believe the suspects are the ones you're looking for. We checked the APB we received this past week, and it was about two people being involved in a robbery and a possible murder, but I don't remember a kidnapping." He paused, then said, "Oh, wait a minute! There was a second APB a few days later with the same MO, plus a kidnapping."

"That would be the one I put out. It must have been the Zanesville police who issued the first one."

"Let me check. Yes, you're right. It was from Zanesville," Sikes said.

"At the time," Dean clarified, "they didn't realize a woman had been in the stolen car."

"That's probably why we had the two APBs," Sergeant Sikes said.

"When we checked the license plate on the broken-down van, we saw it was stolen. The information matched the two hitchhikers we picked up. They are now in our local jail."

"I'm really glad to have those two in custody. It will help us get closer to finding out who our homeless woman is."

"Sheriff Adams, if you would email me all the information you have on how you're involved in the case, I can start the paperwork to get them back to Ohio. I'm sure you know you'll have to contact the Zanesville police to learn what they've been doing about the case so far."

"I understand totally, Sergeant Sikes. I'll do that right away. Thanks for your help."

"Glad we could help. It was kind of funny my partner and I found the abandoned van just a mile or so before the two suspects were found hitchhiking. Not very smart, don't you think?"

Dean laughed, thanking Sergeant Sikes again and saying he would be in touch.

Dean was relieved to have one problem solved with the mystery about Tess. Now she didn't have to worry about being harmed by those two anymore, but he had to make sure he could keep her safe from others, especially the man who inquired about her on Saturday.

He picked up the phone and dialed the number for the Zanesville police. Turning the case of murder and robbery over to them left him with control of Tess.

"Zanesville Police Department. This is Officer Shaw."

"Good morning, Officer Shaw. This is Sheriff Adams with the Jonesboro Sheriff's Department. I called last Wednesday about the robbery/murder case that's under your jurisdiction. Have you been informed about the capture of the two suspects?"

"Let me check with Detective Jones. He's in charge of that case."

While Dean waited for Detective Jones, he went over in his head what he was going to say to Tess about this new development. Should he tell her everything he'd found out so far, or should he leave out the part about the Zanesville police being involved? Tess probably figured out they were involved from the beginning, but she never mentioned it. She knew if they started asking questions about her, she'd have to tell more about her life on the streets. At the moment, they only knew a woman had been in the stolen car against her will.

"This is Detective Jones."

"Detective Jones, Sheriff Adams with the Jonesboro Sheriff's Office. I was calling to see if you'd been informed about the two suspects who are connected with the burglary and murder of the bar owner there in Zanesville."

"We heard the news early this morning. The Indiana Highway Patrol called and said you have the woman who was in the car at the time of the theft."

"Yes, we do, and that's why I'm calling. You see, she could be in danger from another twist in this story. A man called on Saturday, inquiring about her identity. He refused to give his name, saying he was working for a client who wished to remain anonymous until the woman in question was found and identified. I didn't like the sound of his explanation and figured it was time for me to push forward to find out who she really is. According to her, she has been homeless for almost two years—at least that's what she told us."

"We were informed about her. I didn't want to get involved, allowing you to handle the situation. Now I guess we need to move forward. Do you agree?"

"Yes, I do. In fact, I was on my way to tell her I'm not going to allow her to keep us waiting any longer. I'll tell you right now, it's not going to be easy to get what I need from her."

"Why's that?" Detective Jones asked.

"She's smart and knows how to get sympathy. I'm wondering if there's a way to keep her identity for our eyes only, at least until we find out more about her."

"I don't see why not," Jones replied.

"I told this man I'd let him know what we've found out about the woman sometime today, but my gut feeling is he's up to no good. What do you think?"

"I'm going to go with your decision about this, Sheriff Adams. You know her, and I have confidence you're sensing something's not right about this guy. I suggest you tell him that until the law can identify her, we're withholding all information about her from the public. If he pursues it, we'll work to find out who he is. Until then, do what you planned and let us know the outcome."

"I will," said Dean. "I may need your help once we confirm her identity."

"You can count on us, especially if you find out she is from this area."

"Thanks, Detective Jones."

Dean hung up, then called Kevin to let him know he was on the way. He would tell the three of them together about his talk with both the Indiana Highway Patrol and the Zanesville Police Department. Tess needed to know that he, Kevin, and Sara were only doing what was best for her. She had to trust them. If she refused, they couldn't help her make her life livable.

Dean rang the doorbell, expecting Kevin or Sara to open the door. Instead, it was Tess. He could tell she was afraid and wary about why he was coming by.

"Sheriff Adams, please come in," Tess said. "Kevin and Sara are in the kitchen. I'm assuming you're here to tell me news about those two suspects I was with. Have they been caught?"

"Yes, that's why I'm here. They've been found, Tess, but I want to tell all of you at the same time what happened. Why don't I go sit in the front room while you get them."

"I'll do that. Be back in a minute."

He watched her slowly walk toward the kitchen. The stress of all this was getting to her. He needed to find out who she really was, but there was a part of him that knew that once he did, her life would change. He only hoped it would change for the best.

Kevin and Sara came into the front room, followed by Tess. Kevin told the sheriff that he and Sara had prepared Tess for his visit but not for why he was coming. He said Tess had figured it out and knew it probably had something to do with the suspects.

"Sheriff, would you like some coffee?"

"Thanks, Sara; that would be nice. Would it be all right if we all went into the kitchen and sat at the table? I find it helps everyone."

"Is it that bad, Sheriff?" Tess asked, her eyes opened wide.

"It's not that what I'm going to tell you is bad. It's just that you're going to have to be honest with us. It's time to tell us who you are and why you ended up homeless on the streets of Zanesville. No more holding back."

"First, tell me how they found those two who started this whole mess. I wish to God I'd never climbed into that car. It's just I was so cold and tired."

"Tess!" Sara exclaimed. "Please don't say that! I'm glad you got into that car. I'm not glad that they held you hostage, but I'm glad you ended up here with me and Kevin! Don't blame God for doing something you think was bad. Thank God for doing something good, like bringing you here. Just calm down and let the sheriff tell us what happened."

"Sara's right," Dean said. "We're going to get through this, and when it's over, your life will be better for it. I promise."

Tess looked at him, then Kevin and Sara. Her life was changing quickly. All those difficult years, ending up homeless and alone, were about to change. She stopped being angry. If she could get away from people who hated her, then she could do what needed to be done to make her life better.

"All right then," she said, her voice strong and controlled. "I'm ready to tell you the whole story. It's going to take a lot of time, and I might have to take breaks, but I'm ready to let go of this burden. Are you all up to it?"

They all answered yes at the same time, then laughed.

"Here it goes. My name is ..."

Chapter 17

Law Offices of O'Donnell, Young, and Murphy, New York City

Brandon got to the office early on Monday. He wanted to start piecing together the information he had about the missing old woman, hoping to find her before the statute of limitations ran out. He was confused as to how she put that clause in her will, but he knew Chet O'Donnell would help clear it up. Brandon majored in corporate law, so his knowledge of this kind of clause was a bit fuzzy.

Chet O'Donnell poked his head in his office. "Well, Brandon, you're here early."

"Oh, good morning, Mr. O'Donnell. I'm intrigued about this woman's case. With all the information I got from Ross and what you told me at dinner Thursday night, I wanted to find out as much as I could, and quickly. To be honest, I'm surprised this case has me so interested."

"I may have some insight into that. I talked to your dad on Sunday, and I told him about your working on this case. When I told him what it was about, your dad thought you might be interested because of your own family history. He told me that both of your grandmothers died before you were born, so you never knew them."

"I hadn't thought about it, but it's true. They both died when my parents were young."

"He also said you've had an interest in genealogy since you were a kid, which could be another reason why this case interests you."

"I was a nerd growing up. Sports didn't interest me, and you know how important sports are when you're young, especially for a guy.

"I loved the mysteries of the past. As an undergraduate, I majored in anthropology and minored in archeology. It wasn't until my junior year that I took an interest in law."

"I didn't know that; that explains a lot. When I decided to turn this case over to you, I wanted to see how you would handle yourself. I figured if you didn't grumble, try to talk your way out of it, or drag your feet, you were ready for—let's say high-profile cases."

Brandon smiled. "So, you're saying when I find this woman and close the case, you'll seriously consider giving me something more intriguing?"

O'Donnell smiled at Brandon, knowing he was going to be an asset to his company. He hadn't told any of his partners in the firm yet, but he was considering retiring in the next few years. It was time to turn the firm over to younger people. Brandon would be one of his best.

"You get this case closed, and I promise I'll consider you for the next intriguing case."

"You got it, Mr. O'Donnell. I hope you'll let me continue asking you questions about things your grandfather told you about her family."

"I will. Anything I can answer to help find her, I'm willing to share."

"Can I ask you a question now?"

Chet smiled. "Sure, ask away."

"First question—how did you figure out who she is?"

"The mental health facility where she stayed wanted to keep her true identity unknown for some reason. I was able to get enough information from my grandfather's diary about who she might be. My grandfather listed her father's name and the names of his wife and children. When I first saw the report, that's what caught my eye—the name of the woman, especially her maiden name. I knew I'd seen that name before, but I had to dig around to find my grandfather's journals. He kept a journal from the time he was a child. After he died, I spent hours reading them. They're filled with history of life back then and all about my family and my grandfather's law firm. He's the reason I became a lawyer. In time, I'll tell you her birth name. It will be much harder to find her without that."

"How soon do you think you'll be able to do that, sir?"

"I was told within the next few days. The Zanesville police have a strong lead and are in contact with a local sheriff's office near Toledo. As soon as I hear from them, I'll let you know. In the meantime, continue working on what you have so far."

"I'll do that. Thanks, Mr. O'Donnell."

"Brandon, I think it's time for you to call me Chet. The only time you need to call me Mr. O'Donnell is when we're in meetings or working with clients. You've earned my trust and my approval, and I'm glad to have you in our law firm."

"I appreciate that, Mr. O'Donnell—I mean Chet."

"All right then, let's get back to work."

Chet O'Donnell left Brandon's office and headed down the hall to his own. Brandon was feeling proud. Having the privilege of calling his boss by his first name was awesome. He couldn't wait to tell his dad and thank him for what he said to Mr. O'Donnell.

Brandon had no idea what was ahead for him once he found Tess. For now, he would spend the time connecting the dots of where she'd been out on the streets, alone and unknown.

Chapter 18

Jonathan got up Monday morning at six, had a light breakfast, then went to the club to work out for an hour. He liked going early because it was almost empty at that time of day. He used the last thirty minutes of his gym time to swim.

He was a good swimmer, so ten laps around the pool was a breeze. Afterward, he floated on his back to slow down his heart rate and allow his mind and body to relax. Time was running out to claim the family fortune. Since his father's death, other than his mother, he was the lone survivor in line for the money. Just thinking about it made his heart pound.

For the first time in his life, Jonathan thought about the possibility of having a heart attack and dying like his father. He knew that anger was a powerful and dangerous emotion. He also acknowledged that he was very angry.

He tried to calm down by focusing on what he was going to say to Sheriff Adams when he talked to him again.

Since he was still in a stew, he decided to follow through on making an appointment to see his doctor. Hopefully, the doctor could give him something to calm his nerves and reassure him that his heart was fine. Perhaps that would give him some relief.

He climbed out of the pool, showered, and dressed, then left the club to walk the few blocks to his office building. He planned to work harder to distract himself from thinking about his mother. Now wasn't the time to start having anxiety attacks.

The early-morning air held the promise of a cool day ahead. Early fall was his favorite time of the year—warm but cool enough to feel comfortable wearing a suit jacket and a long-sleeve dress shirt.

As he entered his building, a man approached him. At first, Jonathan didn't notice him.

"Good morning. Are you Jonathan Farnsworth?"

"That depends on who's asking," he said, sizing up the stranger.

"I'm sorry. I didn't mean to startle you, but the security desk officer pointed you out to me when you came in."

"It seems I'm going to have to talk to the head of security on the correct protocol for giving out information on those who work in this building." Jonathan's voice was cold. "I don't appreciate being confronted by someone I have never met."

"I'm sorry, Mr. Farnsworth—I'm assuming you are Mr. Farnsworth by the way you're reacting to my question. I should have called your office this morning to set up an appointment, but I was afraid you wouldn't meet with me."

"And why would that be, Mr.—I don't know your name."

"My name is Jeremy Fairchild. I'm your half-brother."

Jonathan turned pale, grabbed the man's jacket, and slowly fell to the floor.

Chapter 19

Tess's heart pounded, and her hands were sweating as she held them firmly in her lap. She stopped talking for a moment and sipped her coffee. Her mouth was dry, and her lips felt numb. She said she would tell them who she really was, but now she wasn't sure she was ready. Fear ran through her body. She knew that from this moment, her life would be changed, but she didn't know if it would be better or worse. They all sat looking at her, waiting with anticipation for the revelation of her true identity.

"My real name is Julianne Teresa Hollister Farnsworth. My maiden name is Hollister, and my mother's father, my grandfather, was Henry Hanes, who started the Hanes Pottery Company in the Zanesville area around 1910, when he was a young man in his twenties. After he and Grandmother Hanes died, my mother inherited his wealth. My grandfather's pottery company became extremely successful, allowing my family to live quite comfortably. After my parents died, I inherited the family fortune. Unfortunately, that wealth has haunted me most of my life."

Tess stopped abruptly. Dean Adams, Kevin, and Sara, eyes wide and mouths agape, were shocked by this news.

Dean was especially stunned. He was speechless until Tess asked him if he was all right.

"I'm just shocked to know who you really are. Everyone who lives in Ohio and the surrounding states has most likely heard of Hanes Pottery. Both my mother and my wife are collectors of the early pottery your grandfather's company made. Wow, I never saw that coming—you, the granddaughter of Henry Hanes."

Tess looked at the sheriff as tears filled her eyes. Memories from her growing-up years came rushing in; she could feel the joy and love her grandfather and grandmother Hanes showed her when she was a little girl. She stayed often in their big house. She was their only grandchild, and they spoiled her. When her grandfather's company grew to become well-known, she was treated to everything money could buy. They provided her own room in what became known as the Hanes Mansion, decorating her room with all the things she loved. She had always loved animals and considered becoming a veterinarian when she grew up, so her room was filled with stuffed animal toys and pictures of animals on the walls. They even bought her a pony. She grew up to become an excellent horsewoman.

Oh, how she missed riding over the rolling hills around Zanesville! When she was a young woman, right before she met her future husband, Herbert, Tess would spend hours outdoors riding her horse, Wings, and sitting along the creek that ran through the property of her grandparents' land. Where had life taken her? Not where she expected.

Sara interrupted her thoughts. "Tess, what's the matter?"

Tess looked at her three new friends and smiled a weak, pitiful smile. These were the people who had made her life less lonely in such a short time. She knew they meant well, but she was having a hard time bringing her thoughts back to the present. Life as a child seemed more comforting than living in the present. All she wanted to do was forget what was happening and go back to her childhood, when life was an adventure and she waited in anticipation for the next step in her future.

She wanted to stop living. Her body and soul were old and tired. She just wanted rest—rest from running away from the emptiness she felt.

"I'm so tired," Tess moaned. "Could we talk about this later? I gave you what you wanted—my real name. I even told you the name of my grandfather. I need to rest a bit while you start the process of finding out more about my life. For now, I just want to forget all about this."

Sara got up, went to Tess, and knelt beside her. She took her weather-beaten hands into her own and spoke ever so gently. "I can't imagine what you've been through in your life, but I want you to know right now, at this very minute, the three of us sitting here have nothing but concern for you and your future. We're not about to let anything or anyone hurt you ever again! Do you hear me, Tess? Never again!

"I'll tell you what. Instead of going upstairs to rest, why don't you go sit in the comfortable chair by the fireplace? I think you just need to rest your eyes for a bit. Come on. I'll go with you and get you settled."

Sara helped Tess up and walked with her to the family room.

Tess loved sitting by the fireplace. The big chair made her feel special. After Tess sat down, Sara pulled up the ottoman for her feet, then grabbed an afghan from the back of the chair and pulled it up around her chin.

Sara sat on the couch to wait for Tess to fall asleep. Before long, she heard Tess's soft, low snoring and knew she was asleep. She walked back to the kitchen where Dean and Kevin sat, talking quietly about what Tess had told them.

"Is she asleep?" Kevin asked.

"Yes. She dropped off within a few minutes. She's exhausted, and I'm worried about her. Did you see the way she looked after she told us who she is? It looked like she just left us here and went somewhere else in her mind. What are we going to do? Do you think we need to call Dr. Young's office and have him see her? I'm sure he could give her something to help her depression. And who could blame her for being depressed? I can't imagine what else we're going to find out about her past!"

"I agree, Sara," Dean said. "She's been through a lot lately, and I'm sure she didn't get medical care while she was homeless. She could have been having episodes of depression for quite a while, and then this latest development pushed her too far."

"Kevin," Sara said, "why don't you go and call Dr. Young's office to see if you can get her in this afternoon. I'd feel better about it."

"I'll go do that now." He got up and left the room, leaving Dean and Sara alone. Dean turned to Sara and saw tears in her eyes.

"Sara, it's going to be all right. You just have to trust me, trust yourself, and trust God. Isn't that the basis of true faith? Knowing that God gives strength to those who believe?

"I'll have to tell you sometime about my situation with faith or the lack of it, but now we need to focus on Tess's state of mind. It's going to take time, but I have confidence she'll get through this."

Sara looked at Dean. Seeing determination in his eyes helped her. For now, their biggest concern was getting Tess help. Faith is a strong motivation, but God also uses the power of healing through modern medicine.

Kevin came back and told them Dr. Young would see Tess that afternoon at three thirty.

"I feel better," Sara said smiling.

While the three of them waited for Tess to wake up, they discussed how to proceed with the information she had given them. Until the fugitives from the murder and robbery case were brought back to Ohio, Tess's true identity was safe with them.

She was now a key witness for the prosecution. Even though she didn't see the murder, she overheard Tom and Sharon talking about it, and Sharon yelling that Tom shouldn't have killed the guy. Even if her testimony didn't convict the two of those crimes, kidnapping would.

Sara heard Tess stirring and went to see if she was awake. "Do you feel better?" she asked.

Tess had a mischievous smile on her face, which said it all. "I do feel better. All I needed was a quick nap. Just let me go freshen up, and I'll meet you in the kitchen." She paused. "You know, Sara, I'm a little hungry. It sure would be mighty nice if I could have some hot tea and one of those sweet rolls we had at breakfast. That's if you don't mind?"

Sara smiled. *Tess is definitely feeling better if she wants to eat. If there's one thing she enjoys, it's eating, probably because she had so little to eat when she lived on the streets.*

Walking into the kitchen, Sara announced, "Well, our queen has awakened, and says she's hungry, so I'm taking that as a good sign."

"Good to hear that," Dean said. "I need to get down to the precinct, so we'll put off finding out more about her past later. Maybe when she gets back from seeing Dr. Young, we can dig deeper into her life. I hope the doc can give her something to relax her. It wouldn't be bad to bring Dr. Young in on her situation. Maybe he can look into her medical background."

"That's a good idea," Kevin replied. "Doctors know they have to keep patients' medical information confidential, but maybe with your help he can find out what we need."

Tess walked into the kitchen, looking wide awake and chipper. "What are you all talking about? I bet it's about me since you all look like the cat that ate the canary."

"Tess," said Kevin, "Sheriff Adams thinks when you see Dr. Young this afternoon, we might have him look into your medical history to help us take precautions on keeping you well."

"Whoa! Just one minute there, folks. I never said I wanted to see a doctor! Who in tarnation came up with that idea? I'm fine, thank you very much! I don't need to see a doctor!"

"I made that decision," Sara said, looking sternly at Tess. "I feel you are depressed and that maybe you have been for some time."

"Who gave you the authority to say how I'm feeling? You had no right to do that, Sara. I will not go, and you can't make me!"

"Tess, I'm going to share something personal with you—something so personal even Kevin doesn't know about it."

Kevin was at the sink, his back to the three of them, but he turned around when he heard what Sara said to Tess. "Sara, what's this about? Have you been keeping something from me?"

"Yes, and I'm sorry."

"I knew it! I can't believe you're going to tell Tess something you haven't told me!"

He was shocked and angry.

"Please, Kevin, let me explain. It's not that I haven't wanted to tell you what's been bothering me, but to be honest, I wasn't sure until recently what my problem was.

"Ever since Tess came into our lives, I've been happier. Since Mom died and I found out I was adopted, I've struggled with feeling sad and lonely and, yes, depressed. I was going to tell you when you got back from your retreat, but with all the excitement over Tess, I didn't. I'm truly sorry, sweetheart. Please don't be upset with me!"

Sara started crying. Kevin put his arms around her and told her it was all right.

Tess turned to the sheriff. "Well, I didn't see that coming, did you?"

Dean sat quietly, sizing up the awkward situation. All this came out because Sara was just trying to get Tess to go to the doctor.

Sara wiped her eyes, then told the three of them, "I saw Dr. Young a couple of weeks ago, and he diagnosed me with mild depression. He gave me medicine, and I'm starting to feel better. If you'll let me take you to see Dr. Young, we can tell him what you've been through. He can make the decision whether you are depressed or have another health problem. So, please, will you go?"

Tess's anger subsided, and she mumbled an agreement, though they couldn't hear her.

"Did you say all right?" Sara asked.

"Yes, yes. I said it, but I'm not happy about it, you hear?"

Sara laughed and gave Tess a big hug.

"It seems it's settled then," said Dean.

Dean got up from the table, stretched his lean six-foot-four body, and headed toward the door. "I think we've all had enough stress this morning, so I say we pick up on Tess's life story at another time. Do you agree?"

They agreed and followed him to the door.

"Sheriff, we'll let you know what the doctor says about Tess," Kevin said.

"I think it's time the three of you started calling me Dean, since it seems we've become friends. What do you say?"

"I think that's a great idea. What do you think, ladies?"

"Dean it is," said Sara. Tess nodded in agreement, then gave Dean a hug.

Dean hugged her back. He started to leave but turned back and looked at Sara. "I want you to know what you said about your depression will stay confidential with me. It was brave to tell Tess about it. Society needs to work harder to see mental health issues as important as any other health problem. I'm here for you if you need me, OK?"

Sara smiled and gave him a hug. "Thank you, and welcome to our family!"

He laughed and whispered in her ear, "Having Tess as a family member is going to be a trip!"

She laughed, giving him a thumbs-up as he walked to his cruiser.

Chapter 20

Jonathan slowly opened his eyes and looked around. His memory was fuzzy as he scanned the room, trying to remember what had happened, but as hard as he tried, he couldn't. He closed his eyes again and took a deep breath, hoping it would clear his thoughts. When he opened his eyes this time, he remembered. His heart started pounding, and he felt sick to his stomach. He was in a hospital.

A nurse walked into his room. "Mr. Farnsworth, how are you feeling?"

"Terrible! I'm sick to my stomach, and my heart's beating so fast it feels like it's going to jump out of my chest."

"I'll adjust your medicine."

She checked his intravenous bag and increased the amount of medicine. "There, that should help you feel better. The doctor has you on medicine to regulate your heartbeat and keep you calm."

"How long have I been here?"

"Since around eight. It's now almost one p.m. You collapsed in the lobby of your office building, and the life squad brought you here. Don't you remember?"

"Not really. Who called the squad?" Jonathan asked, feeling queasy.

"Why, your brother. The two of you were standing in the lobby when you collapsed. Thank goodness he caught you before you hit the floor. Now, try to relax. When you feel up to it, I'll let your brother come and see you. He's been worried about you and keeps asking how you're doing."

"First, he's not my brother, and second, I don't want to see him. He's the reason I passed out. I've never met this man before today. He just walked up to me and boldly stated he was my brother! I want the hospital to keep him away from me, do you hear me? I want to call my lawyer right now. Please give me my phone."

Jonathan's heart monitor started beeping, and he felt light-headed. *What is happening to me?* he thought as he slowly lost consciousness.

When he opened his eyes again, he saw the nurse and a man wearing scrubs and a stethoscope standing by his bed. "Mr. Farnsworth, I'm Dr. Reynolds. How are you feeling?"

"I told the nurse earlier, terrible! What is wrong with me?" Jonathan asked. The heart monitor started beeping, making him light-headed again.

"Mr. Farnsworth, we're trying to find out what's causing your heart to react the way it is. Nurse Johnson was able to regulate your heartbeat, but you need to keep yourself calm. I can't give you any stronger medicine until we find out what's going on. I have you scheduled for tests later this afternoon, but until then, please help by not getting agitated."

Jonathan took a deep breath, knowing he had to control his anger or he would have a stroke or, worse, die. After two or three deep breaths, he felt his heart slow down and go back into a normal rhythm.

"All right, Dr. Reynolds, but the situation that started this morning is making me agitated. Then I get angry. I don't have a calm personality. Being overly calm is not an asset in my line of business."

"And what line of business is that?" Dr. Reynolds asked.

"I'm vice president of one of the most prestigious ad agencies in New York City. Maybe you've heard of Conner Williams Agency? We do advertising for some of the largest retailers in the US and abroad."

"Yes, I've heard of the company. I would think, since it's a high-stress position, you would have learned to keep cool."

"Well, yes. It is a high-stress position, but I've been able to handle the stress until lately. Since my father died from a heart attack about six months ago, it's been hard to stay calm."

"It sounds as if that may be the underlying problem. Our emotions trigger all kinds of reactions. We'll run some tests. Then I can make a diagnosis on how to treat this."

"That's fine—sure," Jonathan mumbled under his breath.

"Nurse Johnson said you wanted to call your lawyer."

"Yes, I need to let him know what happened this morning. I don't have any living relatives, and he's become more than just my lawyer these past six months. I also need to call my office to let them know where I am and cancel my appointments for today."

"I'll let you make those calls if you promise to keep the conversations short and not get into any discussions that will make your heart start racing."

"I promise," Jonathan said, trying to keep calm.

He needed to talk to Derek, his lawyer. The first thing he wanted him to do was find out if it was possible for him to have a half-brother. Then he needed to call his secretary and come up with some kind of excuse for not keeping his appointments that afternoon.

He didn't need the board finding out he was having health problems. There was always someone lurking in the background, ready to slip into his place. His heart acting up could be interpreted as a serious health issue.

Since his father's death, he relied more and more on Derek to help him in every part of his life. If ever he'd had a brother, he would have wanted him to be like Derek—someone he could trust. Now it seemed he did have a brother. He also needed to bring Derek up to date on the news that his mother may have been found. Derek was aware of the statute of limitations in his mother's will. His thoughts jumped to the possibility he really had a half brother. He had known for years his father cheated on his mother, but at the time, it was of no interest to him. He had full confidence Derek would take care of the situation.

Derek picked up the phone after two rings. "Jonathan, I haven't heard from you in a while. I was just going to call you. Are you alright?"

"Derek, I'm in a delicate situation at the present time, and I need your help."

"OK. What can I do to help?"

"I'm at the Lower Manhattan Hospital. They won't release me until they run some tests."

"What happened? I'm leaving now. I'll be there as soon as I can!" Derek grabbed his jacket.

"Don't rush. I'm fine, at least for the time being. I blacked out this morning in the lobby of my office building and was rushed here. It shook me up to wake up in the hospital."

"Was it your heart?" Derek asked, concerned.

"Yes. It's been acting up again, pounding in my ears and racing. I had an episode this morning while I was at the gym, so I made an appointment to see my doctor, but I didn't get there because of this problem."

"What caused you to get upset? Do you remember what it was?"

"What I'm about to tell you has to stay confidential. I need you to do some detective work or hire someone to do it, but discretion is top priority. Do you hear me, Derek? No one is to know about this."

"What is going on, Jonathan? I've never heard you sound so upset! It has to be something big for you to get so upset."

"It is. Trust me. A man approached me this morning after I'd entered the lobby and asked if I was Jonathan Farnsworth. There was something about him and the way he looked that caused my heart to lurch.

"I said it depended on who was asking. Then he told me something that made me so surprised I literally fainted dead away! He said he was Jeremy Fairchild, and he was my half-brother!"

"What? That can't be! I've been your lawyer long enough to know if you had a brother. After your father died, I checked out all possibilities of another relative that could come forward to contest the will. I checked records and births thoroughly. I would have found out if you had any other relatives. This guy has to be lying, Jonathan. Do you think he's looking to blackmail you? Could he know about Delilah?"

"It wouldn't matter to me if someone knew about Delilah. I'm not the married one. She is! And anyway, many of the men at the agency have mistresses. They wouldn't care about her. No, I don't think blackmailing me is what this guy is after."

"If it's not blackmail, what is it?"

"I don't know. That's why I need your help."

"I'll get started this afternoon, but first I need to see you and make sure you're all right. I should be there in fifteen minutes or so. You know how traffic is at this time of day."

"Derek, there was something about this guy that made me think I've met him before. I can't put my finger on it, but he looks familiar."

"Well, we'll get to the bottom of this, but you need to get yourself back on your feet. Time is running out on finding your mother dead or alive. That's our top priority, right?"

"Right, but if we find out this guy really is my half-brother, then we'll have to do something about it. By the way, when I see you, I have another situation that came up this past week. I wanted to wait to make sure the information was correct, but let's just say Mother's luck may have run out. I may have found the old lady." Jonathan smiled, feeling confident that his luck was back.

Chapter 21

Sheriff Dean Adams was up early Tuesday morning. He had decided not to go back to see Tess last night.

Since he hadn't been spending much time with his family, he decided to take a break and spend the evening at home. Heather, who was in her third year of cheerleading for her high school's football team, wanted him to come to one of the Warrior's home games. It pained him to consider that in one more year, she would be out of his daily life and off to college. Joyce worried he put too much pressure on her to fill the void left by Josh, and he shouldn't rely on her to make his life happy.

The morning went by quickly. He caught up on his paperwork and made an appearance at the local town meeting to give his weekly report.

Deputy Richard Harris had been with the sheriff's office for nine years. His upbeat nature was well received by the older folks and most of the teenagers. His only flaw was spending too much time visiting instead of patrolling.

On most days, weather permitting, he did his rounds in the downtown area on foot. The business owners loved to hear his tales about what was happening in the neighborhood, but occasionally, Dean had to get on him for talking too much about police business—something he said could come back to bite them and cause the town council to make a stink.

The situation with Officer Harris made him smile as he compared

Tess and Harris. He was sure Tess would get a kick out of hearing what Deputy Harris did in his daily routine around Jonesboro. She would have a wonderful time telling Richard the perils of running your mouth off, since she had lots of experience in that area. Thinking of Tess, he decided to give the manse a call and see if he could stop by that afternoon. Now that he had her real name, he could look into her past, but he had decided not to yet. He wanted to hear the rest of her story.

Besides talking to Tess, he wanted to keep Kevin informed about the man who called on Saturday asking about the surveillance tape. He hadn't called back, which was surprising since he seemed so determined to find Tess.

"Good morning, Kevin. It's Dean. I was hoping I could see Tess later this afternoon and get back to where we left off yesterday. I didn't try to find out about her after I got back to the office, knowing she'd rather tell us herself."

"She's been anxious ever since you were here yesterday," Kevin replied. "A part of her is glad she told us who she is, but she's scared too. How would three thirty this afternoon work?"

"That's fine with me," Dean said. "By the way, what did Dr. Young say?"

"He was surprised when he learned she'd been living on the streets for over a year. He says she's in good health. She was firm about him not looking into her medical past, at least for now. Sara told him she'd let him know when it would be possible for him to get her medical records from her former doctors."

"Hopefully, that will happen soon," Dean replied.

"We'll just have to hope she'll tell us enough today to get her into some kind of protection program."

"That reminds me, the man who called Saturday about the surveillance tape didn't call back. I'm surprised. On the other hand, I have enough trouble dealing with Tess. I don't need this added problem."

"Don't we all!" Kevin laughed. "At least you don't have to be with her. We try to keep her busy, but it's not easy. You'd be surprised how much energy she has."

"I bet!" Dean laughed.

Kevin continued. "We've been urging her to go to bed early, so we can have some time alone. We may not have kids, but having Tess around makes it feel like we do. Since she's been here, Sara and I have had only a few hours by ourselves, at least in the living areas. The last two nights, we've gone to bed early just to have time alone. Is that what it's like having children?"

"Yes," Dean agreed.

Kevin continued. "I've heard that older folks sometimes go through a second childhood. Maybe that's what Tess is doing. Or she's just lonely."

"You know, Kevin, I can't imagine being homeless and without family. It's been difficult for my family since Josh died, but at least I still have Joyce and Heather."

"Sara and I are so sorry about Josh. I know it's hard, but as you said, you have Joyce and Heather," Kevin replied. "I'll let Sara and Tess know you'll be coming by this afternoon. I hope Tess tells us the truth. I've speculated about what her life was like. I did a search on her grandfather, Henry Hanes, and Tess's name was on the list of family members, like she said. So, we know that much is true."

"I hope she wasn't involved in a life of crime. I don't want to be the one to have to arrest her," Dean joked. "Can you picture that?"

"You'd sure have your work cut out for you!" Kevin agreed.

"Well, I'll see you folks around three thirty."

"See you then."

⁓

When Sara entered the kitchen, she found Tess at the table, reading the local paper.

"What's up, sweet pea?" Tess asked, smiling.

Sara smiled back. "Kevin called. Dean wants to come over this afternoon about three thirty."

"That's OK with me," Tess said.

Sara sat down next to Tess, staring at her.

"All right, enough with the staring, Sara. If you have something to ask, then do it. Just don't look at me that way."

"I'm sorry. I didn't mean to make you uncomfortable, but I'm trying to figure out what's going on in that amazing mind of yours."

Tess's face softened as she reached out and patted Sara's cheek. "You're a sweet kid. If I had a daughter, I would have liked her to be like you. Those big, soft eyes … your tender heart … your trusting soul. But it never happened for me. Instead, I got a son who turned out just like his father—conniving, manipulative, and filled with greed. That's what life dealt me."

Sara tried to hide her shock, but Tess saw it. "That's all right, Sara. I guess I don't come across as the motherly type, but I do have a son."

"Where is he? I would have thought you would have turned to him instead of the streets. Anyway, we should wait until Kevin and Dean are here for this conversation. Don't you agree?"

"I suppose."

"I have a great idea," Sara said. "It's a beautiful fall day, and we've been stuck inside these past few days. How about having our lunch out on the back porch? I'll get Kevin to come home early and cook us up some mean hamburgers. After that, we can walk uptown and get some ice cream. There's nothing better for cheering me up than a chocolate hot fudge sundae with chocolate chip ice cream. Maybe we should start with the ice cream, then the hamburgers!"

Tess laughed, hit the table with the palm of her hand, and stood up. "That's a perfect idea. I'll go and get myself ready while you call Kevin. Why don't you see if Dean wants to join us, if that's all right with you? Then after we have our ice cream, we can come back here and do our talking. I'd just as soon get this over with as soon as possible. The waiting is tough."

"I'll call Kevin, and he can call Dean."

"Okey dokey, sweet pea. I feel better already." Tess walked toward the stairs whistling "You Got a Friend in Me."

Sara laughed and shook her head as she went to call Kevin.

He agreed with Sara's plan and called Dean. Dean liked the idea, especially getting Tess to do something fun. He rearranged his schedule for lunch to allow more time with Kevin, Sara, and Tess. After all, it was work related.

"Richard, I'm going to be out of the office longer than I thought. Do you mind taking your lunch here at the precinct? I'm having lunch with the Richardsons and Tess."

"Hey, that sounds good. You know, Sheriff, I really like that lady, Tess. She has a feisty personality, don't you think?"

The sheriff smiled, agreeing. "If you need me, I'm just a phone call away." Dean decided to walk to the manse. He spent too much time sitting behind a desk, and the manse was just three blocks away, sitting on two acres beside the Lutheran church. The weather was perfect for an early fall day. As he walked by the local businesses, he was greeted by customers and owners who were outside, sweeping their sidewalks or just taking in an opportunity to enjoy the sunshine and cool weather. Knowing most of the local townspeople was the reason he stayed as sheriff of a small town. He had been offered a position in the Columbus Police Department last year. It would have been a nice promotion with a hefty increase in pay, but the idea of being in a large city didn't appeal to him. His family agreed, and they were glad he decided to stay in Jonesboro.

When he arrived at the manse, he saw Sara and Tess outside on the side porch. The manse had been built in 1902 and was a grand home in its day. Even though the church worked hard to keep it in good shape, the house was showing some wear and tear. It had two porches, one on the side of the house and another at the back. The church had recently screened in the back porch. The home was surrounded by beautiful old oak trees and all kinds of bushes and flowers. Over the years, the trees and bushes had grown to make abundant shade.

As he approached, Tess spotted him first. "Well, you're a sight for sore eyes!" she called out, walking down the steps. When she got to him, she reached out and gave him a bear hug.

Dean laughed. "Hello to you too, Tess. I'm relieved you're so happy to see me. After yesterday's tense visit, I wasn't sure you'd be wanting to see me again."

"Oh well, I know you were just doing your job. One thing I don't do is hold a grudge. It doesn't get you far, and it only gets worse the longer you hold it."

"I'm glad you feel that way, and I'm glad we're going to talk earlier than we had planned. I'm hoping it will turn out to be a positive decision. You're become special to us."

"I know that, but some things may be out of your control. We'll deal with that later. For now, I want to enjoy a good ol' burger cooked over a fire, with ice cream for dessert."

Dean and Tess joined Sara on the porch just as Kevin arrived from the church office. "Glad you could come, Dean."

Kevin reached out and shook Dean's hand. "Thank you for inviting me for lunch. We won't have many good days like today left for grilling out, so I'm glad you're taking advantage of it. Joyce has been after me the last couple of weekends to grill out, but, as usual, I spend too much time on the job. My job doesn't help with relationships. Ever since Josh died, I've put in too much time at work. I need to stop it and spend more time with Joyce and Heather."

"How old is Heather?" Kevin asked.

"She'll be seventeen in a few months. It's hard to believe that she'll be a senior next year. She and Joyce have been poring over all the college information they've either sent for or found online. I want her to stay close to home, but she wants to go to an out-of-state school. She has the grades to choose just about any major university, but I'm hoping she chooses one close by. It depends on what kind of scholarships she gets."

"Well, whatever she decides, I'm sure you and Joyce will support her decision. I've been meaning to ask you about Josh. I don't want to cause you any added pain, but I hope you know you can talk to me about his death. I've found out over the years of ministering that just talking about things, especially the loss of loved ones, helps the grief process. I want you to know I'm here for you."

It was one thing for Dean to mention his son, Josh, but for

someone else to bring up the subject brought back that old feeling of anger toward God. He knew Kevin saw his clenched jaw at the mention of Josh and how he quickly turned away and mumbled, "Thanks, but I'm fine," knowing he wasn't. It had been over a year since Josh's car accident, but at times like this, the feeling when he got the news of his death was as fresh as ever.

Dean stopped thinking about Josh when Sara announced, "Kevin, I've got the grill hot and the burgers ready." She handed him the platter of raw burgers.

"I guess that's my cue, Dean. You want to join me at the grill?"

"Sure. Why not?"

While Kevin laid the huge patties on the hot grill and inhaled the aroma of searing meat, Dean was thinking, *Yeah, I'm definitely going to grill out this weekend. We'll have steaks and brats … and I'll ask Joyce to invite the Richardsons and Tess to come over.*

Sara and Tess finished up preparations for their spur-of-the-moment cookout while the burgers sizzled and the aroma filled the air.

"Those burgers smell mighty good, Kevin," Tess said. "I hope you cooked enough for me to have two. It's been a while since I've had a grilled hamburger."

The men looked at Tess and smiled. Her face lit up as she waited impatiently for the burgers to cook. Sara had made a salad and added some chips to the impromptu meal. She also got a jar of Nellie Johnston's homemade sweet pickles from the pantry. One of the advantages of living in a small town and having farmers in their congregation was getting fresh produce in the summer and homemade goodies year-round. Nellie Johnston's sweet pickles got a blue ribbon every year at the county fair. Sara knew Tess would enjoy them.

When the burgers were done, they all sat down at the table. Tess reached out to grab a burger but stopped midway when Kevin cleared his throat. She had forgotten that prayer came first, then food.

Sara took Tess's outstretched hand in hers, and then they all held hands and bowed their heads while Kevin offered a prayer.

"Heavenly Father, we thank you for the opportunity to come together as family and new friends to share a meal. In your eyes, we are all family, your family. It is a blessing to have Tess and Dean with Sara and me today. May you bless us and bless this food that you have provided. We ask this in the name of your Son, Jesus Christ. Amen."

They dropped hands. No one reached for the burgers until Kevin said, "OK, Tess, you can get that burger you've been drooling over."

Tess didn't have to be told twice. She leaned over and took a burger off the plate. Then they settled down to eat and visit on a perfect fall afternoon.

Chapter 22

Tess sat on the sofa next to Sara, her hands clenched together. After returning from their trip for ice cream, it was time to continue her story. She was obviously nervous.

Dean sat across from Tess, while Kevin sat in the chair by the fireplace. Dean asked Tess to sit next to Sara on the sofa. He wanted Sara near enough to reach over and offer comfort.

Dean cleared his throat, ready to start the journey into Tess's past. A sense of anticipation filled the room as they wondered what they were going to find out about her.

"Tess, whenever you're ready, you can start. I'm going to record it, so I can have the information to refer to, and you won't have to repeat it all over again. After we're finished, I'll let you listen to it. That way, you can either add or remove information that makes it clear to us what has been your life up to now. Does that sound good for you?"

"Yes, that's fine with me. Can I stop if I feel nervous or need a break?"

"Of course. This isn't an interrogation. I don't want you to feel like a suspect in a crime. As we've said, we want you to tell us who you are, what your life has been like, and especially what made you run away from wherever you were. For now, this is for our ears only. Does that help you feel less nervous?"

Tess had been holding her breath, but with Dean's assurance, she released the air, then smiled at Dean. "I suppose it will be all right. I trust all of you."

Dean put the small recorder down on the coffee table near Tess and pushed the button. "This is Sheriff Dean Adams of the Jonesboro, Ohio, Sheriff's Department. I'm at the home of Kevin and Sara Richardson. The date is October 18, 2018, and the time is three p.m. The Richardsons, along with Tess, are present. Our purpose is to gather information about Tess, who has been the Richardsons' guest for the past week. All right, Tess, whenever you're ready."

Tess took a deep breath and began her story. "As I told you earlier, my full Christian name is Julianne Teresa Hollister Farnsworth. I was born on July 11, 1940, in Duncan Falls near Zanesville. I have already told you about my grandfather on my mother's side."

"Could you tell us again, Tess?" Dean asked gently. "I need that information for the recording."

"Oh, I forgot that thing was on. My grandfather on my mother's side was Henry Hanes, the founder of Hanes Pottery. Is that good?"

"Yes, Tess. Thank you."

"My father was Clarence Hollister, who was born in South Zanesville. His father was Theodore Hollister, who owned a hardware store in South Zanesville. My father started working for Grandpa Hollister after school and on Saturdays when he was about fourteen. He'd always planned on working with his father after high school and hoped to someday take over the store.

"Father had been out of high school for a few years and had managed to help Grandpa Hollister grow his business, so they were able to open another hardware store in Duncan Falls. That's where my father met my mother, when she and Grandpa Hanes came into the store to purchase some supplies. According to my father, it was love at first sight. After they married, Grandpa Hanes offered my father a job with the pottery company. Since my father had been successful building his father's business, Grandpa Hanes figured he could do the same for his pottery company. And that's what my father did. He went into sales with Hanes Pottery and helped make it one of the largest and most profitable companies in the pottery business." Tess looked at Dean. "Any questions so far?"

"No, not yet. It sounds as if you grew up in a privileged environment."

"I did," Tess affirmed, "and I continued to live in that world of money and position even after I married. But life as an adult didn't go quite as well as my childhood."

Tess told them about her wonderful life, growing up as the only grandchild of Henry and Julia Hanes. She told of her love of horses and how her grandparents showered her with gifts and made her feel like a princess. Her parents sent her to an expensive boarding school when she was fourteen, and she did well in academics and made lots of friends. She came home over the summers and holidays to attend parties and spend time at her grandparents' home. She visited often with her Hollister grandparents, but most of her time was with her Hanes grandparents.

After high school, she attended Oberlin College and received a bachelor's degree in business. She had inherited her father's talent in sales. After college, she worked in the sales department of Hanes Pottery Company alongside her father. Her mother didn't think it was proper for a young woman to be working in a man's world, but Tess loved every minute of it.

She had just turned twenty-three when she met her future husband, Herbert Farnsworth. She was a bridesmaid at a college friend's wedding, and Herbert was a groomsman. They hit it off from the moment they met and embarked on a whirlwind romance. He was in real estate and seemed to be quite successful. He was very handsome and had an outgoing personality that drew Tess's attention. Tess had dated a few men, but none kept her attention for long. Herbert was different. He seemed to understand her wanting to work and have the freedom and independence that most men had.

Tess's father didn't see it that way. When she told her father that Herbert had asked her to marry him, he was not happy. He had done some looking into Herbert's background and found some information that made him wonder about his honesty. When he told Tess about this, she became angry and told him it was none of his business. He told her he had done it to protect her, but she told him she didn't need to be protected. She loved Herbert, and if he couldn't accept that, then she would elope and turn her back on her family.

Her father didn't want to lose his only child, so he backed off. Years later, Tess realized she should have listened to him.

Tess stopped talking. She hadn't realized that Sara had taken hold of her hand while she was telling her story. When she revealed her father's disapproval of Herbert, Tess squeezed Sara's hand tightly, causing Sara to wince.

Tess felt like she was alone in the room. Her face showed her fatigue, making her look older than her seventy-eight years. Reliving her past was painful.

"Tess?" Tess didn't respond to Sara. "I think we need to take a break, don't you?" She reached over and touched Tess's face.

Startled by the touch, Tess jumped forward, then turned and looked at Sara's concerned face. She forced herself to focus on what Sara was saying, realizing she wasn't with her father—she was with Sara, Kevin, and Dean.

"I'm sorry, Sara. What did you say?"

"I asked if you needed to take a break. It's been over an hour since you started telling us about your life, and you look like you're getting tired. So, what do you think—a break for now?"

"I'd like that." Her fatigue could be heard in her voice. "I'd like a cup of coffee and maybe something to go with it."

Sara got up and headed toward the kitchen. Kevin followed, leaving Dean alone with Tess.

The two sat there, not saying a word. After a few minutes, Dean got up and sat next to Tess on the couch. She leaned back her head, putting her hands together and resting them in her lap.

Looking Dean straight in the eyes, she said, "You know, it's been almost two years since I've allowed myself to think about what I was before I ended up homeless and alone. It's like I became a different person out on the streets, and I liked the homeless life better than the real one. In the real one, I had become a hateful, bitter, and angry person. I couldn't find my way back to being the young and happy granddaughter of Henry and Julia Hanes, the girl who had a charmed childhood and thought adult life would be the same. Telling you, Kevin, and Sara, about my past has made me see that life as a homeless woman was better than life as a rich one."

Dean spoke with a gentle but serious tone. "Tess, what you've done or been through in the past is just that, the past. I want you to finish telling us about what happened right before you turned to the streets, and then we'll help you make a new life for yourself. Can you do that? Can you move on and let the pain and anger go? We're here for you right now. I know you have a good heart. It's just been through so much pain and sorrow that it was closed up until you met Sara. She has brought hope and purpose back into your heart, hasn't she? I think Sara is good for you, and, well … I think you're good for her. We both sense Sara is having some personal issues. Once we get you back on track, you might want to see what you can do to help her heal, whatever her pain is. So, how about it? Are you up for the rest of your story?"

She smiled, and her face lit up. She thought about all the good that could come out of this difficult journey if she just believed and had hope. She saw the love of Christ in the lives of Sara and Kevin. They believed in Jesus and wanted her to believe too.

"Yes, I'm up to it, so let's get going!"

Dean smiled at her and stood up. He reached down and offered her his big, strong hand, which she took gladly. With a little tug, she got up, and together they walked into the bright, sunny kitchen.

"Thank you, Sara and Kevin, for giving me the best week of my life in years. And to you, Dean, for helping me take the first step to getting my life back. It isn't over yet, but I want to right the many wrongs I've done so far. And, Sara, I feel a peace in my heart from thinking about this Christ that you and Kevin have such faith in. I hope this good feeling lasts, because I never want to go back to the life I lived before I met all of you."

Chapter 23

Kevin had made a fresh pot of coffee, so they stayed at the kitchen table. Tess seemed more relaxed there. With coffee in front of her and the bright, cheerful kitchen around her, her spirits rose.

"Well, here comes the tough part," she said. "I'm going to reveal the person I was before living on the streets and especially before you found me on your lawn, Sara. I hope you won't judge me too harshly, because I've done that to myself for way too long."

"We're not in the habit of judging others," Kevin said. Sara nodded in agreement. "We are in the habit of listening and witnessing. We want to help you find forgiveness. All you need to do is ask God to forgive you, and he will. Then you work to forgive yourself and move on."

"That sounds honorable, but I've never seen anyone really do that, especially so-called Christians—no disrespect to you folks. It seemed every time I messed up in my past, there was someone waiting to make me pay for that mistake. But as you said, Dean, the past is the past. I need to let go of it."

"That's right," Dean said, turning on the recorder.

Tess started from where she'd left off. "Well, after Herbert and I got married, life was good for the first few years. I continued to work with my father, and Herbert did his real estate business. I never really knew exactly what that was, but I was in love, so I never questioned it. A few months after our third anniversary, Herbert came to me and asked if I could loan him a couple of thousand to help him buy some land to develop a new shopping strip. It was going to be located near one of the many housing developments that had popped up in the area. At the time, I didn't think anything of it. My father and I were bringing in a fair amount of new business for the pottery company, and the board of directors gave us generous bonuses. It was rare at that time for a woman to have large amounts of money in a personal bank account. I gave Herbert the money and figured that was the last of it, but he came to me again a few weeks later and wanted more money. I asked him what happened to the money I'd already given him. He hemmed and hawed around and mumbled that it was taking more than he figured to close the deal. That's when I started to wonder whether he was telling me the truth."

"Did you tell your father what was going on?" Sara asked.

"I wanted to tell him, but I knew if I did, he'd bring up the concern he'd had about Herbert before I married him, so I stayed quiet, at least for a while."

"What happened next?" Dean asked.

"I was in the middle of an extremely important business venture for the pottery company, so I gave him more money and tried not to let it bother me. I figured after the deal my father and I were working on went through, I'd hire a detective to look into Herbert's business dealings.

"The deal my father and I were working on, was with a major retail company, and it took all my attention. The company was located in New York City, and they were interested in selling a new line of pottery we had started. One of my talents, when I worked for my grandfather's company, was looking for ways to incorporate our pottery into everyday life. I realized we could make a line of stoneware dishes that could be used for entertaining and another line for everyday use.

"The deal went through, and our stocks went through the roof, which meant my father and I were given a very generous bonus. By then, I had gotten over worrying about what Herbert was up to. He, in turn, didn't ask for any more money.

"After our fourth wedding anniversary, I found out I was

pregnant. I wanted to be a career woman, but life for women back then was different than today. A woman married and had a family—and that was that.

"I continued to work full-time until two months before our son was born. One day, while I was at work, I doubled over in pain. I called Herbert, and he took me to my doctor. I was told I had to go home and go to bed to protect the health of our baby. It was too early for me to deliver, and staying off my feet was my only option. So, I did—and it wasn't easy since I lived for the challenges of my work. Six weeks later, Herbert and I welcomed our son, Jonathan Hollister Farnsworth.

"I must say, I fell in love with our little bundle of joy. He was a beautiful baby. He had the biggest blue eyes you've ever seen and the fairest skin. His hair was golden brown and curly—just perfect, in my opinion."

Tess smiled as she thought back to the day her son was born. That day was one of the best days of her life.

"So, you have one son. Is that correct?" Dean asked.

"Yes."

"And you don't have any other children?" Dean asked.

"No. Within hours after Jonathan was born, I started hemorrhaging and was rushed into surgery. The delivery of Jonathan had done extensive damage to my uterus, and I had to have a hysterectomy to stop the bleeding. Back then, they didn't have the knowledge they do today for treating bleeding after a birth.

"It was for the best, at least for me. I wasn't naturally maternal, but I tried to be a good mother to Jonathan. Anyway, the years went by, and Herbert and I kept up the appearance of having a stable marriage for the sake of our son and the pottery company. There's just too much to share with you right now about my life during those years. Let's just say, when Jonathan grew up and became an adult, the three of us made mistakes, turning us into people who weren't what you would call *nice*.

"We hid the scars from our pain and sadness by turning to other things to make ourselves happy. We drank, gambled, and had affairs—not me but Herbert and Jonathan. We made our servants' lives miserable, so it was hard to keep help. I can see why now."

"Tess," Sara interrupted, "I can't believe you were ever mean or nasty or hard to work for. You seem like a caring person. I can't imagine you any other way."

"Oh, Sara! What a naïve person you are! I wish you'd been in my life back then. Maybe if you had, I wouldn't have gone through what I did. If only you had been there to give me hope.

"Now, moving on. A few years ago, I found out Herbert had a son from an affair. After my hysterectomy, the doctor told me not to be intimate with Herbert for quite a long time. I think Herbert used that as an excuse and had an affair with the wife of the mayor of—I don't want to mention it—a town near where we lived at the time. It was kept quiet all those years until someone spilled the beans."

"Who did that?" Kevin asked.

"I don't know, but that's when it got back to me. It was the straw that broke the camel's back, and I went into an emotional downward spiral. I was a broken mess, and that's when Herbert and Jonathan tried to use it against me to put me in a mental health hospital.

"However, I decided to admit myself. That way, I would have control over my life and the large amount of money I inherited. They spent months trying to get control of my inheritance."

"Wasn't the money in both your and Herbert's names?" Dean asked.

"No, the money from Hanes Pottery Company was put in my name after my Hanes grandparents died. Grandfather Hanes left a sizable amount to my father and mother, and when they died, those funds were also given to me. Let's just say I have assets way over thirty million dollars. At least I did when I signed myself into Central Foothills Mental Hospital."

"So, Herbert didn't force you into the hospital?" Dean continued.

"As I said, that was his intention. I knew I needed help with my depression, so I decided to check myself in, with the understanding I would continue to be in control of my wealth.

"I was well aware of their scheming ways, so I decided to change my will. I made sure my law firm sent a woman, who just happened to be coming to visit her aunt. After she signed in, I switched rooms with one of my friends at Foothills, and I pretended to be this woman's aunt. The staff members knew the situation with my husband and son. They cared about me. I have to say, I hated leaving—but not Central Foothills.

"Is that when you decided to live out on the streets?" Dean asked.

"Yes. I knew I couldn't leave a trail, like renting an apartment or purchasing a home. If they found me, they'd have justifiable reasons to say I was incompetent. So, I left with nothing but the clothes on my back and a few hundred dollars I'd saved from my allowance that Central Foothills handled. I even left my wallet with my ID, pictures—everything that could identify me if I was found."

"How'd you get away without being seen?" Kevin asked.

"I slipped out one night when the laundry room door was left unlocked. I knew the laundry company's schedule. Every night, their service truck came to take the dirty laundry and leave the clean laundry. This always happened late at night. I watched this go on for weeks and realized the door was left unlocked for about an hour while the delivery people took a dinner break.

"The night I escaped, I waited until a little after midnight. Thank God, the night staff didn't see me, which was a miracle since cameras were everywhere.

"I stole clothes that belonged to the night janitor, and I pretended to be him. I had already memorized his schedule and his habits, so I waited until he went to his supply closet. He always went outside to take a smoke most evenings, and was gone for about fifteen minutes. That's when I grabbed the cart and quickly walked down the corridor, away from the camera so as not to show my face.

"Thankfully, Harry is a short man and wore his ball cap constantly, so unless you looked very carefully, you wouldn't know it wasn't him. I figured by the time they discovered I was missing, I'd be long gone. And I was."

Kevin, Dean, and Sara smiled, thinking of Tess coming up with such a scheme.

"What did you do once you got away?" Dean asked.

"Central Foothills is close to downtown Zanesville, so I headed there. I planned on finding some homeless folks who would welcome me and show me how to live on the streets. I'd read articles about older homeless people being abused by the ones who had been out there for a long time, so I knew I had to be careful. They didn't like anyone threatening their territory. It's amazing how complex the homeless community is. They have their own class system. That's the first thing newcomers learn if they want to survive.

"I figured I'd have better luck if I went under the bridge on State Street, closest to Central Foothills. I'd seen people there but never gave them much thought. Who would have imagined I would become one of them?

"Since it was so late, I hoped most of them would be asleep and wouldn't notice me. I stopped at a dumpster behind an apartment building and looked for something to lie on and maybe an old blanket or rug to cover me. Sure enough, I found a small rug and a flannel sheet that had been ripped almost in two. I didn't want to think about the last time it'd been washed or whose body had lain on it.

"I knew clean clothes, a bed, and fresh food would quickly disappear, but I never thought how demeaning it would be. I wouldn't wish that life on anyone. Well, maybe a few I would." Tess laughed heartily.

"Tess, I'm so sorry you had to go through that experience," Sara said. "There for the grace of God go I. It could happen to any of us."

"Yeah, you can say that again. There I was with assets of millions of dollars, and I'm looking through a dumpster for something to sleep on. Never saw that coming.

"Anyway, that was the beginning of my other life until Sara found me last week. I lived that life just over a year, but a lot happened during that time. I want to move forward for now and get this other stuff taken care of. So, can we move ahead for now?"

"I think we can," Dean replied, "but I need to verify your story. If all the information you've told me pans out, then you'll become a ward of the state, and I can put you in protective custody until the trial of Tom Applebee and Sharon Brown. Is that acceptable?"

"I guess I don't have much choice."

"Not if you want to get your former life back. I know it's not going to be easy, and it will bring up legal questions since you left the facility without consent, but I think we can work that all out. You'll need to contact your lawyer eventually. In the meantime, Kevin and Sara said you can live here, and the story will be you're Sara's long-lost aunt. You'll have to come up with a believable story so I don't have to deal with a bunch of nosy parishioners from the church. Can you do that?"

Tess laughed. "I'm pretty good at telling lies. I know that's wrong, but living on the streets trained me to lie through my teeth to keep from being arrested or having someone find out who I am. So, yes, I can come up with a believable story."

Dean smiled. "I thought you could. So, it looks like we have a plan. I'll start making some calls this afternoon. Besides Central Foothills and the doctors who treated you, I'll need contact information for your lawyer and, if possible, any records from other doctors you've seen over the years."

Tess sat quietly on the sofa while Dean, Kevin, and Sara went into the family room to discuss arrangements for Tess. She felt peace mixed with fear. She didn't know what the outcome of all this would be, but she knew her best interest was in the hands of Kevin, Sara, and Dean.

She did something she never would have expected. She closed her eyes and asked God to help her through this mess. When she opened her eyes, she felt a calmness that moved through her body and into her heart.

She also felt tears on her face—tears of joy. At that moment, she knew God loved her. He had her in his care and would do what was best for her. *Wow, now I see why Kevin and Sara believe in a God who loves all his children! I hope I can make you proud of me, God.*

"Tess, are you ready to give me the information I need to make those calls?" Dean asked.

"I sure am. I'm ready to get this show on the road. You know, I'm ready for Julianne Teresa Hollister Farnsworth to start living again—but you all can still call me Tess!"

Chapter 24

Two days had passed since Jonathan was released from the hospital. His heart rate was staying normal, probably because of the digitalis. All his test results came back negative, meaning his heart was in good shape, other than having tachycardia, a rapid heartbeat. The doctor advised him to take a course called biofeedback, offered at the hospital, to help him control his stress. It had something to do with visualizing his heart rate and breathing to slow it down without medicine. He had an appointment for the next day.

After Derek brought him home from the hospital, Jonathan assured him he would look into the man claiming to be his brother. He knew his office building had a great security system, so it should be easy to get a copy of the surveillance tape.

In the meantime, Derek agreed to check on birth records in the Zanesville area two to three years after Jonathan's birth.

If this man is my half-brother, Jonathan mused, *why would he have waited all these years to look for me? Either he recently learned he had a half-brother and was curious, or Jeremy found out his father's wife had millions and wondered if he could get any of the money.* Either way, it made Jonathan angry just thinking about it. He picked up the phone and called the familiar number.

"Hello." Delilah's voice was sultry and familiar.

"Hello, sweetheart!"

"Jonathan! Where have you been? I tried calling you for two days, but you never called—"

"I've been in the hospital—"

"The hospital!" Delilah interrupted. "What on earth happened? Are you all right? Is there anything I can do for you?"

No, I'm fine at the moment."

"Are you home?"

"Derek brought me home a few days ago."

"A few days ago!" Delilah was furious that Jonathan had waited so long to contact her.

"I'm sorry, sweetheart, but I wasn't allowed to make many calls. Doctor's orders."

Delilah was pouting. "I suppose I'll forgive you. Tell me what happened that was so traumatic that it put you in the hospital," Delilah asked, concerned.

Jonathan told her what had happened.

"Just like that?"

"Yes, but this man tried to buffer the news by saying he didn't want to upset me, then blurted it out. I know I don't have a half-brother ... at least I don't think I do. My dad had his lady friends when I was young, but he would have told me if one of them got pregnant. We were always pretty tight. I remember Mom telling me she had to have a hysterectomy. Then, years later, Dad told me he and Mom couldn't be intimate for months after I was born because of the hysterectomy."

Delilah jumped in. "I had a friend who went through the same thing a few years ago, but intimacy was not off the table for long. Maybe your mother just didn't want to be intimate with your father."

"I suppose. They were never affectionate with each other when I was growing up. Let's just say it didn't make for a very happy childhood."

"Poor dear," she purred, making Jonathan laugh.

"Anyway, there was some talk about Dad and the mayor's wife. I was pretty young at the time and didn't understand any of it."

"So, what's next?"

"Well, I need to get back to the office and take care of a few things.

I don't want anyone knowing about my trip to the hospital, especially the board of directors."

"And what did you tell your secretary? I know what a busybody she is. Why you keep her around is a puzzle to me."

"She may be curious about my private life, but she's a gem in taking care of business. I called her from the hospital, told her I had to go out of town for a few days, and she needed to cancel my appointments. She knows not to ask too many questions about my whereabouts. Anyway, I'll call you this evening. Send me a quick text when you can talk."

"I will, dearest."

"I don't know what I would do without you."

"I feel the same way. Talk to you this evening. I love you!"

"Love you too." Jonathan hung up and finished getting ready for work.

Chapter 25

Offices of O'Donnell, Young, and Murphy, New York City

"Good morning. O'Donnell, Young, and Murphy. How can I help you?" Jennifer Spencer answered her first call of the day.

"Good morning. This is Sheriff Dean Adams from Jonesboro, Ohio. I'm calling about one of your clients, Julianne Farnsworth. I need to speak to the person who's in charge of her legal affairs."

"That would be one of our junior partners, Brandon Keith. He's not in the office right now, but I can have him call you."

"That would be fine. Please tell him it's important he gets back to me as soon as possible. I'm trying to confirm whether the person claiming to be Julianne Farnsworth is for real. We have her in our custody at the present time. She says your law firm is the one she and her family have used for many years."

"I will make sure Mr. Keith knows how important it is to get in touch with you. Is there anything else I can do for you?"

"No, not for now," Dean replied.

"Have a great day, Sheriff Adams."

"Thank you, Jennifer," he replied. *It will be an even better day if the information Tess gave me is true.*

As soon as she hung up, Brandon came barreling through the double-glass doors, lugging a huge cardboard box while holding on for dear life to the bottom. Whatever was inside was causing the box to sag from the weight.

Jennifer stifled a laugh. "What in the world is that?"

Brandon was grinning ear to ear. "Well, Ms. Spencer, this is one of five boxes with information about that missing woman we found out was Julianne Farnsworth. Mr. O'Donnell said I could look through them. You can't imagine how hard it was getting it up here. I'm ready for a nice, relaxing lunch before I tackle whatever's in here."

"You might want to wait on lunch and those files for a sec after I tell you about a call that just came in. The caller, Sheriff Dean Adams, was asking about a woman by the name of Julianne Farnsworth." Jennifer waited for the impact of the name to settle into Brandon's brain. She didn't wait long.

Brandon's eyes widened as he blurted out, "Shut the front door! You've got to be kidding!"

Jennifer broke out laughing. "I thought that might make you happy."

"Who did you say called? How long ago? What did they want?"

"Slow down, cowboy," Jennifer said. "Take a couple of deep breaths and sit down over there on the couch. I'll get the information."

Brandon obeyed. His thoughts raced with all kinds of questions he wanted to ask the caller.

Jennifer quickly returned. "Here's the name, number, and a short message from the caller."

Brandon jerked the note from her hands. "What is this? I can't understand a word of it."

"If you'll wait a minute, I'll tell you what it says. I use shorthand, so let me have it back please."

Brandon could tell that she wasn't happy with him, and he'd better do what she asked. The first thing he'd learned since he began working at the agency was always do what Jennifer said. She basically ran the place.

"Sorry. I shouldn't have acted that way. You're only trying to help."

"Right. So, calm down. The information isn't going anywhere." She quickly transcribed the message.

Brandon immediately grabbed the phone to dial the number.

Jennifer was aggravated. "Brandon, I don't know what I'm going to do with you if you don't stop reacting without thinking first. I'm the one who spoke to Sheriff Adams, and I'm the one who is going to call him. Now, go to your office and wait for me to let you know when I have him on the phone. You got that?"

"I got it. Sorry. I don't know why I'm acting like this."

"It's because you're excited to get a case that has potential. I've worked for this firm for over fifteen years, and I understand how frustrating it is to get all the boring and mundane cases."

"I guess you're right. I have been frustrated. So, before you call Sheriff … what was his name?"

"Sheriff Dean Adams."

"Yes, thank you. Before you make the call, could you give me a few minutes to calm down? I don't want to sound like I'm inexperienced, which I guess I am, but I don't want him to know that."

"You're doing an amazing job for this firm, Brandon. You just need to focus on the cases you're given, no matter how boring they are. Mr. O'Donnell told me just the other day how happy he is with your work."

"Really? Mr. O'Donnell said that?"

"Yes, he did. He doesn't say that about every junior lawyer who's worked here. Trust me, he likes your work. Now, go to your office, young man, and I'll let you know when I have the sheriff on the phone."

Jennifer smiled tenderly as Brandon hurried to his office. *He's so young,* she thought. *I wish I could make him see that, in time, he'll be wishing for those boring and mundane cases. But, for now, I'll continue to help him weave his way among the twists and turns of becoming a seasoned lawyer.*

Jennifer dialed the number of the Jonesboro sheriff's office and was transferred to Sheriff Adams. "Sheriff, this is Jennifer Spencer. We spoke earlier about a woman who says our law firm handles her family legal affairs. You said her name was Julianne Farnsworth. Is that correct?"

"Yes, that's the name of the woman."

"Well, Brandon Keith is handling her legal affairs, so I will connect you with him. Nice talking to you again."

"Brandon," Jennifer said when he answered his phone, "I have Sheriff Adams on line one. If you need my assistance, let me know. Just stay calm and listen to what he is asking before you answer. With what I've heard around the office, this case could be one of our most interesting in a while. Go get 'em, tiger!"

Brandon took a deep breath, then said, "Sheriff Adams, this is Brandon Keith. I was told you're calling to verify if Julianne Farnsworth is one of our clients."

"That's correct, Mr. Keith. Your secretary, Ms. Spencer, confirmed that she is, and she told me you're in charge of the account at the present time."

"That's correct. I was given the account just a few days ago, so I haven't had time to familiarize myself with her background."

"As I told Ms. Spencer, we have Ms. Farnsworth in our custody at the present time, and I'm attempting to confirm the information she has shared with me."

"May I ask why she's in your custody? Has she committed a crime?"

"No, she hasn't, but a crime has been committed against her. At the present time, I can't tell you more about the case. She's being housed with a couple in our community while I confirm what she's shared with us is correct and she is who she says she is."

"So, how can I help?"

"For one thing, you have to keep our conversation quiet. Ms. Farnsworth's life could be in danger, so the fewer people who know her whereabouts, the better for her safety."

"This sounds pretty serious." Brandon was intrigued. "Do you mind if I bring our senior lawyer into our confidence?"

"Yes, that's fine."

"Mr. O'Donnell is the one who gave me this missing person's case. He has known Ms. Farnsworth family for many years and is quite concerned about her."

"Glad to know your firm is working on the case and we can work together to get Ms. Farnsworth in a safer situation."

"Glad for that too. What do you want me to do next?"

"You can talk to your boss about our conversation, but I need all of you not to divulge any information about Ms. Farnsworth. There's a man who is working very hard to find her, and I feel it's not for a good reason. So, I need full confidentiality on the part of your office."

"We can do that. I just found five boxes full of documents and other papers on Ms. Farnsworth's family. This case obviously is no longer a missing person case, but it sounds like it's still a mystery."

"Yes, it's been a mystery for sure, but in the last few days, we've found quite a bit about Ms. Farnsworth."

"That's great news! Do you want me to contact you after I've gone through these boxes?"

"No, not right now. I still have calls to make about Ms. Farnsworth, so just keep what you find until we can go over it together. Thanks so much for your help and for understanding the severity of the situation."

"But I haven't done anything yet."

"Just understanding the situation is helpful. I'll be in touch in the next few weeks, but until then, keep things under wraps."

"I'll do that."

Chapter 26

Once it was established that Tess was who she said she was, Dean Adams turned his attention back to the daily events of Jonesboro, along with his efforts to find the man who called about Tess. He couldn't figure out why the man never called back, since he had been so intent on finding out Tess's true identity. He knew it would take a while for Brandon to go through the boxes of information about Tess and her family. Meanwhile, Tess, Sara, and Kevin settled into a routine.

"Tess, breakfast is ready!" Sara called up the stairs. "Kevin has to leave early this morning because of an important meeting, and he wants to talk to you before he leaves."

"I'm coming! Don't get your panties in a wad!" Tess hollered back. "This blasted arthritis is making me miserable," she murmured as she walked to the kitchen and sat down at her usual spot at the table. Sara was busily finishing up breakfast and didn't notice Tess's slow movements. If she had, she would have told her it was time to see her doctor about the arthritis. Doctors were not on Tess's list of favorite people.

Kevin walked into the kitchen, whistling the song he'd chosen for this coming Sunday's opening hymn. His constant whistling drove Tess up the wall. It wasn't just the whistling; his overly positive attitude annoyed her. Happy people made her nervous. Why, she didn't know, but they just did.

"Tess," Kevin said, plopping down in his chair, "I was thinking about Thanksgiving—you know, that's a week from Thursday—and wondered if there were any traditions you and your family had. Did you do anything that was just about Thanksgiving? We want you to feel at home with us this year."

"Herbert and Jonathan barely spoke to me the last few years they were all at home, so no, there weren't any traditions."

Kevin saw the pain and sadness in her eyes. "I'm sorry. I didn't mean to bring up bad memories."

"Ah, bless your heart, Kevin. That's so nice … thinking about me."

Kevin smiled at Tess's response. "It's hard to believe you have only been here a few months. Sara and I didn't realize how boring our lives were until you came into our lives, and we are thankful for that. You keep us on our toes as Christians. Seeing us through your eyes makes us wonder if we confuse non-Christians by saying one thing and doing another. And might I say, you seem to have picked up a few of our Christian habits."

"I don't know about that, but I've been taking notes of things you all do. I've watched you do kind things. Why, I just saw you yesterday, Sara, being so patient with that old busybody, Mrs. Applebee. How you can stand there and smile and be so nice beats me. If it had been me, I would've told her to mind her own business. She's such a big gossip. The only thing I can think of to cause me to be nice to her would be what you call the Holy Spirit, and it would have to be a huge amount."

Sara and Kevin burst into laughter, continuing until Tess started getting irritated.

"Sorry, Tess," Kevin said. "Just for your information, it's hard even for us to stay positive about people like Mrs. Applebee. So don't praise us too much."

"Well, I still think it takes a lot of willpower to do what you both do."

Tess turned her attention back to her breakfast. She hadn't known what to tell Kevin when he asked her about a Thanksgiving tradition. A memory of her Hanes grandparents' acts of kindness came to her while she was eating. The day before Thanksgiving, they would load up their car with all kinds of food: canned goods, bakery items, fresh vegetables, and, of course, fresh turkeys. Some years, they invited Tess to go with them. Their destination was the local Catholic church in one of the poorest sections of Zanesville. She learned years later that not only did they do all that, but they gave the parish money throughout the year. She always wondered why they didn't do that through their own church, but she guessed they didn't want to bring attention to themselves.

"Kevin, there was a tradition with my grandfather and grandmother Hanes, that I had forgotten about until now. Do you want to hear it?" He didn't answer, so she asked again. "Kevin, did you hear me?"

"What? I'm sorry. I was thinking about something else. So, what is the tradition?"

She told him, then, in the next breath, asked him what he had been thinking about. "You sure looked far away. You know me and my curiosity. I can't think about Thanksgiving after seeing that spaced-out look on your face. Come on, spill the beans. What were you thinking?"

"I was thinking about you and wondering what's going on with the investigation and how much longer this is going to take," Kevin confessed. "I know Dean said he would keep us informed, but we haven't heard anything in over a month. So, that's what I was thinking."

"Kevin," Tess replied, "living on the streets was scarier than this investigation. Having a roof over my head is my safety now. Plus, I have a comfortable bed and loads of food."

Kevin looked straight at Tess. "One thing I've learned about you is that you're a very thankful person, and you show it. There's a sermon in that! Thanks, Tess!"

"You sure confuse me," Tess replied. "One minute I think I've got you figured out, and then—wham!—you go and do something weird, and I'm back to the beginning! Fun times around here whether I want them or not. Well, if we're finished with this little talk, can we get back to eating? I'm hungry."

After breakfast, Tess helped Sara clean up the kitchen. Kevin went to his home office to catch up on a few things before he went to a special church meeting.

For a change, he seemed excited about the meeting, and Tess was curious. For some reason, she thought the meeting had something to do with her. Why, she didn't know. When she lived on the streets, she developed a sixth sense that helped keep her relatively safe. Now, that sense was buzzing in her head, and she didn't like it.

∽

"Sara, do you know anything about the meeting Kevin has this morning? He seemed sort of excited when he left to go to his office. He tells you everything, so you must know what it's all about."

"Uh, I'm, uh, not sure what it's about, but I'm sure it's church related. Why? Do you think it's something else?"

"Well, yes, I do, and I don't know why I'm feeling a bit nervous about it. You see, when I lived on the streets, I had this strange feeling sometimes, and it seemed to come from within."

"I suppose they call that intuition, but some people call it ESP. I personally like to think it's God talking to us, Sara said to Tess." "So, you think something's not right because you're feeling strange?"

"Yeah, that's what I'm saying. What I can't figure out is why I'd be feeling that way now. Oh well. I'll just get my mind on something else. You need me to do anything?"

"No, I can't think of anything."

"Well, it's a nice day, what with the sun shining and all. I wouldn't mind taking a walk down to the sandwich place inside the grocery store. I could get me a bottle of orange soda and sit at one of those little tables. I love watching folks come and go. If you need something, I can get it for you."

Sara looked at Tess and decided it might be a good idea to get her out of the house for a while. "I think that's a great idea. I do need a loaf of bread and a head of iceberg lettuce. That won't be too heavy for you to carry home. Let me go and get some money from Kevin. I'm out of cash right now. I'll be right back."

She hurried down the hallway as fast as she could, burst into Kevin's office, and blurted, "Tess is on to us, and I don't know how to get her to stop asking questions."

"What are you talking about? What questions?"

"Tess said she thought something was up with your meeting and asked if it was about her. I said, 'Of course not,' but I don't think I sounded convincing."

"Why on earth would she think the meeting was about her, even though it is?"

"She told me while living on the streets, she developed a sixth sense that helped keep her safe. I told her it was God's way of telling her she's safe now. I think she believed me, but you know her. She can see through people like they're transparent. Anyway, she's going to the grocery store to get a soda and sit at one of the sandwich shop's tables to watch people coming and going. You know how she loves to do that, so hopefully it will get her mind away from trying to figure out what's up. Quick! Give me ten dollars!"

"Why?"

"I told her I didn't have any cash, and I was going to get it from you."

"I thought you just went to the bank yesterday."

"I did, but I told her that so I could come and tell you what she's thinking about the meeting. Sometimes, Kevin, you are so clueless. I suppose that's because you always see the best in everything. Sorry, I'm just feeling a bit stressed."

"I know, sweetheart. Tess can make even the best situation stressful. Go! Quick, before she comes looking for you. She can read me like a book too."

Sara threw Kevin a kiss, then ran back down the hall toward the kitchen, where she swung around the corner, almost knocking Tess over. Tess was standing with her coat and hat on, tapping her foot impatiently.

"What in the world, Sara! You almost knocked me on my butt. I'm not in that big of a hurry to get to the store. Just give me the money."

"Sorry. I thought I'd left the teapot on and didn't want to start a fire. I can't tell you how many times I've done that."

"You are sure acting strange today," Tess muttered under her breath.

"Did you say something?" Sara asked.

"Nothing important. See you later."

Tess strolled down the sidewalk, enjoying the sun and unusually warm weather for late fall. This would be her first Thanksgiving in many years where she would be with people who cared about her. The folks she spent time with while she was homeless tried to make the holidays a little less sad and lonely, but they, too, were in the same boat. Some of the local churches invited the homeless to come and share a Thanksgiving meal at their church. It was nice to eat hot and tasty food, even if it was for just that day.

Tess forced herself to stop thinking about the past. She just wanted to enjoy the blessing of walking to the store and having the money to buy a soda instead of stealing it.

She sat at the little table in the sandwich shop, watching people come and go while sipping her orange soda. She looked away for just a moment, and when she looked up, there was Mrs. Applebee coming through the door. She tried getting off the stool quickly so as not to be seen, but the stool was too high. The next best thing to do was turn away from the door, hoping Mrs. Applebee wouldn't see her, but she didn't make it. She looked up to see Mrs. Applebee rushing toward her like a wild animal ready to take down its dinner.

"Hello, Tess!" Mrs. Applebee huffed, out of breath.

"Why, if it isn't Mrs. Applebee!" Tess exclaimed. "Fancy meeting you here. I was just relaxing, drinking my favorite soda pop, and watching people coming and going."

"I'm glad to see you, Tess! Is Sara with you?"

"No, she's home. I told her I wanted to get out of the house and enjoy the sun."

"Why, that's exactly what I wanted to do. They say great minds think alike." Mrs. Applebee laughed, snorting like a big old sow.

What in the world happened to make that poor woman laugh that way? Tess wondered. *If her husband had to listen to that for years, it's no wonder he died young.*

"You know, it won't be long before the snow will be flying. I'm just thankful to have a nice, warm, and cozy home to be in," Tess said.

"It's so nice that Pastor Kevin and Sara have invited you to stay with them for a while. I forget, where did you say you're from? My memory is not as good as it used to be."

"I'm from Indiana, a small town called Osgood. It's near Versailles."

"Oh. I thought I heard you were from the Zanesville area," said Mrs. Applebee.

"I do have relatives near there, so that's what you most likely heard. I hear you've been around here all your life. That must be nice," Tess said, hoping to get Mrs. Applebee to talk about herself and quit asking questions. If there was one thing Mrs. Applebee enjoyed doing, it was talking about herself.

"Yes, I was born on a farm right outside of town. My father owned the local hardware store until he retired. Then my husband, Charles, took over the business. After he died, we had to sell it to someone out of the family. None of the grandchildren wanted to run a hardware store. It was a sad day for me, but I survived. I'm now part-owner of the local hair salon. You'll have to stop in and get that beautiful hair of yours cut and styled."

Tess kept saying, "Oh, is that so?" while Mrs. Applebee went on and on with her life story. Finally, Tess said, "Well, it's been a pleasure visiting with you, Mrs. Applebee, but I need to get the things Sara asked me to pick up and head back. I'll see you at Sunday's services."

Tess managed to get off the high barstool, then walked toward the produce section. Before she could get there, Mrs. Applebee rushed up beside her and asked if she was excited about her birthday party this coming Saturday.

Tess stopped dead in her tracks, looked at Mrs. Applebee, and said, "What are you talking about? I don't know anything about a birthday party. My birthday isn't until April, so it isn't mine."

"Oh dear," said Mrs. Applebee. "I think I may have made a huge booboo." She laughed nervously and moved as fast as she could toward the pharmacy. "See you Sunday," she said over her shoulder, moving farther into the crowded grocery store.

Tess got the bread and lettuce Sara wanted. *Where in the world did Mrs. Applebee get the idea that I have a birthday next week?* she mused. *It must be somebody else.* She hadn't told anyone when her birthday was. Many years had passed since she enjoyed celebrating her birthday.

In a fog, she walked the short distance from the store to the manse. She couldn't get the conversation with Mrs. Applebee out of her head. It had been years since she'd thought about her birthday. No one cared when she lived at home with Herbert and Jonathan or when she lived on the streets. The reality that her birthday was Saturday hit her hard. Tears flowed down her wrinkled cheeks. It hurt to remember.

"There you are!" Sara said when Tess entered the kitchen. "I was getting a little concerned. You don't usually take that much time to get a few items from the store. Are you alright? You look a little pale. Do you feel sick?" Sara kept asking questions until Tess stopped her.

"I'm fine except for one thing." Tess was angry. "Are you and Kevin having a surprise birthday party for me on Saturday?"

"Who told you that?" Now Sara was angry. "You weren't supposed to know. It was supposed to be a combined birthday and welcome party."

"Why would the church want to do that?" Tess asked.

"So many people have told Kevin and me how much they're enjoying having you worship with them. They asked Kevin if they could have a welcome party for you after church sometime. He said he thought that was a great idea, and they came up with this Saturday afternoon."

"A church gathering for me? Why, that's mighty nice. I've enjoyed worshiping with them, too, once I got the hang of all the stuff you do. But the birthday thing is all wrong!"

"Now don't go and get all riled up," Sara added. "Kevin found out when your real birthday is, and since it's this Saturday, we decided to do a surprise birthday party along with the church event. What do you think?" Sara smiled, hoping Tess would smile back.

"I told you the wrong date of my birthday for a reason. I didn't want you to know. Well, I guess that didn't work."

"But you told all of us who you really are. You must have known Sheriff Adams would find out when and where you were born. We never would have come up with this celebration if we thought it would hurt you! I can't understand why you're reacting this way, but you must have a reason."

Sara sat down at the kitchen table and folded her hands. She looked at Tess with deep sadness in her eyes. Sara finally conceded. "I'll go and tell Kevin to cancel the birthday party on Saturday. We'll just tell everyone we had the wrong date and laugh it off. Thanks for getting the bread and lettuce for me."

Sara got up and brushed past Tess. She went down the hall to Kevin's office. When she entered, he could see that she was upset. "What's the matter, sweetheart?"

She sat down on the love seat and told him what had just happened with Tess. She still couldn't figure out why Tess was so upset. She also wanted to know who spilled the beans. But when she thought about it, maybe this was a blessing in disguise. How embarrassing and upsetting it would have been for everyone, especially Tess, if she'd reacted so negatively at the gathering.

"What do you think happened that would make Tess act this way?" Sara asked.

"I don't know, sweetheart; it doesn't sound like the Tess we think we know."

Kevin sat beside Sara and pulled her into his arms. She laid her head on his chest and listened to the beating of his heart. It always comforted her. Throughout their marriage, she always knew she could go to Kevin, no matter what the problem. He seemed to know what to say to make her feel better.

"Let's go talk to her together," Sara said. "I just want to know what is going on, and I don't want to do it by myself."

"I agree. We'll do it together," Kevin said. "That's the way she sees us, doing things together. Right?"

"Right! I feel better already. Thanks, honey. You always know what's best! Well, maybe not always but most of the time." She smiled at Kevin.

He stood up, pulled her up from the couch, and gave her a kiss.

"You know what?" she said, wrapping her arms around his neck. "I'm going to make your evening very special after we get this situation taken care of with Tess."

"Oh, really!" He laughed and kissed her again.

She kissed his ear and whispered, "I've missed it being just the two of us. I love Tess, but it has not been easy finding alone time."

He laughed, untangling himself from her arms. He grabbed her hand and pulled her down the hallway toward the kitchen, laughing and hooting like a kid. When they got to the doorway of the kitchen, Tess was still standing there, her arms folded. She didn't look any happier than when Sara left.

"What is going on with you two? Here I am, waiting for Sara to come and tell me how angry you are with me. Instead, the two of you are acting like teenagers. So? What's going on?"

Kevin cleared his throat, looked sternly at Tess, and burst out laughing. He looked at Sara, and she started laughing too.

Tess was dumbfounded. *Well, they've gone and lost their minds,* she thought. *What in the world did Sara tell Kevin?*

Kevin and Sara stopped laughing. They could see Tess was getting angry.

"Come sit down by the fireplace, Tess," Kevin offered. He took her weathered hand and guided her to her chair.

As soon as Tess sat down, the tension she'd had all morning melted away. *Why, these sweet, caring souls wouldn't do anything to hurt me. They're the ones who continue to love and care about me.*

Tess looked at Kevin and smiled. He smiled back, relieved to see her calming down a bit.

"We just want to find out why you don't want to have a birthday party. That's all. Nothing else."

Sara jumped in. "I thought you knew by now how much we care about you. So, your reaction hurt me deeply." Sara's eyes filled with tears.

"Well, I suppose I did overreact. It's just when I found out about the party, anger burrowed deep into my gut. It was as if I was back home living with a cold and indifferent husband and a selfish, narcissistic son. The anger was so strong I couldn't breathe. Please forgive me, Sara."

Sara got up from the couch and sat by Tess. She took Tess's hands, lifted them to her lips, and kissed them. Tess didn't know what to do. Nobody had ever done that. Just the feeling of her hands in Sara's lifted her spirits. She and Sara smiled at each other through their tears, then began to laugh. It was a joyful laugh, filled with love. If there ever was a time Tess might believe in this thing called the Holy Spirit, it was now. Her soul filled with warmth and happiness. She started singing a song she had heard the first Sunday she attended church with Sara and Kevin. She liked the melody, but the words now had meaning as well.

> And God will raise you up on eagles' wings,
> Bear you on the breath of dawn,
> Make you to shine like the sun.
> And hold you in the palm of God's hand.

"Tess, I didn't know you had such a beautiful singing voice!" Kevin exclaimed. "You should think about singing in the choir. I'm sure they would love to have you."

"Don't even think it!" Tess said, giving Kevin one of her stink eye looks. She then said, "We've had tears, singing, and laughter, folks, but I guess I need to fess up why I'm so angry about this party stuff."

"You're right," Kevin said, "and please, the truth. No more keeping secrets."

"I will. I'll tell you the truth. But I don't want to see any pity in your eyes. So, can I trust the both of you to listen and not react?"

"Yes." Sara smiled.

"We won't react, at least for now," Kevin added.

"OK then, here it goes. When I was growing up, my parents and grandparents spoiled me rotten, and that included birthday celebrations. They'd go all out. They'd invite friends and their families; they'd even invite the neighbors. It was always a grand event."

"That must have been fun!" Sara said.

"It sure was. Mother loved to bake, so she'd make my favorite, chocolate cake with chocolate icing. And she decorated it beautifully. Even after Herbert and I were married, Mother would make my birthday cake."

"I'm confused, Tess. You're telling us how happy your birthdays were, so where's this going?"

"Just hold on. So, these celebrations stopped after my grandparents and parents died. Herbert didn't even try to keep my birthdays special. I missed celebrating with my family, but I just pushed those feelings down inside me. It was just another day when my birthday rolled around. Then something happened the birthday right before I committed myself to Central Foothills."

She stopped talking. In her mind, she stepped back to the morning of her birthday two years ago. She was standing in the kitchen of her home in Zanesville. Gloria, her friend since childhood, sat at the round oak table that had belonged to her Grandmother Hollister. They were laughing about the time they got caught smoking Grandfather Hollister's Cuban cigars out behind the horse barn.

"I can't believe you're having another birthday," Gloria said. "It seems like it was just yesterday we were planning your marriage to Herbert. Let's see … I think you said your forty-eighth anniversary is coming up in June. I know things have been strained between the two of you for years, and I imagine when you heard the news about his love child, that must have been traumatic."

"Tess, are you alright?" Sara asked.

Kevin took hold of her cold, shaking hands. She looked directly into his eyes but appeared not to see him. Her gaze moved to Sara.

Suddenly, her body jerked. She blinked, her eyes focusing on Sara. She seemed to have been in a trance.

"Tess, you're back!" Kevin was relieved.

"What in heaven's name are you talking about? Of course, I'm here." She shook her head, clearing out the cobwebs from two years ago. She hadn't realized she'd stopped talking until Kevin's voice broke into her thoughts. *How long have I been, as Kevin said, away?*

"You looked miles away, Tess," Sara said.

Tess began talking again. She told Kevin and Sara about her friend Gloria.

"What did Gloria tell you?" Sara asked.

"She told me that Herbert had a child with the mayor's wife of a small town not far from where we were living, a few years after Jonathan was born. She assumed I knew. She always wondered why I hadn't said anything to her over the years. When she realized I didn't know, she felt awful. Poor Gloria was almost in tears, but I assured her I was fine. I should have known Herbert was messing around. I guess I didn't want to know, but I never dreamed he had a child with this woman."

"Wow, I didn't see that coming," said Kevin. "I imagine you were not just upset but embarrassed by the situation it put you in. What did you do after Gloria left?"

"I went and poured myself a glass of whiskey and waited for Herbert to come home. When he did, I told him I just found out about the child he and the mayor's wife had."

"How did he react?" Kevin asked.

"He looked at me with pity, and I just lost it. I threw my glass of whiskey in his face and walked out of the room. I grabbed my purse and car keys and left. I didn't come home until after midnight. When

I walked into the darkened house, it hit me hard. How could I have been such a fool not to have known about the child?"

"Don't beat yourself up, Tess. It wasn't your fault." Sara tried hard not to show how angry she was. *How dare that husband of hers treat her that way. If Kevin had done that to me, I would have done more than throw whiskey in his face. But then, Kevin would never do what Herbert did.*

"Sometimes we're aware things are being done that shouldn't be done," Sara offered, "but we sort of put our heads in the sand, if you know what I mean. I've done that before because I didn't want to face what I suspected was happening. You may have suspected something was up with Herbert and this woman, but you worked even harder for your father at the pottery company to keep those thoughts away."

Kevin's face turned red with anger. "Sara's right. The only thing you're guilty of is not kicking Herbert's sorry ass out of the house."

Tess's face lit up when she saw his red face. She threw back her head and laughed until the tears ran down her face. It was funny enough to see his red face, but for him to swear was even funnier.

"You've made my day, Kevin Richardson! I never thought in a hundred years I'd hear that word come out of your mouth!" She laughed until her stomach hurt. "I feel better than I have in months, and I have you to thank. Whew, that felt good!"

"I'm sorry I said it," Kevin responded, "but it just slipped out so easily. I will definitely have to ask forgiveness for that slip of the tongue." He looked a bit sheepish, but he laughed too.

"I hope you know that even Christians sometimes use words they shouldn't, and this was one of those times. At least it made you laugh."

Tess went over to Kevin and kissed him on the top of his head. "You are such a sweet man. I'm so glad to have you in my life."

"So, are we on for the surprise birthday party that isn't a surprise anymore?" Kevin asked.

"You betcha!" Tess said. "Let's get ready to party hardy!"

"Where did you hear that?" Sara asked. "I haven't heard that saying in years and never expected a woman your age to even know it."

"I may be turning seventy-eight, Sara, but I've had a few parties that definitely were hardy. In fact, some of the celebrating would turn your face a bit red."

"What on earth did you …? No, don't tell me. I don't want to know." Then she laughed. "OK, tell me the cleanest one, if there are any."

Tess threw back her head and laughed again, feeling the weight of the past slowly lifting from her soul. Deep inside, a burst of warmth moved through her. *Maybe this is the year I'll finally be freed of all the emotional pain I've felt for more years than I care to acknowledge. A celebration of friendship and life … wow!*

Chapter 27

Jonathan sat at his office desk on a Saturday morning, staring at his calendar opened to the month of November. *Where has the time gone?* he thought as he rubbed his tired eyes. He thought for sure he would have found his mother by now. Even if that had happened, what was he going to do to get her to change her will and designate him as the heir of her money?

Frustrated, he got up, walked down the empty corridors to the executive kitchen, and started a pot of coffee. The quiet helped him concentrate on what needed attention. As the largest ad agency in New York City, there always was something that needed his input. Today wasn't any different.

While he waited for the coffee to brew, he thought about all that had happened since Daniel Graves brought him the surveillance video of the gas station in Jonesboro.

When the coffee was ready, Jonathan filled a large mug and headed back to his office. He anticipated the finality of catching his mother. All the sleepless nights and stressful days, and even the money he'd spent to find her, were going to be worth it. He was excited just thinking about $30 million.

But it hadn't work out as he planned. His life took an even crazier path when Jeremy showed up at his office building. Because of the situation, all the leads about his mother had gone cold.

He finished his first cup of coffee and went back for another. On his way back to his office, his phone started ringing. By the time he reached it, the caller had hung up but had left a number, which turned out to be a law firm in New York City. No one answered when he called, so he left a message.

Jonathan heard the elevator stop and footsteps heading toward his office. Getting up to investigate, he spotted Derek with a bag of bagels. Jonathan was surprised. "What are you doing here? We weren't supposed to meet until this afternoon."

"I know, but I wanted to talk to you as soon as I could about some very interesting news," Derek replied.

"Really!" Jonathan took the bagels from Derek. "Do you want a cup of coffee?"

"Sure! I'll get it." Derek knew his way around. He and Jonathan met frequently at his office after everyone had gone home or on weekends.

While Derek went for his coffee, Jonathan felt excitement growing about Derek's information. Was it about his mother or maybe something about his half-brother, Jeremy? Whatever it was, it must be important for him to show up without calling.

Derek entered the office and sat down by Jonathan's desk. He grabbed a bagel and loaded it up with cream cheese and lox.

"OK, share this earth-shaking news before I explode!" Jonathan demanded. "Would this news be about O'Donnell, Young, and Murphy law firm?

"How did you know that?" Derek asked, surprised.

"Because they called right before you got here. I missed the call, but they left their number and a message asking me to call them back."

"And what did they say when you called back?"

"Nothing. Their voice mail kicked in, so I asked them to call me back and tell me why they were calling. You must know, so what is it?"

Before Derek could say anything else, Jonathan's phone rang again. Jonathan answered quickly."

"Hello, Mr. Farnsworth. This is Brandon Keith from the law office of O'Donnell, Young, and Murphy. A few days ago, our office received a call from your lawyer, Mr. Beecher, inquiring about your mother."

"Yes, Mr. Keith, that's correct."

"Mr. Beecher said your mother's location is unknown to you and you were hoping we might know that information. Is that correct?"

"Yes, that's correct. It dawned on me recently that maybe my mother had been in contact with your firm since she disappeared. I know she and her family have used your firm for years, so I instructed Mr. Beecher to call your office in hopes you might help me find her." Jonathan tried hard to sound like a son desperate to find his lost mother.

"Mr. Farnsworth, I can understand your situation about not knowing where your mother has been, but our firm cannot divulge the whereabouts of your mother at this time. I'm sorry."

"So, you're telling me you know where my mother is, but I can't be told that information?"

"Yes, that's what I'm saying. Your mother gave our firm strict instructions for not letting anyone, including you, know her whereabouts—at least for now."

"Being the only living relative of my mother should give me the right to know where she is!" Jonathan's heart started racing, and he felt dizzy. He opened the top drawer of his desk to get his heart medicine, swallowing it without water. Then he breathed deeply to calm himself.

"Mr. Farnsworth, did you hear me?" Brandon asked.

"Yes, I heard what you said, and take my word, I will find my mother—with or without your firm's help."

Brandon was not going to let this arrogant man get to him. "I hear what you're saying, Mr. Farnsworth, but without your mother's approval, you will not find her or talk to her."

"I don't like your tone, Mr. Keith. I will have my lawyer contact one of your firm's partners and find a way around my mother's wishes. Until then, do not contact me!" Jonathan slammed down the receiver so hard it bounced off the holder and hit the floor.

Derek, seeing how upset Jonathan was, tried to calm him down.

"Jonathan, I promise, as soon as we get through the Thanksgiving holiday, I will talk to one of the senior lawyers at your mother's firm, and we will find out where she is. In the meantime, why don't you come and have Thanksgiving with Nancy, me, and the kids. She's always after me to have you come for a visit."

"I don't know, Derek. Ever since this thing with my mother, I find it hard to socialize. Nothing personal."

"Just come for the meal," Derek encouraged. "You don't have to stay long."

"I have to admit, it's hard being alone for a holiday. All right, I'll come, but just for the meal and maybe a drink or two." Jonathan felt happy for the first time in months.

"Great! Well, I'm out of here, buddy."

Derek and Jonathan walked toward the elevator. "Derek, you truly are a friend to me. When this whole mess is over, we need to celebrate. Start thinking about what we can do."

"I'll do that, Jonathan, and you know this friendship works two ways. You're a good friend to me too."

The elevator arrived, and Derek stepped in, waving goodbye to Jonathan.

Chapter 28

Kevin went back to his office, leaving Sara and Tess to talk about the upcoming celebration. He sat down at his desk and put his head in his hands, running his fingers through his hair. He was exasperated with Tess. *What are we doing?* he thought. *How in the world did we get caught up in the life of a total stranger? It seems like six months have passed, but in reality, it's only been two months.*

Looking up at the ceiling, he asked, "God, why have you brought this complex person into our lives? We truly care about her, but she's turned our lives into a soap opera."

He rubbed his eyes and reached for the phone, punching in the now familiar number. As usual, Deputy Harris answered and transferred the call.

"Hello, Kevin!" Dean said with warmth in his voice. He had grown to like and respect Kevin over the past few months. At first, he was a bit uncomfortable around him since he was clergy, but now he was relaxed and considered Kevin a friend.

Dean and his family were now attending Kevin's church. When they first started going, he was uncomfortable. He was still angry at God for letting Josh die. Listening to his former pastor talk about God's love and healing power for those who had lost a loved one made him sick to his stomach. Since meeting Kevin, and attending his church, he was starting to feel less anger toward God.

"What can I do for you, Kevin?" Dean asked.

"Well, I have two things I want to talk to you about. First is to make sure you, Joyce, and Heather are coming to Tess's surprise birthday party. And second, has anything new come up about her situation?"

"First question—yes, we're coming. Wouldn't miss it. And no, nothing new about her situation other than what I told you a few weeks ago."

"She hasn't asked lately about who's looking for her. As you know, that isn't like her."

"After we found out it was her son who called our office, it's been hit or miss on getting straight answers."

"She doesn't say much about him," Kevin said, "but I can tell she's worried about what he's up to."

"I'm still waiting to get approval to investigate Tess's son further. It seems we need a just cause for looking into his private life."

"Well, I suppose that's a safety net. I sure wouldn't want people looking into my life."

"I hear you!" Dean was thinking about the wrong things he and his buddies did when he was a young man. Thankfully, none were illegal, but they still made him uncomfortable.

He continued, "All I know at the present time is his name, where he works, and his marital status."

"We haven't told Tess he called your office to see if she was the woman in the surveillance video," said Kevin. "We think the less she knows, the better—and better for us!"

Dean laughed, knowing exactly what he meant.

"Thanks, Dean. See you at Tess's surprise party. Oh, by the way, it's not a surprise party anymore."

"Let me guess; she found out and is now making your life difficult."

"Amazing! You understand that!" Kevin laughed too. "What a complicated and, at times, endearing soul our Tess is. Well, I'll let you get back to work. See you soon."

"Sure thing. And don't let Tess get to you and Sara. She's just lucky it was your lawn she landed on."

Kevin hung up, smiling.

თ

Saturday morning arrived with the sun shining brighter than it had in days. Sara and Kevin had been given a small gift—breakfast alone. Tess's presence had changed more than their morning routine.

Sara was cleaning up the breakfast dishes when Tess walked in. She turned around in time to see Tess yawn and stretch her arms. "Well, good morning, sleepyhead," she said. "It looks like someone slept well."

Tess yawned again, rubbing her eyes to focus on Sara. She sat down at the table, propping her head up with her hands, and yawned again. Then she laid her head on the table.

"What in the world is wrong with you?" Sara asked, pouring a cup of coffee and placing it in front of Tess.

"Yawning can have another meaning, and that meaning is I slept rotten last night. I think it's all this business about that blasted party today. I know I told you and Kevin I was OK with it, but I'm starting to have second thoughts."

Sara was annoyed. "Tess, you'll enjoy yourself once you get to the party. Look at it this way—you'll most likely get presents, you'll be the center of attention, which you like, and you'll have your favorite dessert, chocolate cake with chocolate icing. What could be better than that?"

"Well, I suppose. I don't want everybody making a fuss over me. I never know what to say when that happens. So ..."

Sara sat down at the table. She absentmindedly brushed toast crumbs into her hands. She wasn't paying attention to what Tess was saying until she stopped talking.

"So, what, Tess?"

"So, I was trying to figure out how you or Kevin could be with me all the time at the party. Just in case I need help."

"Help with what?" Sara asked.

"I just told you! Weren't you listening?"

"No, not really," Sara replied.

"Then what were you thinking?" Tess was frustrated with the whole conversation.

"To be honest with you, I was thinking about what we'd do if, at the last moment, you chickened out and didn't go to the party."

Tess looked at Sara, her face softening. Of all the people she'd met over the past few months, Sara was the one she felt closest to. She reached over and took Sara's hand. "Sweetie, I promise, I will not chicken out on you. You have my word!"

Sara's face brightened. She leaned over and kissed Tess on her wrinkled cheek. "That makes me happy! Now, what were you going to say before we got sidetracked?"

"I wanted to make sure you or Kevin could be with me at all times at the party this afternoon."

"Why?"

"Because I get tongue-tied when people make a fuss over me. I've been that way all my adult life."

"If that's what you want, and it will get you to the party and make you happy, then that's what we'll do! So, does that work?"

"Yes!" Tess said with a big grin.

"Well, that's settled. Now let's go check out your clothes and see which outfit you want to wear this afternoon."

"Oh yeah, I didn't think about getting dressed up!" Tess said, followed by an offensive word. Oops! That just slipped out. Sorry."

Sara sighed. Her shoulders slumped forward, and she shook her head. "I know it's hard not to swear, but please try very hard not to swear at your party. If you feel the need to, just excuse yourself and go outside and say it to the wind or to the ground or anywhere but at the party."

Tess saw the seriousness on Sara's face. Without meaning to, she laughed.

"Tess, I'm not kidding! This is not funny!"

"OK, I'm sorry. I really mean it." Tess tried hard to stop laughing.

Sara turned around, stomped down the hall to the downstairs bathroom, and slammed the door.

"Oops! I'm in big trouble now," Tess said to herself.

She went upstairs to her bedroom and sat on the bed. She knew she needed to pray and mean it.

"God, it's me, Tess. Sara is the one who prays for me most of the time, so I hope you'll hear me without her here. She says you know me and everything about me. She says you love me no matter what I've done or how bad I am, which you know is a lot! I don't know why I laughed at Sara. What a nasty thing to do, and after all she's done for me! What in the world is my problem?"

Tears fell on her folded hands. Without intending to, she got off the bed and knelt down with her head on the bed. She cried for the emotional pain in her heart, the anger that never went away, the loss of her family and friends, and especially the loneliness.

She continued to pray. "I don't want to destroy Sara and Kevin's faith in me. I need you to show me how to stop being difficult. If anyone can do that, Sara says you can! So, please help me out. Thank you, God. Oh, and amen!"

She struggled to get up off the floor, then went downstairs to make amends with Sara. She went down the hall and knocked on the bathroom door.

"What do you want, Tess?"

"I'm sorry I laughed. I don't know what came over me. Your face looked so serious, and I was thinking how it would look if I was swearing at the air and the ground. I just found it funny. I wasn't making fun of you; I just found the whole image hilarious. That's all it was, and I'm truly sorry."

Tess turned and walked back upstairs to her bedroom. She quietly closed her door and reached under the bed for the suitcase Sara and Kevin had given her soon after they took her in. She lifted it up and put it on the bed, then took what was in the dresser drawers and put them in the suitcase. When she picked up the warm flannel pajamas Sara had given her just last week, she realized what she was doing—running away again, just like she ran away from Herbert and Jonathan. How many times was she going to run away from her pain?

There was a soft knock on Tess's bedroom door. She opened

it, and there stood Sara. Her cheeks were red from crying, but the familiar sweet smile Tess had come to love was there.

Sara looked over Tess's shoulder and spotted the suitcase open on her bed. She walked past Tess and lifted the new flannel pajamas Tess had placed in the suitcase. Then she gently laid them back down. "Well, if that's what you want to do, we're not going to stop you. Where are you going to go? Are you going back to being homeless and living alone out on the streets?"

Tess sat down next to the suitcase. "I was going to leave so as not to be a burden to the two of you. It seems the harder I try to be good and kind and helpful and not make you both embarrassed with my antics, the worse it gets. So, I was leaving to give you back the lives you had before I came and turned things upside down."

Sara sat down next to Tess. "I'm not going to lie, Tess. Our lives have been changed since I found you, but most of the time, that change has been wonderful and made us realize we needed someone like you in our lives. You've been like a tonic to me. Before you, I struggled with depression, but now I'm sleeping better, I'm laughing more, and Kevin says he hasn't seen me this happy in a long time. So, your being in our lives is worth all the turmoil that goes with it. Now, put your things back in the drawers, put that suitcase back under the bed, and let's pick out a nice dress for your party today. What do you say?"

"I say let's do it!"

❧

The parking lot of Trinity Lutheran Church was almost full when Sara and Tess arrived.

"Wow, that's a lot of cars!" Tess said. "You suppose they're all here for me?"

"Of course they're here for you. Maybe you don't know it, but you're liked more than you realize. Even the people who attend the contemporary service wanted to help celebrate your birthday."

"Well, that's a big surprise!"

Before she parked the car, she asked Tess if she wanted to be dropped off at the door.

"No. I don't want to go in there alone."

"That's fine. I just didn't want you to have to walk too far."

"I'll be fine." Tess's voice revealed a slight quiver.

Sara reached over and squeezed her arm. She parked the car in the pastor's parking space, then got out and went to help Tess out of the car. She opened the car door, expecting Tess to grab her arm for leverage, but instead, Tess sat frozen in her seat.

"Hey! It's going to be OK. Once you get in there and see how happy everybody is, you'll relax."

"But what if I panic?"

"Don't think about it. Think about all the gifts you most likely will receive. I bet you'll get money or gift cards. You know how you like to have cold, hard cash," Sara teased. "I remember the first time I gave you twenty dollars to get an orange soda at the grocery store. Your eyes lit up like a Christmas tree! Every time I think about that, I smile. You were even more excited when I told you to keep the change, so think about that."

Tess got out, and Sara led her to the double-glass doors. When they got there, both doors were opened by two well-dressed young men. Smiling at Tess, they each offered an arm and escorted her to the front of the room, where a massive altar chair was waiting for her. After she sat down, a little girl, about five years old, ran up and presented her with a bouquet of flowers tied with blue ribbons, Tess's favorite color. She looked around the room and saw Dean Adams and his wife and daughter. Smiling broadly from the back of the room was Deputy Harris, still in his uniform.

"Why, I do declare!" she exclaimed.

She couldn't believe how many people had come out to see her.

Sara stood at the back of the room, holding her breath. *What in the world am I going to do if Tess gets so nervous she bolts out of here?* "Please, God, don't let that happen! Let this special child of yours have a memorable birthday for a change!"

"May I have your attention!" Kevin called out. "Please, everybody, could you quiet down for a moment?"

The sound of happy voices stopped, and everyone sat down at the beautifully decorated tables. Sara looked at Tess. She was smiling from ear to ear. All the fear had been erased and replaced with pure joy.

Sara let out her breath in a sigh of relief. "Thank you, God, for hearing my prayer and easing Tess's fears."

"We have gathered this afternoon," Kevin began, "to welcome our recent attendee to our church services, Tess Farnsworth. I think most of you know by now that Tess is Sara's long-lost aunt.

"Sara, would you like to tell your reaction when you first met Tess?"

"Oh my ... yes, of course."

Sara quickly walked to the front of the room and gazed into the crowd of smiling faces.

"I don't know where to begin," Sara said, hesitantly. "They say to start at the beginning, so I guess that's where I'll start. We met a few months back when she showed up on the doorstep of the manse. It was cold that morning, and she wasn't wearing a warm coat, just a light jacket. She stood there shivering. I didn't think twice but invited this total stranger into my home. Now, look at that sweet face." Sara pointed in Tess's direction. "Wouldn't you invite her into your warm home?"

Sara made a downcast face at Tess. Everyone laughed, including the honoree. "Well, I asked her what she wanted, and without any forewarning, she blurted out she was my aunt Tess!"

Sara felt a bit guilty about lying to these wonderful church people, but it had to be done to keep Tess safe.

"I couldn't believe it!" Sara continued. "How could this be? Well, after many hours of talking with me and Kevin, Tess convinced us she was for real." Sara smiled at Tess.

At this point, Kevin stepped back in. "There is so much more to the story, but for now, let's get to celebrating Tess coming to our church and, of course, her birthday."

Everyone started clapping.

"Yoo-hoo, Tess!" Mrs. Applebee yelled above the clapping. "How old are you?"

The clapping subsided, and all eyes were on Tess. *Oh, no* thought Sara. *What is she going to say? Please, please be nice, Tess.*

"You know, Mrs. Applebee, a lady never tells her true age, so I'm as young as I feel, and today I feel sixty! And that's the truth!" Tess laughed.

The room filled with laughter. Mrs. Applebee may have been trying to put Tess on the spot, but it didn't work. Tess knew how to handle nosy people like her. Not only did it put Mrs. Applebee in her place, but it endeared her even more to her new friends and church family. Sara was so proud of her!

The party lasted to almost dinnertime. Tess spent most of the time sitting in her big chair, enjoying all the attention. She got up long enough to hit the buffet table and, when it was time, to blow out the candles on her favorite cake. The invitation for Tess's party said no gifts, but that didn't stop most of the guests. A small table had been placed near the front entrance for anticipated gifts. Sara noticed that, once in a while, Tess would glance over at the gift table to see how many packages and cards had been placed there.

Halfway through the party, Sara slipped away from visiting with a group of older ladies to check on Tess. "How's it going?"

"Oh, Sara! This is the best thing that has happened to me in years! I'm having the time of my life!"

"Now, aren't you glad you came?"

"I sure am. The best is yet to come though."

"What's that?" Sara asked, puzzled.

"Why, that table over there, the one by the front entrance. Isn't that for me?"

Sara looked at the table, loaded down with festively decorated packages. "Yes, those packages and cards are for you. After the party is over, we can take them back home, and you can open them when you want. I don't think anyone expects you to do that now."

"That's a relief!"

Just as Sara started back to the group of ladies, she heard music.

"Tess, that's Mrs. Applebee playing the piano. She's actually pretty good, don't you think? Oh! Now she's singing! Oh my, she's horrible!" She and Tess started laughing.

"Well," Tess said, "she plays fine, but her singing sounds like a cat got its tail underneath a rocking chair. Poor old thing. She laughs like a snorting pig and sings like an injured cat, but she's enjoying herself. Maybe she's not that bad after all."

"Why, Tess, what a nice thing to say about gossipy Mrs. Applebee."

"I think this party is making me mellow!" Tess replied, giggling.

Tess left Sara and went looking for Kevin. When she found him, she asked if they could talk in private.

"Of course. Let's go into the sanctuary. No one's in there right now."

He was pretty sure she was having a good time, but with her, he was never 100 percent sure. "So, what's up?"

"Kevin, you know how angry I was when I first heard about this get-together."

"Yes."

"Well, I feel blessed that this all happened, and I ... I want to tell the folks how happy they've made me. Do you think I can do that?"

He smiled, then gave her a big bear hug, almost lifting her off the floor.

"I guess that's a yes."

"Of course it's a yes! Here's what we'll do. You go back to the party, and I'll get everybody's attention. Then you can tell them, in your own words, how much you appreciate the party. And don't forget to thank them for the gifts."

When Kevin and Tess came back to the social room, Kevin said, "Folks, can I have your attention please? Before you leave, Tess has something to say to all of you. So, may I present our guest of honor, Tess!"

Everyone quieted down, and all eyes were on her.

Tess looked out at the smiling faces of the people who had gathered to welcome her and celebrate her birthday. She was nervous, but she needed to tell these caring people how amazing they were.

"I can't believe it's only been a few months since I arrived in

Jonesboro. When I attended my first service at your church, I have to admit I was sure nervous. I hadn't been inside a church for a long time. From that first moment until right now, all of you have made me feel welcomed. Thanks for accepting me just the way I am, warts and all. Thank you!"

The crowd clapped, and many of the people came up and shook her hand or gave her a welcoming hug. Tess's soul bubbled up with joy.

Everyone had left, except for a few ladies cleaning up in the kitchen. While Tess and Sara got their coats, Kevin loaded the car with the dressed-up packages and the bulging box of cards, then went back to the social hall. He had a few things to do for the next morning's service before going home. Sara and Tess drove the short distance home. When they pulled into the driveway, Tess blurted out, "That was so much fun! I can't wait for next year's birthday!"

Sara shook her head, laughing at Tess. "You are such a hoot, Tess Farnsworth!"

"I will take that as a compliment, Sara Richardson. Now let's get inside so I can open all those gifts."

Chapter 29

The aroma of roasting turkey woke Tess up. She sat up in bed and rubbed her eyes to clear the images of her dream.

In her dream, she was ten years old. She and her parents were spending Thanksgiving with her mother's family in the country outside of Zanesville. Thanksgiving Day had arrived with the first snowfall of the season. She jumped out of bed, ran to her parents' room, and shook them awake, exclaiming there was snow and yummy smells coming from downstairs. Oh, how excited she'd been, knowing the day would be happy and filled with good food and family time!

"Tess! Breakfast!" Sara called up the stairs. Tess threw off the blankets and slipped her feet into the warm, furry house shoes Sara had bought her. She went down the hall to the bathroom near her room and peered into the mirror. The face looking back was old and worn from years of sadness and stress. *Where is the young girl who loved simple things like first snowfalls and smells from holidays past?* she mused. *Gone. That's where.*

Sara walked to the bottom of the stairs and called again, "Tess, did you hear me?"

"Yes, I heard you! We all heard you!" She made her way slowly down the stairs, step by step.

"There you are," Sara said as Tess walked into the warm kitchen. It smelled not only of roasting turkey but also cloves, ginger, and cinnamon from the pumpkin pies Sara had baked for today's celebration.

"I don't know what your family did for breakfast on Thanksgiving, but we just have a light meal."

"That's fine," said Tess. "I'm not hungry."

"There are lots of cookies and sweet breads if you want something a little more filling. People from church give us homemade goodies throughout the holidays, so you won't want for sweets, that's for sure."

Tess, still half-awake, remained silent.

"Are you alright?" Sara asked, concerned.

"Oh, I'm sorry, sweet pea. I'm …"

"You're what?"

"To be honest, I'm still thinking about a dream I had right before you woke me up."

"I hope it was a pleasant dream."

"It was. I dreamed I was ten years old, spending the Thanksgiving weekend with my parents at Grandma and Grandpa Hanes's home in the country. It had snowed the night before, and I couldn't wait to get outside to make a snowman." Tess smiled at the thought of playing in the snow.

"Why, that was a pleasant dream. Let's hope your first Thanksgiving with Kevin and me will measure up to that." Sara gave Tess a big hug. "Go sit down, and I'll get your coffee."

"No, I can get it. You go ahead and keep doing what you need to do for the big meal. What time are we eating?"

"We usually eat around two."

"You said Kevin's family was coming today." She hadn't met any of Kevin's family, but she had heard about them.

"Yes!" Sara replied. "We have Kevin's brother Frank and his family, his sister, Kendra, and her family, and his mother and father. We usually have the whole family with us every other year. That way, the in-laws can spend Thanksgiving with their families the other year."

"That's nice," Tess said. "I thought Kevin had two brothers."

"He does. His other brother, Josh, lives in Chicago and doesn't come home very often. He's always been a bit of a loner." Sara chopped up celery for the dressing while she talked. "Kevin's parents are excited to meet you. We told them the same story we told the church people about you, so they shouldn't ask you too many questions—at least I hope not."

"What does that mean?" Tess asked.

"Oh nothing. It's just that Kevin's mom can be a bit nosy, if you know what I mean."

"Mrs. Applebee nosy or just curious nosy?"

"Oh, heaven's no—not Mrs. Applebee nosy! His mom's too sweet for that. I just meant she's interested in people in a good way. Just forget I said that. Now, finish your breakfast and go get ready."

After Tess finished her breakfast, she started up the stairs when Sara said, "Put on that powder blue dress I bought you. You look so pretty in it. Kevin said it makes your eyes sparkle."

"What in heaven's name? Sparkling! I'm too old to have sparkling eyes," she mumbled as she went up the stairs to put on her blue dress.

Kevin came into the kitchen, munching on a cookie Mrs. Sandburn had made. "Mmm, these layered cookies are to die for!" he exclaimed. "Man, does it smell good in here!" Kevin walked up behind Sara, putting his arms around her waist. He nuzzled her neck, giving her goose bumps. She laughed but didn't tell him to stop.

"I know," she said, enjoying Kevin's attention. "Smell is one of the senses that helps us enjoy our food, along with sight. It gets the old taste buds revved up for what's to come."

"You sound like Julia Child," Kevin said as he gently kissed his wife's soft neck.

"Well, it's true. The cooking shows tell you—you eat with your eyes and your nose first."

She picked up a sweet onion and began to chop it. Her eyes began to water. "Phew! That's stinging my eyes."

Kevin pulled away from the warmth of Sara's body. She turned around, put her arms around his neck, and planted a big kiss right on his adorable lips. He returned the kiss with more passion than she expected.

"Wow! That was amazing! Must be the sexy smells that have your motor running," she teased.

"Do you know how beautiful and sexy you are?" He tried to kiss her again, but she lovingly stopped him.

"Thanks for the compliments, but if you and your family want to eat by two, then you need to let me get back to cooking."

"OK, I'll stop for now. 'But you must remember this, a kiss is just a kiss, a sigh is just a sigh, the fundamental things apply as time goes by.'"

Sara's eyes softened, and her heart did a flip when Kevin started singing one of their favorite songs from the old movie *Casablanca* in his masculine baritone voice.

"That's not fair," she said, laughing and throwing her kitchen towel at him. "You know what that song does to me. Oh fudge ... you *do* know what that song does to me! Now that's enough! Go away!"

As Kevin moved toward the hallway, he asked, "By the way, where's Tess?"

"She's upstairs getting ready. I told her to put on that pretty blue dress that you said brings out the sparkle in her eyes."

"I like that one on her. Do you think she's a bit nervous about meeting my family today?"

"It's hard to tell with her. She can be a little unfriendly, but I'm sure she'll have a wonderful time. Don't worry, sweetheart. Now, go find something to do while I finish up the stuffing."

The doorbell at the manse rang promptly at one o'clock. Sara yelled for Kevin to get the door while she went in search of Tess. She had to admit she was a little nervous about Tess meeting Kevin's family. With all of them having big personalities, they could be a bit overwhelming. It had taken her years to feel comfortable around them. She found Tess in the dining room eating a cookie.

"Tess, Kevin's parents are here. Do you want to come and meet them?"

"Do you think they'll like me? Is my dress all right? What do I say to them? I don't know about this, Sara. I'm a bit nervous."

Sara went to Tess and hugged her tight. "They are going to love you! You look beautiful in that dress, and it's normal to feel a little nervous meeting people for the first time. So, come on. I'll be with you the whole time."

Sara and Tess heard Kevin's laugh and words of greeting as his parents entered the foyer of the old but comfortable manse. Sara's heart was always warmed when she saw Kevin's parents. Since her own parents died, they had become her adopted parents. She hoped they would accept Tess and show her the same love they gave her.

Sara hugged her mother-in-law first, then her father-in-law. Both of Kevin's parents were attractive. They kept themselves in shape. His dad loved to play golf, and his mom was into tennis. Keeping up with them was a challenge.

"Mom and Dad Richardson, I want you to meet my aunt Tess." Sara put her arm around Tess's waist and guided her toward Kevin's parents. She could feel the tension in Tess's body.

Dear God, please help Tess relax. You know how nervous she is right now. Just send down your love and strength to get her through the meeting of new people today!

Kevin's mom reached over and gave Tess a big hug. "Tess, it's a pleasure to meet you!" she exclaimed. His dad shook her hand, smiling broadly.

"We hope this will be the first of many times we'll see you! Next time Kevin and Sara come to visit, they'll have to bring you along."

Tess smiled and said it was a pleasure to meet them too. Sara removed her arm from Tess's waist, relieved the first round of introductions were finished.

Kevin hung up his parents' coats, and they all went into the family room to wait for the rest of the family. His siblings were always running late, so he knew there was plenty of time for his parents to visit with Tess before the rest of the gang showed up.

Sara returned to the kitchen to continue working on Thanksgiving dinner.

Finally, the doorbell rang again.

The rest of Kevin's family arrived at the same time. Hugs and laughter abounded while everyone took off coats and made their way to the family room. Tess sat quietly in her favorite chair by the fireplace. When there was a pause in the conversation, Kevin introduced her to the rest of his family. Like his parents, the women gave her hugs, and the men offered warm handshakes. The nieces and nephews said a quick hi, then rushed off to the kitchen to greet Sara and see what goodies they could eat before the big meal.

"So, Tess, what was it like meeting Sara for the first time?" Kevin's father asked.

Tess froze. She wanted to run out of the room and hide in her bedroom for the rest of the day, but she knew she couldn't.

She turned to a quick prayer. *It's amazing,* she thought. *Here I am praying again to a God I'm not sure even exists. Prayer has helped in the past, so why not now?*

Dear God, it's me again—Tess. Could you find it in your heart, if you have a heart, I sure don't understand this thing called the Trinity and who's who. Anyway, can you help me out? I know I'm not Christian material, but I'm trying real hard to be that person. I just want to make Sara proud of me as her aunt, even if it's not true. I really do wish I was her aunt. Sorry, I got off track again. Well, anyway, can you help me or not?

Tess looked up and spoke confidently to Kevin's father. "It's been the best thing that's happened to me in years, and another thing, you've raised a wonderful boy! I have never in my whole life been welcomed and accepted by anyone like Kevin and, of course, Sara. Why, they opened their home to me, a total stranger, and then they opened their hearts."

Tears stung Tess's eyes, and she was beside herself with embarrassment. *What in the world is the matter with me? Why, here I am, meeting Kevin's family for the first time, and I'm so emotional over it. They must think I'm touched in the head.*

Kevin's father told Tess how proud he was of Kevin. The he added, "Tess, you're a welcome addition to Kevin and Sara's family, and I'm thinking to our family too. I'm so glad you found your way to Sara."

Before Tess could respond, Sara came into the room and

announced dinner was ready. Everyone got up and headed toward the dining room. Kevin helped Tess up from her chair and said quietly, "You know, I'm sure it's hasn't been easy meeting my family for the first time. They can be a bit overwhelming, but you maneuvered your way around my father's questioning with poise and confidence. Now, are you ready for a feast?"

"Are you kidding?" She laughed. "I've been ready since before sunup!"

Kevin escorted Tess to her appointed chair next to Sara. Everyone was talking at the same time, and it took Kevin two tries to get their attention.

"Another Thanksgiving for our family to be together to celebrate our blessings, and they are truly many," said Kevin, looking first at Sara, then at Tess. "I would like to make a toast before we pray—to Tess. We are so blessed to have you here with us this year. Our lives have been changed, but that change has been the best! Here's to Tess."

All the adults raised their wine glasses and said, "Here, here!"

Looking at Tess, they waited for her response. She looked at her glass of wine and said, "Do you have any bourbon in the house? That's my go-to drink."

Chapter 30

Jonathan entered his office building early Monday morning, feeling refreshed and somehow energized. Being with Derek and his family for Thanksgiving helped him focus on his purpose in life—or what was left of it.

The elevator was filled to capacity, making him wait for the next one. Jonathan thought it was unusual to see so many people this early in the morning. Maybe everyone was like him, wanting to get going for these last weeks before a new year began.

As he entered his office complex, Doris, the receptionist, greeted him. Doris had been the receptionist for Connor and Williams Agency for over fifteen years, and in that time, she'd never seen Jonathan smile at her.

"Good morning, Doris." Jonathan said with a smile.

"Did you have a nice Thanksgiving?"

"I did. How about you?" *This is strange*, she thought. *I'm having an actual conversation with the cold and aloof Mr. Farnsworth.*

"I did. My friend Derek invited me to spend Thanksgiving with him and his family. I'd forgotten how much I missed being with someone for Thanksgiving."

"Why, that was nice of them," Doris commented. "I'm so glad you had a nice time."

He was taken aback by her friendly demeanor. *What a pleasant person Doris is, and to think I've never noticed that until this morning.*

It seems the time with Derek and his family has definitely had an effect on me.

"I certainly did, Doris. Thanks for asking. I'd better to get to work. Have a good Monday."

Jonathan was still smiling as he walked toward his office. He decided to send Doris a bouquet of flowers for her desk.

The phone was ringing when he got to his office. He threw his coat and briefcase on the chair by his desk and quickly answered.

"Hi, Jonathan. It's Derek. I wanted to tell you how much Nancy and I enjoyed having you here for Thanksgiving."

"Derek, I was just thinking about you and your family and how gracious you were for inviting me."

"I'm glad you had a good time. Anyway, the reason I'm calling is to tell you that I was thinking about the situation with your half-brother, Jeremy, and I thought you might consider meeting him to find out why he took this long to find you."

"I was thinking about that too," Jonathan replied. "After you confirmed he really was my half-brother, and doesn't seem to want anything from me, I'd like to know more about him."

Jonathan's heart started to speed up. He took a deep breath, hoping to relax enough to slow it down.

"How about I get in touch with him and set up a dinner appointment at the club for the three of us?"

"I like that idea. And since you're my lawyer, you can set the tone on why we're meeting. Hopefully, that won't make him feel intimidated."

Derek noticed that Jonathan sounded stressed. "Are you alright, buddy?"

"Sort of. My heart started beating faster at the mention of Jeremy. I guess thinking about him makes me think about my mother, making me angry. I'm fine. So, I'll wait for you to call for our dinner plans with Jeremy. And please say hi to Nancy and the kids for me."

"I will," Derek said.

After talking to Derek, Jonathan picked up his phone and called his favorite florist in Manhattan to order flowers. Doris was the first person people saw when they entered the office, so he wanted something to make her happy—and visitors as well.

"The Flower Pot. How can I help you?"

Jonathan recognized Jenny's voice. "Good morning, Jenny. It's Jonathan Farnsworth. How are you?"

"Mr. Farnsworth! I haven't heard from you in months. How are you?"

"I'm fine." Jonathan smiled. "I hope things are going well for the Flower Pot."

"They are, and thanks for asking. Now, what can I do for you?"

"I'd like to order your best arrangement for this time of year for our receptionist, Doris Taylor. She's so important to our company, but sometimes we've forgotten to let her know. So, I've decided to fix that."

"What a nice thing to do. Is there a price range?" Jenny asked.

"Not really—just make sure it says wow!"

Jenny laughed. "I can definitely do that. Who do I bill for this?"

"Please bill it to me and make sure you add a 20 percent tip for you."

"Why, thank you, Mr. Farnsworth! I'll get this out this afternoon. Oh—what should the card say?"

"Say, 'Thank you for all that you do for us at Connor and Williams. Sincerely, Jonathan.'"

"Got it! Good to hear from you, and have a great week!"

Jonathan felt good about doing a kindness for Doris.

When he was a little boy, he picked wildflowers from the field behind the family home to give to his mother. Her favorite was jack-in-the-pulpit. She loved them, and at that age, he tried very hard to make her happy.

His mood quickly changed from feeling gentle and caring to angry. He forced himself to think about how happy he had been with Derek and his family at Thanksgiving. He didn't want to go back to the hatred and anger he had toward his mother. For the first time in months, he didn't want his mother to pay for taking him out of her will. He was changing—it seemed for the best. With that thought, Jonathan turned back to his work, hoping better days were ahead.

Chapter 31

Dean stood on the top step of the stairs leading to the massive red door of Trinity Lutheran Church. He wasn't sure he wanted to do this, but Joyce said it was time to put Josh's death behind them. She was tired of seeing him sad. She grieved for Josh, too, but she knew they needed to move on. Josh would always be missed, but he wouldn't want them to continue grieving for him.

Dean opened the door and walked into the silent foyer. It felt cold and impersonal without the warmth of heat and the friendly worshipers. The atmosphere matched his mood; grief flooded over him like water rushing down a hillside after a heavy rain. He turned to leave, but then he heard footsteps coming toward him.

Just as he got to the door, Kevin saw him. "Dean, are you coming or going?"

"Actually, I'm not sure."

"Why's that?"

"Remember when you said if I ever wanted to talk about Josh, to let you know?"

"I do. Is this the time?"

"I think so, but … maybe not. I'm having conflicting feelings right now." Dean stood with his hat in his hands, feeling like a lost puppy.

"Let's go to my office. It's warmer and brighter than this dark foyer."

They walked down the long aisle of the sanctuary to Kevin's

office. Kevin was right about the office being better than the cold foyer. The church building was more than a hundred years old, and the original fireplace in Kevin's office still worked. A gas insert had been installed in the fireplace, making it easy to use and less messy. The fire was on, making the room warm and cozy.

Dean sat down in the chair by Kevin's desk. After they both were comfortable, Kevin calmly asked, "How can I help?"

Dean cleared his throat, folded his hands in his lap, and froze. He couldn't utter a word.

"Dean, if you feel uncomfortable talking to me, that's understandable. I imagine it feels strange, since you're the one who usually asks the questions."

Dean laughed. "That's one reason why I like you, Kevin—you're insightful. And you're right. I'm the one asking, not answering as sheriff."

Kevin smiled. His natural personality was one of nurturing and compassion.

"Well, I try not to get too personal with my questions, so I'll let you lead on this."

"Thanks, Kevin. I appreciate that."

Dean relaxed, knowing Joyce was right. This needed to be done.

After he shared the details of Josh's death and how he'd been carrying around his anger for over a year, he felt better. The hurt in his heart wasn't as painful. Tears filled his eyes, and before he realized it, he was crying.

Kevin stood beside him and put his hand on his shoulder, quietly praying for him.

Dean could hardly breathe; his sobs shook his whole body. Finally, his tears subsided and gradually stopped. Feeling like a different man, he looked up at Kevin and knew God had blessed him at that moment. The pain he'd been carrying for so long had left, and he felt lighter in spirit and happier than he'd been in months.

Dean stood up, and the two men hugged as brothers—brothers in the Lord Almighty. Together they walked back through the dark foyer that wasn't so dark anymore.

Before Dean opened the big door, he turned to Kevin. "I don't know what to say."

"You don't have to say anything," Kevin answered. "You've said it all, and God heard and answered. The horrible pain you've carried for all these months is gone."

"I agree, and I'm ever so thankful! Next time we see each other, let's have a cup of coffee and talk about what's next for Tess. She's now at the top of my priorities. If God does for her what he's done for me, she's in for some great moments."

"Absolutely!" Kevin agreed. "The healing has started, but we need to keep talking."

"I know," Dean agreed. "Please say hi to Sara and Tess for me."

"I will. Tell Joyce and Heather hello for us. I'll see you soon."

Dean whistled as he hurried down the stairs. He walked to his cruiser, ready to face whatever life gave him, knowing God was there with him every step of the way.

∽

Kevin came through the back door, expecting to see Sara preparing lunch. Not finding her there, he walked down the hallway toward the family room. He met Tess coming out of the family room, reading Sunday's church bulletin. She saw Kevin and smiled. "Hey there, sweet pea! What's up?"

"Do you know where Sara is?" Kevin asked.

"Can't say that I do. I'm not her keeper, you know."

"Sorry. It's just that she's usually in the kitchen getting lunch at this time."

"You're forgiven, sonny!" She patted him on the cheek and headed for the kitchen. He followed, still wondering where Sara was.

"Maybe she went to the store to get something for lunch," Tess suggested, opening the refrigerator. She peered inside, looking past anything that was healthy, and grabbed an orange soda.

"I suppose, but she usually tells me when she's leaving the house." Kevin whined like a little kid.

"For cryin' out loud! So your wife's not where she usually is at this time of the day! Deal with it! Do you always keep such a tight rein on the poor girl?"

"No, of course not! I'm not that kind of husband. She has her freedom to come and go as she pleases. We just try to respect each other. That's all."

"Why don't you just call her to see where she is? That way, you can either get yourself something to eat—for me too—or wait for her to get home."

"You're right. I'll do that." Kevin dialed Sara's cell phone, and she quickly answered.

"Hi, honey. Just making sure I didn't forget that you weren't going to be home for lunch."

"Is it that late?" Sara asked, looking at her watch. "I didn't mean to stay out this long."

"That's fine, sweetheart. Don't rush home. I can get lunch for me and Tess."

"No, I'm on the way."

"OK, if you're sure you don't need more time."

"No, I'm finished. I'd planned on going to the post office, then grabbing a few things at the store for dinner, but I ran into Joyce Adams, and we got to talking. She's such a sweet person. We decided we'd get together for lunch this Friday … and take Tess. She needs to get out of the house."

"That's fine, honey. Do you want me to start anything for lunch?"

"No. We're having leftover meatloaf sandwiches. Tess loves them. You could set the table and get drinks ready."

"OK, I'll do that. See you in a bit."

"Bye."

Kevin told Tess that Sara was on her way home, and he was going to set the table and get the drinks ready.

"Let me do that, sonny boy. You sit down at the table and tell me what your day has been like."

"Why, thank you, Tess. I'm glad you're interested. Actually, the morning was pretty ordinary for a Monday until Dean Adams stopped by."

Tess waited for Kevin to say more, but he didn't.

"So?"

"So, what?" Kevin countered as he put out the placemats and silverware.

"So, why did Dean stop in?"

"Oh sorry, I can't tell you that. What I discuss with people who come to see me is confidential."

Tess stopped what she was doing and looked at Kevin. "You go and tell me Dean Adams, who I consider a friend, stopped by to see you, and you can't tell me why?" Tess was agitated. "That's like knocking a shave and a haircut and leaving out the two bits. You can't do that!"

"I'm sorry, Tess, but that's the way it works. What if I go and tell you what Dean shared with me in confidence, and you tell someone, and that person tells another, and before long, it's all over town. By that time, the story has changed numerous times. If that happened, no one would trust me or want to talk to me. So, that's why I can't tell you."

Tess's hard look penetrated Kevin's very soul, making him scared to death of what was next. He held her stare, and eventually, she smiled and gave him a pat on his back.

"Why, I'm proud of you! Look at you, keeping confidences and all. You're a good person, Kevin Richardson, and I'm glad to be your friend and aunt! Well, not technically, but nobody knows that but you, me, and Sara. Anyhow, I won't ask any more about Dean."

"Thank you. I'm glad you understand."

Sara walked into the kitchen, carrying two bags of groceries. Kevin went to help her, while Tess finished getting the drinks.

"Tess, there was enough meatloaf left from last night's dinner, so we're having one of your favorites—meatloaf sandwiches."

"Oh, you are a sweetie!" Tess exclaimed. "I do love a meatloaf sandwich. When I was living on the streets, they were hard to come by. The only way was to sneak back to the open kitchen for the homeless when they had meatloaf night, and 'pretty please' them to death for another sandwich. I got pretty good at making them have pity on me, being an older woman and such. Why, they'd give me two meatloaf sandwiches! Of course, I never ate both of them. I'd give one to my friend Rose."

"Who was Rose?" Sara asked.

"You mean I haven't told you about Rose?"

"No, you haven't. I would have remembered."

"Well, Rose and I met after I'd been on the streets a few months. She was a drinking woman, about my age. Well, she'd been in jail a few months for disorderly conduct, and I didn't meet her 'til later. Let me tell you, when she drank, she was as mean as a skunk. Anyhow, after she got out, she came back to where she'd been living. By then, I'd been there awhile."

"I still can't believe you lived on the streets," Sara said. "It makes me sad all over again when you tell these stories. I'm just so thankful for finding you."

"Not as thankful as I am!"

"Sorry. I didn't mean to interrupt. Please go on."

"Well, we just seemed to hit it off from the start, and we stayed friends until she died, not long before my situation with those two nutcases who took me on a joyride." Tess was riled up, ready for a fight with whoever got in her way.

"That must have been difficult, losing Rose," Kevin commented. "Sounds as if the two of you were good company for each other. I'm so sorry."

"I'm sorry too!" Sara put her arms around Tess and squeezed her tight. Tess grunted at the hug, but enjoyed the affection.

"I was really sad when she died—and lonely too. Tess confessed. She was the only good thing that came out of living on the streets."

"How did she die?" Kevin asked.

"She died of a heart attack. None of us knew she had heart problems. Living the way we were living, we never knew if we had serious health issues until we either ended up in the hospital or dead, whatever got us first."

"I hate to ask, but what did they do with her body?" Kevin asked.

"One of the social workers who checked up on us every week told us that Rose had a son and daughter. The daughter lived in Columbus, and the son in Boston. They found them through the information the police had on Rose when she was arrested. Seems she'd been arrested quite a few times."

"Poor thing," said Sara.

"Did the children know where she was?" Kevin asked.

"No, not really. They just knew she was homeless and wouldn't let them or anyone else help her with her alcoholism. She likely had mental issues too. You'd be surprised how many of the homeless have that."

Kevin had taken a course at the local university on how to work with homeless people with mental health issues. It opened his eyes not just to their homelessness but also to how many had mental problems contributing to their situation. He never in a million years would have thought he'd be using that training with Tess, his own homeless person.

"Anyway," Tess continued, "the daughter was contacted, and she identified her mom. As far as I know, Rose had a funeral and was buried in a place where the family could visit her grave."

"Did you and her other friends from the homeless community go to her funeral?" Sara asked.

"No, we were left out of the loop. I guess the family members were too embarrassed about her living situation. I sure wish I could have said goodbye to her. She was a good friend and helped me adjust to living homeless. I'll always be grateful to her."

Tess's face showed sadness and loneliness. Even though Kevin and Sara knew she was happy with them, they could tell sometimes she thought about her friends from the homeless community.

"Hey! Let's get away from all this sad stuff and get to eating these meatloaf sandwiches! I'm getting hungrier by the minute." Tess was back to her ornery self.

They continued to eat, lost in their own thoughts, when Sara brought up the subject of Joyce Adams and the lunch date.

Kevin jumped in. "That's right. You said the two of you made plans to meet for lunch on Friday. Didn't you say you were going to invite Tess to go with you?"

"When were you going to share that bit of information with me, Miss Sara Jane?"

Sara laughed at Tess for using her middle name. "You sounded just like my mom when I was little and got into trouble. She used my middle name to let me know she meant business. How did you know my middle name is Jane?"

"Kevin told me when we were trying to figure out what story we were going to tell about who I was. He was asking my real name at the time—which I didn't share—and I asked what your full name was. Was that all right?"

"Of course it's all right. I was just surprised. That's all. Other than Kevin calling me Jane once in a while, no one else uses that name."

"Well, missy, I might have to use it again if you go and misbehave."

Tess had formed a strong bond with Sara, wishing again she truly was her aunt. "OK, Ms. Sara Jane, I'm ready for my dessert."

Sara smiled, shaking her head at Tess.

While they ate their dessert, Kevin told Sara that Dean Adams had stopped in to see him.

"Yeah, and he wouldn't tell me why." Tess was still indignant about it.

"I told you, Tess, that is privileged information between Dean and me."

"I know. Don't go and get your tighty-whities all in a bunch, unless you wear boxers," Tess chortled, hitting the kitchen table with the palm of her hand.

Sara laughed. Kevin didn't find it funny at all, making it even funnier.

"Oh, lighten up, Kevin! Tess is just having a bit of fun with you." Sara leaned over and whispered in Tess's ear that Kevin wore tighty-whities, causing Tess to laugh louder and longer.

"All right, the two of you, stop it! And, Tess, it's none of your business what type of underwear I wear!"

Sara and Tess started laughing again, but they stopped before Kevin got mad.

"We're sorry, dear." Sara reached over and patted Kevin's hand. "It's just sometimes when you get into your pastor mode, you sound so formal and reserved. Tess is just a curious person like me. Right, Tess?"

"Yes, that's right. I am."

"You usually tell me what people tell you, and I never tell anyone what was said. Right?" Sara asked.

"Yes, you're right, but I don't know if I should let Tess know."

"Tess is family now. She knows how important it is to keep anything she hears us talk about to herself."

"That's right. I wouldn't want to hurt anyone by spilling the beans."

"So, I see no reason why you can't let her hear what Dean said this morning."

"I suppose … but, Tess, you have to promise you will keep anything I tell you confidential. Do you hear me? I mean it."

Tess knew Kevin meant business, and anyway, she wouldn't want to hurt Dean. "First of all, I like Dean a lot. He's a good man. Secondly, who would I be telling this to? I only talk to the two of you—and maybe Alice once in a while at church. So no, I will not tell anyone."

"OK then, I'll tell you," Kevin said.

"Joyce told me she's been worried about Dean since Josh died last year. Was that what Dean talked about?" Sara asked.

"Yes. He wanted to talk to somebody but didn't know who. So instead, he carried it with him until he started having emotional issues. That's when he knew he needed to talk to someone."

"How'd Josh die?" Tess asked.

"He was killed by a drunk driver who'd been arrested more than once for DUIs. Each time, the guy got away with just a fine and a slap on the wrist because his father was on the city council."

"That's not fair!" Tess exclaimed.

"You're right. It took killing someone to put the scum in prison."

"What did you tell him, Kevin?" Sara asked.

"I told him I was glad he decided to talk to me, and we set up another time to continue working on his issues."

"I'm happy for that." Sara smiled at Kevin.

"Sounds like you've got this, sonny boy! I sure wish you were my son. Even though I have a son who's worthless to me, it would be tough losing a child. No wonder he's so protective of Heather. She's such a sweet kid. She always comes and says hi to me after church. Hey! Speaking of church, I read in last week's bulletin that this coming Sunday is the first Sunday of Advent. What is that about?"

Kevin replied, "I saw you reading the bulletin and wondered if you had noticed the mention of Advent."

"Oh, Tess, you'll love Advent!" Sara said. "It's the fun time of getting ready to celebrate the birth of Jesus. We decorate the church with wreaths and garland. The ladies' guild does such a great job of putting up the Christmas tree and Chrismon ornaments, and the white candles with Christmas balls around them on the windowsills make the sanctuary look so beautiful! This is my favorite time of year for the church!" Sara was practically dancing around the kitchen.

"You said it was the first Sunday in Advent. How many Sundays are there in this church year thing you're talking about?" Tess asked.

"Well," Kevin explained, "it's the first of four, and then we celebrate Christmas. You know what? Christmas falls on a Sunday this year. I love it when that happens." Kevin started getting excited too.

"What's with the two of you? Sara's nearly dancing, and now you're grinning from ear to ear."

Chapter 32

Jonathan arrived at the club a few minutes before seven for his dinner meeting with Derek and Jeremy. All day, he'd kept himself busy trying not to think about seeing his half-brother again. Derek had found out a lot about Jeremy. He and his family lived in Duncan Falls, just outside of Zanesville. Jonathan remembered going to Zanesville with his mother when he was around ten years old. They would visit an older woman who his mother helped from time to time. The woman had worked in her grandfather's pottery company and was now down on her luck. His mother gave her food and some money for her rent and utilities.

Strange … he'd forgotten about that. He'd also forgotten how kind his mother could be. He remembered her as cold and angry most of the time.

She and his father fought constantly the last few years he lived at home, helping him make the decision to choose a university in New York to get away from both of them.

He was deep in thought when Derek called his name.

"Jonathan. Jonathan!"

"Derek! I'm sorry." Jonathan gave Derek a quick hug. "I was thinking about my mother. Anyway, where are we meeting Jeremy?"

"I told him to go ahead and be seated at our table, and we would meet him there."

"Good idea. I need a little time to prepare myself before seeing him again."

Jeremy arrived at the club and told the hostess who he was meeting for dinner. She escorted him to the reserved table and asked if he would like a drink. When his drink arrived, he sipped it, taking in his surroundings.

The men's club dining room reeked of old money. He didn't know whether he was envious or put off by what it represented. Before he could think any further, Jonathan and Derek showed up. He stood up to greet them.

"Jeremy, nice to meet you in person," said Derek.

"Likewise," Jeremy responded.

"You, of course, remember Jonathan."

"Yes, I'm sorry about how we met the first time, Jonathan. Please accept my apology."

Jonathan looked into Jeremy's eyes and saw something that reminded him of his father. The difference was Jeremy's eyes reflected kindness and compassion. His father's eyes had held aloofness and greed. *Just like mine*, he thought.

"Jeremy, please sit down," Jonathan said, reaching out and shaking his hand.

Jeremy was nervous. He just wanted Jonathan to know why it was important for them to meet. Now that it was happening, he struggled to find the right words. He cleared his throat and said, "I found out I was your father's son about three years ago. It came as a shock, but I'd always felt there was something not right. Then one day, right before my mom died, she told me the man I'd thought was my father was not. She told me who my father was. She didn't want to go to her grave with that secret."

Jonathan sat stone faced while Jeremy shared his experience.

Derek jumped in. "How did you feel when you found out?"

"I was stunned but not shocked," Jeremy responded.

"So, it only confirmed your suspension about your dad not being your biological father," Jonathan said through clenched teeth.

"Yeah, that's about right."

"Why did you wait all this time to find me? Why now? It's been almost three years, for crying out loud. It seems that you would have wanted to know sooner than this." Jonathan was obviously angry.

Derek quickly intervened, knowing Jonathan's anger wouldn't solve anything. "Jonathan, I'm sure Jeremy just wanted to find out who you were. If it took a few years. Well, maybe it's because he was confused about what to do."

"Derek's right. I didn't know what to do. Mom died a few months later, and I was taking care of her estate and all the other things I had to deal with. My dad died of lung cancer the year before, so it was just me. I'm an only child, like you."

Jonathan saw the pain and frustration Jeremy was going through and calmed down.

"I'm sorry, Jeremy. I didn't mean to get angry. None of this was your fault. So, I'm thinking you must be around forty?"

Jeremy smiled, saying he was right about his age. Jonathan smiled too.

Derek said, "Well, gentlemen, why don't we order dinner? We can talk more about where the two of you want to go with your newly found relationship."

Jonathan and Jeremy agreed.

"Jeremy, I always wanted to have a brother, and now I do."

Jeremy breathed a sigh of relief.

"Me too. Thanks for understanding. I hope I can live up to what you imagined a younger brother would be."

"From what I've seen so far, I'm confident you will."

Chapter 33

Sara, Kevin, and Tess had just finished Saturday-morning breakfast when the phone rang. Sara answered.

"Good morning. This is Chet O'Donnell with the law firm of O'Donnell, Murphy, and Williams. Could I speak to Julianne Farnsworth, please?"

Sara's heart did a flip-flop. *How does he know Tess is here?*

"I'm sorry, but there's no Julianne Farnsworth living here. Are you sure you have the right number?" Sara mouthed to Tess, "Do you know a Chet O'Donnell?"

Tess jumped up and grabbed the phone out of Sara's hand. "Chet! How are you? It's been ages since I've heard from you. I hope this is a good call and not a bad one."

"Julianne, it's so nice to hear your voice! Yes, it has been far too long since we spoke. Why did the lady who answered the phone say I had the wrong number?"

"Well, Chet, you see, they don't hear my real name, Julianne, spoken much. They call me Tess."

"I didn't know that. Would you feel more comfortable if I called you Tess?"

"Yes, I would. Now you most likely know what my situation is since you have the right telephone number and all."

"One of our junior law partners has been doing a fantastic job for you, Tess. He's also been in contact with the local sheriff there in Jonesboro—Dean Adams. I hear the pastor and his wife, there in Jonesboro, have been doing a marvelous job of keeping you safe. We're grateful for the care they've given you."

"So, you're telling me you've known where I've been for some time? That's the first I've heard of it, and I'm not happy about it!" Tess said. "I know Dean Adams has been taking care of my safety, but he never mentioned he'd been in touch with you and your firm."

"Tess, please don't be angry or upset with Sheriff Adams. He's just trying to keep you safe from Jonathan. That's all."

"I suppose you're right."

"I know I am. Now, could you give the phone back to Sara or Kevin, whoever wants to talk to me?"

"I will, but first answer my question about whether this is a good call or a bad one."

"Let's just say that it's not totally bad but a concerning situation. Now, let me talk to Sara or Kevin. They can tell you all about the situation after I've spoken to them."

Tess turned around to hand the phone back to Sara, but Kevin took it instead.

"Mr. O'Donnell, this Kevin Richardson. Tess has mentioned your law firm a few times. I'm surprised though that Sheriff Adams didn't inform your office we were trying to keep Tess calm by not telling her who knew her whereabouts."

"I'm so sorry, Kevin. May I call you Kevin?"

"Yes, of course, but I wish you hadn't called. We've worked hard to keep her busy enough to not worry about what Jonathan's up to. Now, this changes the situation."

"I'm sure it has, but Sheriff Adams and I thought it best to bring Julianne—or should I say Tess—up to date on what Jonathan is doing to find her. Sheriff Adams was confident that this would be a good thing for Tess."

"I do trust Dean Adams, so if he says it's fine, then I guess it's OK."

"Please tell Tess that Jonathan does know where she is and who all of you are, but he hasn't done anything so far to try to contact her or have someone else do it for him. Actually, he seems to be busy getting to know the half-brother he recently learned about. Anyway, tell her what I've shared with you. Sheriff Adams said he would stop by today sometime and talk to all of you about this new development."

"Glad to hear that."

"And please tell Tess we here at our firm have her best interest in mind. I will talk to her at another time. Nice talking to you, Kevin."

"I will, and please let me know if anything new happens with Tess's son."

"I will."

Kevin had barely hung up the phone when Tess was on him like bees on honey. "What'd he say? Did he tell you anything about Jonathan? Does he think Jonathan's going to try to get me and take me back to that mental health facility?"

"Tess, calm down. The only thing he said about Jonathan was that he now knows where you are, but for the time being, he's done nothing. So relax. Please!"

"All right, I will, but you better tell me if you find out he's trying to do anything underhanded to get at my money."

"I will. I just told you that!"

Tess looked at him with those skunk eyes and huffed out of the room. Sara started to go after her, but Kevin asked her to wait a few minutes to give Tess time to calm down. There'd be no reasoning with her in the mood she was in.

"Do you believe Mr. O'Donnell?" Sara asked.

"I do."

"I just want Tess to enjoy Advent and not be worrying what Jonathan's up to," Sara said.

"We'll make sure of that." Kevin said. "God will help us give Tess a wonderful Christmas."

∽

When Sara and Tess entered the church foyer Saturday afternoon, they were met with the smells and sights of the Advent season. Wafting throughout the sanctuary was the scent of fresh evergreens, waiting to be hung.

"Wow! Those sure smell good!" Tess gushed. "It reminds me of when I was a child and Grandpa Hanes and I would go and cut down our Christmas tree to go in the big foyer of his and Grandma's house. Those sure were good times, and I miss them!"

"I know. Doesn't it smell wonderful?" Sara agreed. "I only remember a few times when my family had a real Christmas tree. Mom got tired of having to vacuum up the tree needles, and that's when we got an artificial tree."

"Herbert and I had real Christmas trees for the first twenty years of our marriage. We had them cut and delivered to us by a tree farm employee. It wasn't as fun as cutting down your own."

"You will be happy to know Kevin and I have a real tree every year for Christmas. In fact, we were just talking about doing that. If you want, you can go with us."

"I'd love to! When can we go? I hope you're not the kind of people who wait until Christmas Eve to decorate your tree. I want to see and smell it as long as I can."

Sara laughed at her enthusiasm.

They left the sanctuary and followed the sound of voices coming from the social hall. Alice Wagner saw Tess as soon as she and Sara entered.

"Tess, it's so good to see you." She rushed up, giving Tess a warm hug. She then reached over and hugged Sara.

"Are you going to help us decorate for Advent?" Alice asked. "I know you are, Sara. You do such a nice job decorating."

Turning back to Tess, she asked, "Did you know that Sara has a degree in interior design? She helps out with decorating the church through all the seasons of the church year. You have a real talented niece."

Tess looked at Sara and smiled. "I do know, Alice. That's why the manse looks so stunning." Tess felt proud of Sara. In her heart, Sara was her niece, and some day, when this thing with Jonathan was over, she planned to tell Sara she wanted to be a part of her life until that life ended.

The rest of the morning was spent making the church look festive.

After a light lunch, laughing, and enjoying each other in Christian fellowship, Tess and Sara went back to the manse. Tess settled into her favorite chair by the fireplace and thought, *I can't wait to see how this Christmas is going to turn out.* Within minutes, she was fast asleep, dreaming of Christmases past, where life was simpler and filled with anticipation of good things to come.

Chapter 34

Jonathan woke up happier than he'd been in years. He jumped out of bed, stretched his arms high above his head, then went to the kitchen to put on the coffee.

After retrieving the morning paper, he briefly looked at the headlines, then tossed it aside. His high-rise apartment had a small breakfast nook that looked over Central Park. It cost him a load of money to purchase it, but it was worth every penny. Every season of the year gave him a view of New York's finest scenery, from early-spring wildflowers to winter's picturesque scene like a Currier and Ives painting. He seemed to have it all—except happiness, which continued to elude him.

For some reason, he was restless this morning. *What's happening?* he wondered.

It all started when he spent Thanksgiving with Derek and his family. Jonathan was surprised to realize he was jealous. For the first time in many years, he longed for a family.

Again, he thought about his mother's kindness toward the older woman who lived in Duncan Falls. Tears filled his eyes, threatening to fall. *Real men don't cry,* he thought. At least that's what he had been told as a kid.

He remembered a box of old family photos he'd brought home after his father died. At the time, he wasn't interested in looking at them. He'd had his fill of dealing with his parents' problems. But now, something was compelling him to find the pictures.

Each apartment in his building had a small storage unit in the underground parking garage. He slipped on his house shoes, put his coat on over his pajamas, and headed down to the parking garage. It had been months since he'd looked in the storage unit, but he was sure the box of pictures was near the door.

When he raised the door, there they were.

He recalled when he was a kid, his mom would remind him every so often to save the family pictures if the house caught on fire. He smiled. With all the expensive surroundings they lived in, she told him to save the pictures first.

Jonathan lugged the bulky box to the elevator, hoping not to run into anyone, especially Mrs. Crosby. What a nosy, gossipy old woman! How many times had she told the other tenants about his lady visitors? Too many for sure.

Fortunately, no one was in the elevator. Once inside his apartment, he put the box on the kitchen island, then put on a fresh pot of coffee. While the coffee perked, he decided to get a shower. While in the shower, Jonathan started humming a song his mother sang to him when he was a little tyke, "The Itsy-Bitsy Spider."

> The itsy-bitsy spider went up the waterspout.
> Down came the rain and washed the spider out.
> Out came the sun and dried up all the rain,
> And the itsy-bitsy spider went up the spout again.

He started laughing. The stress he'd been carrying around for so long had lifted. Jonathan knew he wanted to find the kind of happiness Derek and his family had. Maybe starting with the pictures was the first step.

After getting dressed, he went back to the kitchen, poured a fresh cup of coffee, and settled in at the kitchen table with the box of photos in front of him.

The first picture he pulled out was of him with his parents at their home in Zanesville. He looked about eight years old. His parents were smiling. His dad's arm was around his mom's shoulder, and each parent had a hand on his shoulder. Smiling, he dug into the box and pulled out several batches of pictures, each handful causing his spirits to soar higher, bringing him just a bit closer to his mother—Mom.

Time passed. Jonathan stayed at the table, looking at the past through the family pictures. Many were of his grandparents, and some were of his great-grandparents. Sometimes he smiled at the images; other times he felt sad. When he came across more recent pictures of his parents or himself, he tossed them aside. He didn't want to look at the unhappiness on their faces.

When the pile of discarded pictures grew higher than the happy ones, he knew it was time to stop. As he returned the pile of discouraging photos to the box, one slipped out and landed right in front of him.

He picked up the photo, realizing he'd never seen this picture of him and his parents on the last Christmas they spent together. The three of them were standing in front of the nine-foot-tall, beautifully decorated Christmas tree in the foyer of the old family home. He stood between his mother and father. Their arms were around him, and they were all smiling. Wondering when the photo was taken, he turned it over and read the date—12-25-2013. *That was just five years ago. We looked happy. What happened?*

The phone rang, startling him.

"Good morning! How are you on this bright, crispy morning?" Derek sounded happy.

"Hey there, buddy. I'm good. What's up?"

"Nancy and the kids want to put up the tree this evening, and we thought it would be fun if you would join us for dinner and help trim the tree. What do you say?"

Jonathan was surprised at the invitation. Loneliness washed over him. "Why, I …"

"Now don't tell me you're busy. I know for a fact you're not." Derek laughed as he waited for Jonathan's response.

"How do you know that? Are you spying on me?"

"No, you told me when we talked last, so no excuse for not coming tonight."

"All right, I'll come. What time?"

"We don't want the kids up beyond their bedtime, so how about five? Does that work for you?"

"It does. See you then, and, Derek ..."

"Yes?

"Thanks!"

"No problem. See you at five, my friend."

Jonathan hung up, anticipating the evening ahead. He looked once more at the photo of him and his parents five years ago, then tossed it on top of the sad and neglected photos. Pausing a moment, he picked it up and gently placed it on top of the happier photos. Finding some twine, he tied up the stack of photos he wanted to keep handy, then put all the others back in the box. An idea was forming about his mother. He knew where she was now, so what if ...

Chapter 35

Sara went looking for Tess and found her in her usual place—sitting by the fireplace. "Are you ready to go?" she asked.

"I suppose, but I have to say I'm a little nervous about this morning. What did you say goes on at the Advent service? I don't want to go and do anything wrong and have someone laughing at me."

"Tess, the services are no different than all the other services you've been to. The only difference is we have the lighting of the first Advent candle. I told you, there will be four of them over the next four Sundays."

"So, who lights these candles?" Tess asked. "Do you suppose I could do one? That'd be fun, sort of like lighting a birthday candle but only one. Hey, it is like a birthday candle! We're waiting for Jesus's birthday!"

Sara laughed at Tess's idea, but it could happen if she and Kevin were with her. They always picked families to light the Advent candles. "I'm sure the church would be fine with that. I'll talk to Kevin about it, but let's go before we're late."

They entered the sanctuary by the side door near the church parking lot. The sanctuary was nearly full when they walked in. It always surprised and sometimes made Sara angry to see so many people start coming back to church during Advent and Holy Week. She knew she shouldn't feel that way, but she did.

"Wow! Would look at that!" Tess exclaimed. "Where'd all these people come from? It looks like the whole town showed up today. Do they know something I don't?" Tess asked, sounding surprised and a little excited.

"No, Tess. This happens every year at Advent and Lent. My mother used to say, 'Looks as if they came out of the woodwork.'"

"Good saying. I guess God's up there feeling pretty happy to see so many of his earthly children getting ready for his boy to be born. It must make you feel good too. Right, Sara?"

Sara mumbled something under her breath, then grabbed Tess's arm and steered her to their usual seat, only to find it occupied. It was on the tip of her tongue to tell the occupants those were hers and Tess's seats, but she stopped. Instead, she smiled and welcomed them to church.

Grabbing Tess's arm again, she guided her all the way back to the only place left to sit, the last pew on the right.

"Kevin's going to think we're not here if we sit way in the back."

"Look around, Tess. There's no other place to sit, so hush up and read today's bulletin!"

"You don't need to bite my head off, for crying out loud!" Tess spoke louder than she meant.

Old Mr. Jenkins, who was hard of hearing, looked over his shoulder and shushed her. Sara looked at him and said, "Oh hush up, yourself!"

This wasn't like Sara at all. Tess leaned over to ask her if she was OK as the introit began.

Kevin walked to the lectern and greeted the congregation. He made a point of greeting those who were visiting for the first time and said he hoped they would make this their home church. After the announcements, he invited Dean and Joyce Adams and their daughter, Heather, to come and light the first Advent candle.

"Why, look there, Sara! Dean and Joyce and Heather are lighting the candle. I'm so glad they're coming here now, aren't you?"

"Yes. Now please be quiet!" Sara whispered.

Tess decided it was best to just let go of whatever was bothering Sara and enjoy the rest of her first ever Advent Sunday.

The choir's anthem was so good even Tess clapped. Most Sundays, she wasn't much interested in their songs. They never had a melody she could get excited about, but today's music was pretty snappy.

Kevin had an interesting sermon about a man named Joseph who was betrothed to a young woman named Mary, who was going to be Jesus's mom. Other than using some fancy words that Tess wasn't sure what they meant, she enjoyed the sermon.

When it was over, she, Sara, and Kevin went back to the manse. The first thing out of Tess's mouth was, "Sara, what was wrong with you at church this morning? I've never seen you so grumpy, and it sure bothered me."

"What's Tess talking about, Sara?" Kevin asked.

"It's the same thing that bothers me every year, Kevin. Those hypocrites who come back to church during Advent and then again at Lent! I just get so angry!"

Tess was stunned to hear Sara say those things. *Why, Sara's the sweetest, most loving and caring young woman I've ever known.*

"So, what gives, Sara? Are you saying it's wrong to go to church only at Christmas and Easter? Is that what you think? Don't you think God's happy when one of his kids takes time to put him first at all? Do you think he cares if it's only a few times a year? I don't think so; I think he's thrilled to death! You've told me and shown me what a loving and giving and healing God we have. But now you're telling me there are strings attached to this relationship with God. I thought he loves us no matter what, and even if we mess up, he still loves us. So, be happy they've come back again this Christmas season. Love conquers all is what you've been telling me, so let that love take away your anger, sweetie."

Sara listened to Tess's little sermon and realized the student had become smarter than the teacher. "Tess, you've become very wise while living with us. I am overwhelmed by your understanding of what the real story of God's love is. Thank you for reminding me. You're absolutely right. God is more interested in what's in a person's heart. I will ask for forgiveness from him … and from you, dear Tess."

Sara hugged so tight that Tess couldn't breathe. Then they both laughed. Kevin watched, shaking his head and smiling at his two best girls. "Ladies, let's go out for lunch today. What do you say?"

"We agree!"

Kevin took Tess's arm, then Sara's, and the three of them left, laughing and truly enjoying the beginning of Advent.

Chapter 36

Jonathan's Friday was turning out to be a good day. He had acquired a new account for an up-and-coming cosmetic store called Face to Face. He was confident that this account would help him look good to the president of the agency. Besides landing the new account, he'd also booked a flight to Toledo for the next morning. He admitted to being nervous about his decision to go see his mother, but he knew in his heart it was the right thing to do.

The next morning, Jonathan was up early. His flight to Toledo was at 9:00 a.m., and he needed to get to the airport an hour and half before his plane departed.

He arrived at seven thirty and headed to the VIP lounge. That was one of the perks of his position with the company. He made a cappuccino at the coffee bar, then settled in a chair by the huge window to watch the planes arrive.

When he was a kid, his dad would sometimes take him to the Columbus airport to watch the big jets come and go. Watching airplanes take off had always been one of his loves. Two years ago, he got his pilot's license, but he hadn't used it for some time. The only thing he'd done outside of work in the past five years was start an affair with Delilah. But he didn't want to think about that now. Instead, he thought about the previous evening.

He had enjoyed spending the evening with Derek and his family. After dinner, he and Derek went into Derek's office to relax.

"How are things with you and Delilah?" Derek asked.

"To be honest, she's wearing me out. Her constant calling and begging me to come and be with her has worn thin."

"I've never liked your affair, but as a friend, I've tried to keep my comments to myself."

"I appreciate that, but I've known all along how you've felt about Delilah."

"It sounds as if you're thinking about ending the relationship. Am I right?"

"Yes," Jonathan said, putting his head back on the soft leather chair. "I just don't know how to do it. I've never had this kind of relationship before. Do you have any suggestions?"

"Well, from what you've told me, no matter what you say, she's going to make a scene, so just tell her in as few words as you can and leave. If you stay, she'll have a tantrum, and sadly, most men just give in."

"Hmm. Are you sure you haven't done this yourself?" Jonathan smiled. "I don't mean you've been unfaithful to Nancy. I just mean your suggestion sounds so ... reasonable."

"To be honest, I got involved with a married woman at the first law firm I worked for. I was young and cocky, and she was drop-dead gorgeous—and knew it. One night, after we'd worked late on a case together, she came on to me, and, of course, I went for it."

"How long did the affair last?"

"Thank goodness only a few months. I realized it was a mistake and quickly ended it. She cried and begged me to not leave her, but I did what I'm telling you to do, and that was that."

"It must have been uncomfortable working in the same firm."

"It was, but thankfully I was offered a position here in New York. I vowed not to ever get involved with a married woman—and not with an unmarried woman either," Derek said.

Jonathan laughed, then changed the subject. "I have something I want to run by you and see what you think."

"This sounds serious."

"It is, but I'm not sure if I should go through with it."

"Does it have anything to do with your mother?"

"Yes, how'd you know?"

"Just a lucky guess. I recall at Thanksgiving you talked a lot about your family, but I've noticed a drastic change in you since then. It's almost as if you're mellowing toward your mother."

"I have, and I think it's because of being with you, Nancy, and your kids. When I saw the love you have for your family, it stirred up feelings about my own family. I started remembering some good times with my parents, and, yes, there were good times."

Derek smiled. "I've wished for some time that things would get better for you. I knew you and your father both seemed to need power and control in your lives, especially over your mother."

"You're right. Dad and I did—at all costs. That's what destroyed my relationship with my mother! I'm weary of this pain inside me. I want it to stop. It's destroying me!"

"So, you've done something to change this feeling, right?"

"Yes. I've booked a flight to Toledo for tomorrow morning and rented a car to drive to Jonesboro, where my mother is living."

"I'm not sure that's a good idea, Jonathan. It seems too spur of the moment, even for you. You need to take in consideration the problem with the local sheriff. You know for a fact he's keeping tabs on you. Aren't you afraid he'll find out about you being in Jonesboro?"

"I've taken care of the sheriff situation," Jonathan assured his friend.

"Just be careful," Derek said. "Anyway, why are you doing this?"

"I want to see what mother's been doing for the past few months. I know you think I have an alternative motive, but I don't. I just want to see her from a distance and determine if she's changed in any way."

"How can you find that out from just watching her?" Derek asked.

"I know she's changed these last few years. After all, she was homeless for quite a while. I need to see her and decide if I have any good feelings for her."

"And if you do, what then?" Derek asked.

"I'll take that step later. So, will you at least wish me luck?" Jonathan asked with emotion.

"I suppose so. Just let me know if you need anything."

"I will; I promise."

⁀

Jonathan's flight was announced, interrupting his thoughts about last night. He and the other passengers from the VIP lounge boarded first. After finding his seat in first class, he settled back for the hour and a half flight to Toledo. He used the time to make notes on what he was going to check out in the Jonesboro area. He'd found very little information about the town, as nothing much happened there.

The plane touched down a little earlier than scheduled. He went directly to the car rental desk and picked up his leased car. Not wanting to be noticed by anyone, especially the sheriff's department, he asked for a white sedan with an Ohio license.

He had chosen a hotel near the airport. After checking, he went to the concierge's desk for suggestions on where to eat. She asked about his preferences, then suggested a few nice restaurants in walking distance.

After lunch, Jonathan programmed the map app on his phone for the drive to Jonesboro. Since it wasn't that far, he took his time, looking at the barren fields that just a few months ago were full of ripened corn and soybeans. Memories of similar fields near where he grew up flashed across his thoughts.

The day was sunny and warm for early December. Ohio was notorious for overcast gloomy weather, making this day unusual. The sun warmed the interior of the car, so he opened the windows just a crack to let the cool air in. His mood brightened as he drew closer to Jonesboro. He wondered if it was because he would see his mother or simply the pleasant memories from his childhood.

The town of Jonesboro looked like a typical small community in rural Ohio. A main street went from one end of town to the other, with side streets named after families who had lived in the area for generations. He smiled when he saw a side street near the edge of town named Skunk Hollow.

Jonesboro's population was around fifteen thousand. It was certainly not a large town, but it was big enough to have six churches, two small grocery stores, a Walmart, and numerous gas stations. Driving through downtown, he saw antique stores, a shoe store, two ice-cream parlors, and other mom-and-pop-owned variety stores. The town's Christmas decorations made everything look festive and cheerful. It was Saturday, and people were out shopping or just enjoying the unusually warm day.

He rounded a corner and noticed a coffee shop on the other side of the street. Since it was almost three in the afternoon, he decided coffee would be nice. After parking, he walked the short distance to the shop named Cup of Joe. Upon entering, he paused long enough to inhale the aroma of freshly brewed coffee. Behind the counter, the barista smiled at him. She was young and looked to be in her early twenties. Like so many young people, her hair was dyed pink, and she had an assortment of piercings.

"Hi! What can I get you?" the young lady asked.

Before he ordered, he took a minute to look over the list of the many different hot and cold drinks available. "I'll have a tall coffee of the day, black, and one of your blueberry scones, please." Jonathan smiled at the young lady.

When his order was ready, he took it to one of the high-top tables near a large window looking out onto the bustling Main Street. The shoppers popped in and out of stores, while the children ran up to look at the toys and winter gear displayed in the storefront windows. Ohio didn't normally get much snow, but that didn't discourage the children from asking Santa for sleds and outdoor paraphernalia to play in the anticipated snow.

Jonathan read his emails while he had his coffee and scrumptious scone. He looked up to see a nice-looking man, appearing to be in his early forties, enter the coffee shop. Normally, Jonathan didn't pay much attention to people coming and going, but this man seemed different.

The young barista quickly went to greet the man. "Hello, Reverend

Richardson. What can I get for you this afternoon? Do you want your regular order?"

"Hi, Corey. Actually, I'd like to have a spiced hot tea today. Give me the cinnamon orange."

"Anything else? Greta made fresh blueberry scones this morning. Do you want one?"

"That sounds pretty good. Could you put two more in a bag for me to take home to Sara and Tess? You know how much Tess enjoys her sweets," Kevin said with a laugh.

"I bet she's excited about Christmas. I know she's been without a family for a few years, so finding Sara has been such a good thing."

"Yeah, we're happy she found us, and Sara's happy to have her in our home. Of course, she can be a handful, if you know what I mean."

Corey laughed, having waited on Tess many times. She knew Tess had a mind of her own.

Jonathan took in the conversation with interest, realizing this was the minister that his mother, now called Tess, was living with, along with his wife, Sara.

After Kevin left, Jonathan asked the young woman where Trinity Lutheran was. She told him it was farther down Main Street on the corner of Main and Meadowlark. Jonathan thanked her and left the shop.

He was excited to know he would see his mother in the morning. Kevin Richardson seemed like a nice, caring man. He could imagine his mother was happy with her newfound family. *If only I could find that kind of caring with her,* he thought. *Maybe I can.*

Jonathan knew he'd have to change his feelings toward her. Could he do that? It seemed his mother was allowing God into her life now. He could understand that, living with such a lovely couple like Kevin and Sara Richardson. *If God could change my mother, maybe there's hope for me,* he mused. *Why am I even thinking this way?* Whatever it was, he continued to think about the possibilities of a better life, a life where, instead of trying to control situations and other people's lives, he would think about others instead of himself.

He'd been sitting in the car for thirty minutes, thinking about a different kind of life that included people who would love him and care about him and didn't want something from him.

He pulled out of the parking lot and turned left toward the church. The houses thinned out at this end of town. Then he saw it—a beautiful stone church with a tall steeple and exposed bell that most likely could be heard far and wide. On the back side of the church was a newer addition and a newly sealed parking lot with handicap spaces near the back door.

He wondered how his mother's health was. Being homeless for such a long time had most likely compromised her health. He hoped she was able to walk and get around. Here again, he was thinking kindly about his mother.

He wondered where the pastor's home was located. Maybe the address was on the church sign out front. He drove around the block and came back to the front of the church. Nothing on the sign. He was ready to pull away when he noticed the sign had a website address. Of course, churches now had websites. He Googled it, and sure enough, there was a note about a Bible study group that met at the manse each Wednesday night during Advent.

Jonesboro was so small he decided to find the house on his own. After driving around for ten minutes, he found the street, then the manse. It was a large brick home with two porches. Each had a swing. He imagined his mother sitting in one of them—happy, not the mentally worn-out woman he last saw in the mental health facility.

He parked at a distance from the manse so as not to be seen. The sun filtered through the large maple trees that now stood naked. Sara had decorated the front porch with all kinds of beautiful Christmas decorations. On the front lawn was a large nativity with all the bells and whistles. He noticed baby Jesus was missing. He'd heard from a Catholic friend that many churches left out the baby Jesus until Christmas Eve, when he was placed in the crèche.

Now that he'd found the church and the manse, he drove back toward the downtown area. On one of the side streets, he saw a library, and across the street was the local sheriff's department. Chills ran down his back as he thought about Sheriff Adams. He knew Adams had eyes on him. "Please don't let him find out about me being here," Jonathan pleaded out loud. *Who am I saying this to?* he wondered. Then his thoughts turned into a prayer. *All right, I guess I am saying this to you, God. If you really care about me like Christians say you do, then help me out. I don't know what's happening to me. I only know my heart's hurting! Please help me with my mother ... my mom.*

Chapter 37

Tess had enjoyed last Sunday so much she decided this Sunday she'd get ready early. Sara had said they needed to leave earlier to get their regular seats before someone else sat in them. That was fine by her. She loved all the beautiful decorations around the sanctuary, especially the nativity figurines, which almost filled the right side of the pulpit. She had noticed last Sunday that baby Jesus wasn't in his crib, so she asked about it. Sara explained it was traditional for some churches not to put baby Jesus in his crib until the Christmas Eve service.

That made her even more excited about Christmas Eve and Christmas Day.

"I'm ready when you are," Tess told Sara.

"Wow!" Sara was amazed.

"You said you wanted to get there early so nobody would steal our seats."

"Tess, I didn't say steal. I said take."

"The same to me. You just want it to sound nice."

Sara laughed at Tess's honesty. "All right, get your coat, and don't forget your hat. Last week, you forgot it, and you complained about your head being cold."

"Rub it in. Ever since you talked me into getting my hair cut shorter, my head gets cold more often."

"I'm sure having your hair shorter has nothing to do with your head being cold," Sara teased.

"I liked my long hair," Tess mumbled under her breath.

They arrived at the church thirty minutes before the service started. Again, there were more people in the sanctuary than normal, but thankfully, their places were empty. After taking their seats, Sara looked around the sanctuary. She never tired of admiring the beauty of Christmas. Besides, it being a special time in the Christian life, it spilled out into just about everything in people's lives. From the bright and colorful decorations to the religious symbols, the birth of Jesus our Savior was proclaimed. She had to admit that she still got excited about Christmas presents.

A few members of the church came up to Sara and Tess, wishing them a Merry Christmas. Mrs. Applebee was one of them. She reached over Sara and gave Tess a big hug. Tess grunted but didn't say anything. Sara knew Tess wasn't fond of Mrs. Applebee, but since her birthday party, she had noticed that Tess was kinder to her. Now that she thought about it, Tess seemed nicer to everyone.

⁂

Jonathan parked on one of the side streets, near the church's front entrance. He wore dress slacks, a button-down shirt, and a sports jacket. Trying to figure out what to wear had been stressful. Here he was, a high-powered executive in a dog-eat-dog job, and he couldn't decide on what to wear to a small-town church.

He arrived early, hoping to find his mother and observe her before the service began. His heart started pounding, and his ears were ringing. He knew what that meant.

He asked the usher, who was greeting people at the door, where he could find a drinking fountain. He was directed down a hallway off the sanctuary. He found the fountain in front of the restrooms. After taking his medicine, he wandered farther down the hallway to a large room with closed double doors. He assumed it was their social room. He looked through the closed doors, then returned to the sanctuary. He was surprised to see the sanctuary was filled almost to capacity. He climbed the stairs to the balcony, hoping to find a seat by the railing so he could find his mother in the crowd.

Jonathan's eyes spanned the congregation, stopping at the sight of two women standing in the third row. *The older woman with the short, curly white hair has to be my mother*, he thought. His heart pounded harder. *Please, God, don't let me faint! I just want to see my mother—that's all.*

The two women were talking to a woman who was tall and a little on the masculine side. He could hear her laughter all the way up in the balcony. Smiling, he thought it sounded like a pig snorting.

The woman leaned over the younger woman and gave his mother a hug. From where he sat, he could see his mother's face, and he could tell she definitely wasn't enjoying the hug. He smiled, noticing she looked younger than when he saw her last.

The service began, and the other woman returned to her seat. After standing for the introit, Pastor Richardson invited the congregation to pass the peace, whatever that was.

A well-dressed, middle-aged woman standing next to him grabbed his hand and said, "May the peace of God be with you." He wasn't familiar to her, so she included a welcome to church.

After being seated, a family of four approached the pulpit for the lighting of the second candle for Advent. A cute little girl, about ten or eleven, lit two of the four candles. Her younger brother voiced his displeasure at not being allowed to light the candles. The congregation laughed, while his parents were obviously embarrassed. Jonathan smiled, wondering if Derek's kids would have acted the same.

The choir sang their anthem, scripture was read, and then the ushers took the morning offering. Jonathan took a hundred-dollar bill from his wallet and put it in the offering plate. The usher looked at his offering, leaned over, and said, "Bless you, sir," then patted him on his shoulder.

Pastor Richardson talked about a woman named Elizabeth who was related to Mary, the mother of Jesus. It seemed when Mary went to visit Elizabeth and told her that she was pregnant with Jesus, the baby inside of Elizabeth leaped for joy. Her child would be born six months before Jesus. The scriptures said the baby's name would be John, who later became known as John the Baptist.

Jonathan listened intently, enjoying the story but not sure if it really happened.

After the service was over and most of the people had left, Jonathan lingered to watch his mother a few minutes longer. The young woman with his mother went to talk to the choir director, leaving her alone. As she bent to pick up her purse, she looked up toward the balcony, where Jonathan continued to observe her. He didn't expect that to happen, so he quickly turned away.

Afraid she might walk to the front of the church, intent on seeing who he was, Jonathan quickly went down the stairs. As he turned back for one more look, he saw his mother standing motionless at the end of the pew, as if she was in another time—long ago when things were happier for her and her little boy.

Monday morning, Jonathan was back to work. Concentrating on all the small fires he had to put out was giving him a headache. He got up from his desk, went to his personal coffee bar, and made himself a French vanilla latte. As he waited for it to brew, his phone rang. Derek wanted to know how the trip to Jonesboro went and how Jonathan survived the church service.

"So, how'd it go? Did you get to see your mother?" Derek asked.

"Actually, it went quite well."

"How did she look after two years?" Derek was anxious to hear his friend's answers.

She looked happy. I'm not sure what I was expecting, but what I saw was a sense of peace on her face."

"Now, how could you see peace in your mother just by looking at her?"

"Derek, I'm telling you the truth. My mother looked happy, and relaxed, and contented. That's what I saw, even at a distance."

"OK, don't be defensive. I'm just surprised. That's all."

"Sorry. I guess I am sounding defensive. It's just that seeing her so happy made it hard for me to be angry. My feelings are all mixed up right now. It didn't help that I enjoyed the service and so much more of what happened while I was there."

"Why don't you come for dinner tonight, and you can tell me and Nancy all of what happened in Jonesboro? How's that sound?"

"That sounds great!" Jonathan replied. "See you this evening."

As he hung up, a sense of peace engulfed him. Maybe that was what his mother was feeling. What was this emotional pull he was feeling toward her? Whatever it was, it was strong and wonderful and confusing, all at the same time.

Chapter 38

Tess sat at the breakfast table, lost in thought. Kevin and Sara talked about the day and what they would be doing, not noticing how quiet Tess was. Sara asked Tess if she wanted to go do some Christmas shopping and have lunch at her favorite restaurant, Mom's in the Kitchen.

"Tess, did you hear me?" Sara asked again.

"What'd you say, Sara? I was thinking about something and didn't hear you. Sorry."

"Are you alright? You seemed far away."

"Yes, I'm fine … just thinking about something strange that happened yesterday after church."

Sara smiled at Tess. "It must have been pretty interesting to keep you from listening to Kevin and me."

"It was—and it was strange."

Kevin, his travel mug filled with coffee and ready to leave for his church office, stopped at the mention of something strange and sat back down. "What happened, Tess?"

Tess looked at him, then Sara. Her face was pale, and her eyes reflected sadness that neither Kevin nor Sara had seen since the first few days she was with them.

"It was after the service. Sara had gone to talk to Mr. Davis about the music for Christmas Sunday, and I was getting ready to join her when something strange happened."

"What?" Sara asked, concerned.

"It was as if a voice inside me said, 'Look up at the balcony—right now!' And I did. Looking down at me was this man. He was middle-aged, had a thick head of hair, and was tall, over six feet, but being so far away, I'm not sure. Anyway, he was nicely dressed. The strange thing was he turned away just as I looked up at him, as if he didn't want me to see his face. Don't you think that's a bit odd?"

"Tess, we told you there are more people attending services during Advent than normal. You even mentioned that to Sara," Kevin said kindly. "He was probably one of those people."

"I suppose you're right, but I can't put my finger on it. Something about him seemed familiar."

"You've met so many new people, Tess. Maybe you've seen him around town or at the grocery," Sara offered, hoping to reassure her. She noticed that besides being upset, Tess acted afraid. "Did this man make you feel threatened?"

"No, it's not that. It's just … well, never mind. I'm being unreasonable." Suddenly, Tess changed her tone. "Let's go Christmas shopping! It will be fun and will help get my mind off my silly thoughts."

Kevin got up, gave Tess a quick kiss on the cheek, then left for church. Sara said she'd be ready to leave in about ten minutes, then left the kitchen. After she left, Tess thought again about the man in the balcony. There sure was something about him that seemed familiar. *Stop it, Tess! Think about how fun it's going to be to go Christmas shopping.*

She got up and went to the family room to wait for Sara.

Chapter 39

Jonathan's week passed quickly. His clients were gearing up their advertising material for Easter. Some were even preparing for Memorial Day and Fourth of July.

Derek called to see if he wanted to do a little Christmas shopping. Jonathan really didn't have anyone to shop for, but he decided it would keep his thoughts occupied. They planned on meeting for drinks and dinner around five, then going to a few stores not far from Derek's home.

Jonathan arrived at the restaurant right on time; Derek was already there working on his first drink.

"Hey there, buddy!" Derek greeted his friend.

Jonathan knew he was lucky to have Derek as a friend. Along with being an excellent lawyer, his friendship had gotten him through some rough times since his mother disappeared.

Jonathan ordered a martini, and before saying anything else, he told Derek he'd broken up with Delilah. Derek said he was proud of him. Their conversation quickly turned to Jonathan's trip to Jonesboro.

"So, you're still moving forward with your plans to go to Jonesboro again this Sunday?"

"Yes, nothing's changed there. What has changed is the way I'm feeling."

"How's that?"

"I'm not sure. I just know I'm not angry anymore. It's as if the anger vanished. Like a cloud of smoke, it's gone."

"Wow! That's amazing, Jonathan!"

"I know. I can't believe I was so angry. I—God forbid—I thought about physically harming her! How could a son feel that way about his own mother?"

"You won't like this, but when I first met you, I saw a man consumed with power and money. I wasn't sure I wanted to be your lawyer, but then I saw a side of you that showed kindness and gentleness."

"I'm glad you saw the other side of me and took the job."

"Me too."

"Do you think there's hope for the kindness and gentleness to come back? Do you think it may be happening now?"

"Yes, I do. I don't know what's causing these changes, but I do know I'm happy for the change. Now, let's put this subject aside and think about something enjoyable, like Christmas."

"I agree," said Jonathan.

Their dinner arrived. While they were enjoying their meals, New York City was getting its first major snow of the season.

Jonathan arrived at the airport on Saturday, going through the same process as the week before. He spent the time on the plane figuring out what he would do after the church service. Last Sunday, he made the mistake of staying afterward. It was strange how his mother decided to look up toward the balcony and caught a glimpse of him. Thank goodness he turned before she saw his face. Even though he wore glasses instead of his contact lenses and he'd grown out his beard, he still worried she might recognize him.

Being homeless had changed his mother's appearance from her time in the mental health facility, but she seemed happier. She smiled and laughed when the masculine lady said something to her. He hadn't seen her show any joy for years.

Had he changed since he saw her last? Until now, not much. For the past year and a half, he'd been filled with anger and revenge. That was when he started the affair with Delilah, thinking it would help ease his anger and frustration. The relationship worked for a while but started to fall apart after he found his mother.

The flight attendant announced the plane was landing in Toledo. Repeating last week, he got his rental and checked in at the hotel. After lunch, he went back to his hotel room, planning to take a quick nap, but changed his mind. He just couldn't relax.

He had planned to eat at a local restaurant near his hotel for dinner but decided instead, to drive to Jonesboro. On the previous weekend, he'd overheard a young couple talking about an Italian restaurant called On the Grapevine that had just opened in Jonesboro. He found the address and phone number, then called to make a reservation. There had been a cancelation, so he could have that time slot at 6:00 p.m. *That worked out great*, he thought.

He arrived in Jonesboro early and drove around town. The downtown streets were bustling with Christmas shoppers. Snow had fallen the night before, turning the town into a winter wonderland.

Jonathan found the restaurant and parked at the far end of the parking lot. When he entered, the smell of garlic shouted, "Italian!" Of all the restaurants he'd patronized over his many years in New York, Italian was his favorite.

A waiter took him to his table, gave him the menu, and asked if he would like to start with a glass of wine. He asked the young man what wine went well with lasagna. The waiter suggested a red wine from Sicily called Primitivo. Jonathan, a wine connoisseur, was impressed with the waiter's suggestion and ordered a glass. While he waited for his meal, he sipped his wine, and began to relax.

Turning his attention to his surroundings, he was surprised with what he saw. The restaurant's upscale and authentic décor would go well in a big city like Manhattan.

What a pleasant small town Jonesboro is, he mused. *I can see why my mother likes it here. Living in a place where people know and care about each other—that's rare today. Nothing like New York City, for sure.*

When his dinner arrived, he delved in with gusto, not realizing how hungry he had been.

Amid the wine, the soothing music, and the fantastic food, Jonathan started again to want a loving relationship and a family who cared about him. He decided living in a small town like Jonesboro would be nice.

Wow! Where did that come from? he wondered. *It must be the food and the intimacy of the restaurant's relaxing environment.*

After his meal, the waiter inquired if he would be having dessert. Jonathan seldom had dessert, but tonight he felt laid back and more relaxed than usual.

"What are the choices?" he asked. The waiter shared the long list of desserts.

"They all sound delicious," Jonathan said, "but I think I'll stick with my Italian cuisine and have the tiramisu."

"Good choice, sir. I'll be back shortly with your tiramisu."

The waiter had just left when the front door to the restaurant opened and in walked Kevin and Sara Richardson—and his mother. *What are the chances of this happening?* Jonathan thought. *I never imagined they would come to a place like this. It's too expensive and ritzy for a clergyman and his wife, but there they are, almost right in front of me.*

He panicked! His heart jumped in his chest, pounding in his ears. He feared he would faint right there in front of Kevin, Sara, and his mother.

At that moment, his waiter appeared with his tiramisu.

Then a strange thing happened. The pounding and racing of his heart subsided, the sense of fainting disappeared, and a calmness took over his body. The room filled with a burst of white light. He shut his eyes from its brilliance. A voice whispered in his ear: "It's all right, my son. Don't be afraid." When he opened his eyes, the room was back to what it had been.

A sense of peace enveloped Jonathan as if a greater power had connected with him.

∽

Kevin escorted Sara and Tess to their table and pulled out their chairs for them. As usual, Tess had to make a big deal of it.

"For crying out loud, Kevin, I'm still capable of pulling out my own chair. I'm not that feeble yet."

"Tess, Kevin's using his manners. You should know that. I'm sure you've dined in some expensive, fancy restaurants."

"Sorry, Kevin. Sara's right. I've forgotten how manners work. And yes, I've eaten in many expensive and ritzy places in my day. I can't believe how the way I lived on the streets continues to hang on to me. Anyway, let's get to the good part of this evening—eating!"

Kevin and Sara smiled at each other. Life with Tess kept them on their toes.

Their server greeted them and asked for their drink orders. Tess wanted to try something new, so she asked their server what she would suggest. The sweet young lady asked Tess if she liked iced tea, and Tess replied yes. She told Tess they had peach, raspberry, and mango teas, along with strawberry and regular lemonade.

"Man, that's a lot of choices! Let's see. How about that peach-flavored tea. I like peaches."

The young lady smiled at Tess, then said, "They can put sliced peaches in the drink if you'd like."

"Why, that sounds wonderful, dear!" Tess exclaimed.

They settled in, talking about Christmas and the last two Advent services. Kevin had asked the church board if it would be all right if he, Sara, and Tess lit the Advent candles the Sunday before Christmas. He told them Tess was excited and compared lighting the candles to lighting candles on a birthday cake for baby Jesus. When they heard that, they laughed and agreed.

Their dinners arrived, postponing any more discussion about church. As each of them turned their attention to their meals, Tess took a moment to look around the restaurant. There were young and old people—well dressed and casually dressed, families and couples—all seeming to enjoy themselves.

Suddenly, Tess's eyes fell on a middle-aged man seated a few tables away from them. She dropped her fork onto her plate, attracting Kevin's and Sara's attention. They were alarmed to see fear on her face.

"Tess, what's wrong?" Kevin asked.

"See that man over there at the table by the window, sitting by himself? Do you see him?"

"Yes, I see him. Do you know him?"

Kevin waited for her to answer, but all she did was stare at the man. Her face was white as a sheet; her hands trembled. Sara asked if she was feeling ill. Tess didn't answer. She just kept staring at the man.

When Kevin took Tess's trembling hands, she looked at him and said, "That's the man who was looking at me from the balcony on Sunday. No, it can't be! It just can't be!"

"What can't be, Tess? You're not making a lot of sense here. Why are you so upset about a man who was looking at you Sunday? We told you he's probably one of the Christmas and Easter visitors."

"That's my son! That's Jonathan!"

"Are you sure? He doesn't look anything like you described him to Sara and me. And why would he come to Jonesboro and decide to eat in a public place, knowing the police are keeping tabs on him."

Kevin didn't know what to make of the situation. His choices were to confront the man or give Dean Adams a call. The man Tess said was her son didn't seem to be in a big hurry to leave. If it really was Jonathan, wouldn't he leave? He must have seen them come in.

"What are you going to do, Kevin?" Sara asked, her voice shaking.

"I don't know!"

"Kevin!" Tess said. "Go over and confront him! Tell him he's not welcomed and to get out of here—now!

"Is that what you really want me to do? Tell him to leave? Aren't you a little curious why he's here in the first place?"

Kevin looked straight at Tess. He knew her curiosity was stronger than her fear. He started to get up to go talk to Jonathan, but Tess stopped him.

"Don't tell him to leave just yet. Find out why he's here. Then ask him to leave."

"Kevin, shouldn't we call Dean before you talk to him—just as a precaution?" Sara asked.

"I suppose it wouldn't hurt. Go ahead, but ask him to stay in his car," Kevin told her. "We don't want to make a scene right here. It would embarrass all of us."

Kevin got up and walked toward Jonathan's table. His heart raced, and his palms were sweaty. *He silently prayed, Dear God, if there ever was a time I need your guidance, it's now. Give me the courage and the words to say and do what's best for Tess and, yes, for her wayward son, Jonathan.*

Kevin stood in front of Jonathan's table, his voice shaking as he asked, "I think I know the answer to my question, but I'm going to ask anyway. Are you Jonathan Farnsworth?"

"Yes, I am, and you are Kevin Richardson, pastor of Trinity Lutheran Church here in Jonesboro. Please sit down," Jonathan said, his voice warm and gentle.

Kevin sat down in the chair across from Jonathan, hoping God had heard his quick prayer. He took a deep breath, then came right out with it. "Let's not beat around the bush. Tess is sitting over there with my wife, and she's scared to death. She thinks you're here to hurt her. Are you?"

"No, I'm not—not now."

"What do you mean *not now*?"

"May I call you Kevin? I'm not sure how I'm supposed to address a clergyman."

Kevin smiled and told him it was fine to call him by his first name.

"These past two years have been filled with more than enough stress, grief, and, yes, anger for a family to go through. You only know me by what my mother has told you, and I'm sure she's given you an earful of what a lousy and mean son I've been. And she's right! I have been—until these past few weeks, when something strange has been happening to me, causing me to feel confused and delighted all at the same time."

"Before you go any further with telling me why you're here and what happened in the past with you and your mom—or even your life—I had Sara call Sheriff Adams, and he's on his way here."

"I figured that would happen, and I'm ready to deal with that and everything else that's going to take place in the next few hours and possibly weeks. I know you don't trust me, and you have every right not to, but I'm telling you the truth. I have no plans to hurt my mother in any way! Please believe me."

Kevin saw grief in Jonathan's eyes but also a desire for redemption for his life and his feelings about his mother. At that moment, Kevin knew God had done what he asked, giving him courage and the right words to say to Jonathan. He trusted God to make sure things would be fair for both Tess and Jonathan.

Kevin's phone rang. Dean Adams was calling from his police cruiser to ask what Kevin wanted him to do with the situation. Kevin asked him to wait a few minutes longer; then he'd call and let him know what to do.

"That was Sheriff Adams."

"So, what is your next move, Kevin?"

"I'm going to go back to my table, tell Tess you're not here to harm her, and tell her and Sara to go back to the manse. Then you and I will go outside and speak to Sheriff Adams."

Kevin went back to his table, where Tess and Sara were waiting anxiously to hear what he and Jonathan talked about. He told them what was said, including the part where Jonathan swore he wasn't there to harm his mother in any way, and they were going to meet Dean in the parking lot as soon as Jonathan paid his bill.

"I need the two of you to go back to the manse when you're finished with your dinner. I'm going to suggest to Dean that he, Jonathan, and I go back to my office at the church and talk about this … this … whatever this is and figure out what happens next."

Tess didn't say a word, which was not like her at all. Kevin asked if what he was going to do was all right with her. She mumbled something under her breath that he couldn't hear.

"I'm sorry, Tess, but I didn't understand what you said. Could you say that again?"

"I said it's fine. I just want to know if my son is telling the truth, that he doesn't want to harm me physically or, God forbid, put me away again so he can say I'm incompetent and get hold of my money! That's all."

"Dean and I will get to the bottom of this. Now, you ladies finish up your dinners and go home."

Kevin leaned over, kissed Sara, and gave Tess a kiss on her head. Then he left to meet Jonathan at the door.

"I'm not hungry anymore, Sara. Can we just go home?" Tess asked.

"Sure. I've lost my appetite too. We'll have our dinners boxed up, and we can take them home."

"I'd like that. Thanks."

"You're welcome, sweetie. Listen, I trust Kevin to get this all figured out. And you know what? Jonathan may be telling the truth. He may be having a change of heart, like you."

"What are you talking about—a change of heart like me? What do you mean?"

"It means when we first met, you didn't believe in a loving God. You didn't put much stock in religion, and you sure didn't want to attend church!" Sara smiled, thinking about their first few weeks with Tess.

"But you started to change. You allowed me to pray with you, and now you pray on your own. You've changed so much, Tess, in such a glorious way! I believe you've found the Lord in your heart! Now, why don't you give Jonathan the benefit of the doubt? Maybe God has been working on him, and he's not even aware what's happening."

As Tess looked at Sara, her eyes filled with tears. The tears flowed down her cheeks onto her hands. Sara was right. She had changed for the better. She now felt love in her heart and a desire to be a better person. Now she needed to give Jonathan the same chance as Kevin and Sara had given her, a chance for new beginnings with God in their lives.

Wiping the tears off her cheeks, she took one of Sara's hands and patted it. "You're right, sweet pea. I need to give my son, my Jonathan, the benefit of the doubt. Maybe God has been working on him, and he's not even aware it's been happening."

Sara put her arm around Tess's shoulder, and the two of them got up to leave. Before Tess walked out the door, she turned around to get one more glimpse of her son, her boy, Jonny.

After Jonathan paid for his meal, he and Kevin went outside to meet Sheriff Adams. Jonathan was nervous. After all, his actions toward his mother had brought in law enforcement from Jonesboro and the New York police.

As they approached the cruiser, Kevin stopped long enough to put his hand on Jonathan's shoulder to reassure him. Jonathan felt strength from Kevin. *Maybe this will work out*, he thought.

Dean got out of his cruiser and walked toward Kevin and Jonathan. "I'm assuming you're Tess's son, Jonathan. I'm Sheriff Adams. I can't say it's a pleasure to meet you under these circumstances."

"Yes, I'm Jonathan. Why do all of you call my mother Tess? Her name is Julianne."

Kevin smiled. "Your mother told us from day one to call her Tess. Even after we found out her real name was Julianne, she still told us—and quite firmly—she wouldn't answer to anything but Tess."

"I wonder why." Jonathan said. "Her middle name is Theresa. Maybe that's where she got the idea to be called Tess. Anyway, I'm sure you've noticed she has a mind of her own."

Kevin and Dean laughed.

"I was thinking that the three of us could go to my church office and discuss what to do next. Is that OK with the two of you?" Kevin asked.

"I just got off duty, so it's fine with me. Is this something you'd be comfortable with, Jonathan?"

"That's fine, Sheriff. I have nothing to hide."

"I have to tell you that while I waited for you and Kevin, I put in a call to NYPD just to make sure everything was in order with you. I'm sure your lawyer told you we asked the police to keep an eye on you. I'm sorry about that, but you did, after all, put out some red flags regarding your mother, and they were not in her best interest."

"Yes, I knew. I would have done the same thing if I'd been in your position. But, Sheriff—and you too, Kevin—I hope I can change your opinion of me and how badly I've behaved on the subject of my mother."

"I can't speak for Sheriff Adams, but I'm willing to hear your side of the story. Just be aware—we are very protective of Tess. She's made her way into many hearts since Sara found her. I just want you to know."

"Same here on feelings about your mom," Dean agreed, "but I'm not as trusting as Kevin on your motives toward your mother, past and present. I guess it's because of the kind of work I deal with. Anyway, let's go to your office, Kevin."

Kevin and Jonathan got into Jonathan's rental, Dean in his cruiser, and they drove the short distance to the church. The church was dark except for a few security lights in the parking lot and by each door. The custodian had plowed out the parking lot and cleared the sidewalks of the snow in preparation for services in the morning. They entered the church through a side door. The church was ominous in the dark, but when Kevin flipped the light switch, the hallway became bright and welcoming.

They walked down the hallway in silence, Kevin leading, Jonathan in the middle, and Dean bringing up the rear. Kevin unlocked his office door and turned the lights on, illuminating the room. Jonathan was surprised to see such a cozy and pleasant office. What he had been expecting he wasn't sure, but not this, a room filled with bold colors and leather furniture—very masculine. Everything in the room worked together, as if Kevin had a decorator. *This church must have money to have a professional decorator do the pastor's office,* he mused.

Kevin moved another chair in front of his desk, motioning for Dean and Jonathan to sit. He sat at his desk where he could look at both men at the same time. Jonathan admired Kevin's beautiful and rich-looking desk. He admitted to himself that he was a little jealous of Kevin's desk and his office, even though he had the best office with the best view of Manhattan.

"So, how do we even begin this? What would you call this, Dean—an inquiry?"

"No, it's not an inquiry. Jonathan hasn't been arrested. Let's call it getting answers about why he's here in Jonesboro."

"OK, that sounds nonthreatening. Do you agree, Jonathan?" Kevin looked at him, hoping he would agree.

"That's fine. As I said earlier, I have nothing to hide. So, what do you want to know?"

Dean asked, "Is it true you found out your mother took you out of her will days before she disappeared, and you were angry? And that you found out the stipulation in her new will stated if she wasn't found in two years after she disappeared, all the money would go to an orphanage in Zanesville?"

Jonathan hung his head and waited a full minute before he looked up at both men. "Yes, that's all true," he admitted.

Dean continued, "So, it's true you hired a private detective to find your mother."

"Yes again."

"I have to admit, Jonathan, so far, you've been honest and upfront with us. Don't you agree, Kevin?"

Kevin leaned back in his chair, looking like a character out of a who-done-it novel. "I agree wholeheartedly, Dean, and to take his answer further, I think he really has had a change of heart, and it seems recent."

"Now what?" Jonathan asked. "You both agree what I've told you is true, so do I have to continue with this interview, or can I now tell you the real reason I'm here in Jonesboro?"

Dean's cell phone rang, and he left Kevin's office. While he was gone, Kevin fidgeted with the papers on his desk, trying to keep from asking Jonathan any more questions without Dean's presence.

"Well," Dean said to Jonathan, "that was the NYPD getting back to me. According to them, you haven't done anything in the past six weeks to cause them to be suspicious of you.

Jonathan leaned back in his chair. He ran his hand through his thick hair, looked up at the ceiling, then laughed softly.

The tension of the past few hours slipped quickly away. Looking at Dean and Kevin, Jonathan smiled the biggest smile he'd shown in years. A wave of joy and gratitude flowed through him, wiping away the pain and anger he'd carried for many years. Whatever it was that kept coming at him, he hoped it wouldn't stop! While this was happening to Jonathan, Dean and Kevin experienced an energy pulsating throughout the room.

Jonathan's reaction to Dean's news surprised both men. Seeing Jonathan's smile and the change in his demeanor shocked them and gave them joy, all at the same time.

"I think, gentlemen, we've encountered what some Christians call a visit from the Holy Spirit!" Kevin said.

Dean and Jonathan had never experienced anything like what they were feeling. Call it what you want, but it was amazing! The sensation of pure joy and redemption flowed through them. Kevin had encountered the Holy Spirit many years ago. He'd been struggling with the choice of going into the ministry or teaching English literature at a small college near his home. It happened while he was alone, on his knees, asking God for an answer; suddenly, his body was filled with joy! God answered him, assuring him that he was to go and preach and teach and love all those who would listen. This feeling was what he'd heard about all his life, the Holy Spirit. He hadn't experienced the Holy Spirit again until now.

Dean and Jonathan didn't know what to make of it. Dean struggled at times to understand the story of Jesus's birth all the way through his crucifixion and resurrection, let alone this thing called the Holy Spirit.

Until a few weeks ago, Jonathan didn't believe in religion at all. Now here he was, sitting in a minister's office with the local sheriff, being filled with this thing called the Holy Spirit. *Come on,* he thought, *this is not me!*

"I don't know about you, but I feel pretty happy right now," Kevin responded. "Listen, guys. It's late, and we're all tired. How about we finish this up after church tomorrow?"

Dean and Jonathan agreed.

"Jonathan, I hope you're still coming to church tomorrow. I want to hear, as commentator Paul Harvey used to say, the rest of the story." Kevin smiled at Jonathan.

"I plan to come, but I'm worried my mother won't like me being there."

"You let me take care of that. I think, deep down inside, she wants to get her son back."

Dean and Kevin hugged Jonathan before he left for his hotel in Toledo.

"I'm still confused about what happened in your office, Kevin. I'd like to talk to you later about it."

"I know, Dean. The Holy Spirit is a tough one to explain, even to the seasoned Christian. We'll go over that after we get this situation with Tess and Jonathan under control. Oh, and since Sara took Tess in my car, could you drop me off at home?"

Dean laughed. "I guess I didn't think about that. Sure, no problem."

Before Kevin got out of Dean's cruiser, he said, "Get some rest, and I'll see you at church in the morning."

When Kevin arrived home, he was surprised that Sara and Tess were still up. He should have known Tess would want to know what went on.

"Why are you ladies still up?"

"Do you think I could just go to bed and not find out what Jonathan's up to? I didn't just fall off a turnip truck, Kevin. So, what did he say? Did he fess up that he and his father wanted me committed and declared incompetent so they could get control of my money? Did he—huh?"

"Tess, just settle down. I'm not going to go over what went on with Jonathan and Dean right now, not at this hour. Both of you go to bed, please. We'll talk about this tomorrow, I promise."

"I think I have every right to know what my son has been doing and what he told you and Dean. I don't think I'll be able to sleep at all. Anyway, good night."

"Stop a minute, Tess. I don't want you to lie awake all night, so here's something that should help you sleep. Your son, Jonathan, was honest to Dean and me about what's been going on while he tried to find you. He shared that something amazing has been happening to him these past six weeks, and it's all positive!"

"Do you believe him, Kevin? You know how much he's wanted my money and what lengths he'd go to get a hold of that money. He's like his father, conniving and ruthless! I don't trust him one bit."

"I believe him, Tess. I really do. Have a little trust in me and Dean—and also God. I'll see you in the morning."

After Kevin and Sara went to bed, Sara tried hard to get Kevin to tell her what was said with Jonathan and Dean, but Kevin refused.

"Sara, I'm telling you like I told Tess, I'll share everything tomorrow. Now, let's get some sleep. I'm exhausted."

"I'm sorry, sweetheart," Sara said, snuggling up to him. Her body, warm and soft, helped Kevin calm down.

He whispered, "I love you, Sara," as they both fell asleep.

Chapter 40

Jonathan arrived at the church early. He was greeted by the same man who made a point to welcome him back. Jonathan thanked him and took the bulletin handed to him. Before going up the stairs to the balcony, he stopped and looked into the main sanctuary. It was fifteen minutes before the service would start, and the sanctuary was almost full. He debated whether to go sit in the balcony again or find a seat in the main sanctuary.

Since his mother saw him last evening and she knew he was coming to church, he decided to take a leap forward and sit nearer to the front. He wanted to get another look at her, even if it would be her back.

While he looked at the bulletin, his mother and Sara entered the sanctuary from the side. The old, homely woman with the strange laugh ran up to greet his mother just like last week.

What in the world does that woman want from my mother? Jonathan thought, smiling. His mother was not like the woman he remembered last time he saw her. *Come to think about it, I'm not like the man I was just six weeks ago!* he mused. He hoped Kevin could help untangle all the new feelings and emotions he'd been having.

Before his mother and Sara sat down, she saw him, stopped, then gave him her skunk-eyed glare before sitting down.

Without meaning to, Jonathan laughed out loud, recalling her giving him that look when he was a misbehaving kid. Apparently, Tess heard his laugh. She turned around and glared at him. He gave her the biggest smile his face could muster up. Startled, she gave him a slight smile back, then turned around as the organ music signaled the service was beginning.

After Kevin's announcements, a family of five walked up to the altar to light the third candle of Advent. *Such a nice-looking family,* Jonathan thought. *Most likely, I'll never have a family,* he mused. *At my age, the chances are slim, but maybe I will marry someday.*

Kevin's sermon was another interesting story to Jonathan. Joseph and Mary had to travel from a town called Nazareth to another city named Bethlehem, where a census was taken. Joseph was from Bethlehem, related to a man named David. *David is someone I'd like to read about. Sounds as if he lived an interesting life,* Jonathan thought.

After church, he waited to talk to Kevin. Dean came up and introduced him to his wife and daughter. When Dean started to tell his wife and daughter who he was, Jonathan's heart did a quick jump. He was fearful of being known as Tess's son. But Dean introduced him as Jonathan, a friend of Kevin's. They had no reason not to believe him, relieving Jonathan's anxiety.

Dean's wife and daughter excused themselves to go talk to another family, leaving Dean with Jonathan. "How are you holding up?" Dean asked, showing concern.

"I have to admit I'm really nervous right now."

"I'm sure you are, but try to stay calm. Your mom's probably nervous too."

About that time, Kevin came up to the two of them and reached out to shake their hands. He could feel Tess's eyes penetrating his back.

Kevin continued talking to Jonathan and Dean, and the three decided to meet that afternoon around two at the manse. Kevin told Dean he wanted him to continue being a part of the conversation with Jonathan, since he was going through his own spiritual journey.

Kevin thought about inviting Jonathan home for Sunday lunch, but he changed his mind. He wasn't ready for the possible fireworks Tess might set off.

While Sara and Tess waited for Kevin, Tess tried her hardest to hear what the three men were talking about.

Dean and Jonathan walked out of the sanctuary together, and Kevin joined the ladies.

"What did he say?" Tess asked suspiciously. "What did Dean say? He's the sheriff, so he had to say something about Jonathan spying on me."

Tess's words made Kevin angry, but he knew she was just afraid of Jonathan doing something to make her go back to the place she feared the most—the mental health facility.

Instead of answering her questions, he put an arm around her and Sara and guided them to the outside door.

Before he got in his car, he told them Jonathan and Dean were coming to the manse around two that afternoon. Tess was shocked, but she agreed to hear Jonathan out before making any judgment about his intentions for her future.

Kevin was worn out already. "Well, God, let the games begin," he muttered, then smiled, thinking of Tess. Whatever happened from this point on was a mystery, but he knew God would work it out.

✑

The doorbell rang exactly at two o'clock. Kevin opened the door to both Dean and Jonathan. Kevin laughed. "How'd the two of you manage to get here at the same time?"

"We met at the church and came in my car," Dean said.

"That was a nice gesture. Come on in, fellas. We're meeting in the family room for now. Later we'll move to the dining room for a dessert break."

Jonathan and Dean followed Kevin. When they entered the family room, they saw Tess sitting in her favorite chair by the fireplace. She turned her gaze away from the roaring fire and smiled at Dean but gave only a slight nod to Jonathan.

Kevin spoke first. "We're here, Tess, to let Jonathan tell his story about the past three months, when Sara found you on our lawn."

At the mention of finding Tess, Jonathan jumped in. "I know there are questions you want to ask me, but I'm really curious how my mother got on your front lawn."

Before Sara could answer, Tess replied, "Jonathan, you don't deserve any answers about me or where I've been for the last two years. In fact, you don't deserve anything except my anger over how you and your father treated me for many years! All the two of you wanted was my money! Isn't that true, Jonathan? You wanted my money!"

Kevin was angry at Tess's outburst. He was determined to allow Jonathan to tell his story without Tess interfering. "Tess, that's enough! You promised Sara and me you would be fair and allow Jonathan to tell his story—all of it! So let him!"

The look on Tess's face stunned them. Her demeanor changed in a flash. Instead of more anger, tears ran down her face. She sank farther into her chair, as if she was trying to disappear.

Sara jumped up and went to Tess, hoping to comfort her.

The men didn't know what to do, especially Jonathan, since he was the source of Tess's pain. He got up from his chair and walked toward the foyer, planning to leave. Suddenly, Tess called out to him. "Stop! Please don't leave. I love you, son!"

Jonathan turned around. His mother looked at him with tears in her old eyes. "Jonathan, there's so much you and I need to talk about. The most important is mending our relationship."

Jonathan walked back into the room and stood there, not knowing what to do next. But Sara did. She went to him and hugged him with all her might. The tension in the room disappeared.

Jonathan knelt in front of Tess. She reached out and touched him gently on the cheek, wondering where the years had gone and how he, her son, had drifted so far from her.

"Mother, I'm so sorry for what happened to you and for the years you've gone without love from me and Dad. I know I can't make up for that time, but at this moment, I'd like to work as hard as I can to win back your love!"

Tess reached out and hugged him, stroking his head, remembering when he was a little boy putting his head in her lap. How much she wanted her son back, to love and be loved by him. Tess looked up at Dean, Kevin, and Sara and said, "This is a surprise even for me. I never thought I'd be with people who love me, and I have my son kneeling in front of me, saying he's sorry. This thing with God just keeps getting better. I'm still struggling to understand his ways, but I'm learning."

Kevin was speechless. Never in a million years would he have thought Tess would be the one to initiate mending her relationship with Jonathan. God even surprised him. *Thank you, God!*

"I think this is a good time for dessert," Kevin announced.

Wiping the tears off her cheeks, Sara agreed and went to the kitchen.

Tess asked, "Could we sit at the kitchen table? Since I've been here, that's where the best conversations have taken place. What do you all think?"

"Hey, if that's where you want to talk, Tess, then that's what we'll do," Kevin agreed.

They all went into the kitchen. Without hesitation, Tess sat down in her usual seat. Before the rest sat down, she asked Jonathan to sit across from her so she could look at him face-to-face. He smiled and did as she asked.

While the coffee perked, Kevin, Dean, and Jonathan decided they wouldn't go over what they'd talked about the evening before, since Kevin had filled Tess and Sara in on the important parts that morning.

There was a lull in the conversation while they waited for the coffee and dessert. When the coffee was ready, Kevin got up and helped Sara. After they sat down, the conversation turned to casual talk about Christmas and Tess's excitement over lighting the last Advent candle next Sunday. Jonathan asked what that was about, and they told him his mother saw it as birthday candles for baby Jesus. He smiled, remembering how childlike she could be.

After they finished their dessert, it was time to get to back to the reason Jonathan was there.

While Tess took a quick bathroom break, Jonathan told the others that no matter what happened that afternoon, he knew things were going to work out for him and his mother. Sara patted his hand to let him know she agreed.

Tess returned, signaling the time for Jonathan to tell his story.

Kevin said, "Before we start, I'd like to pray. Is that OK with everybody?"

"I was thinking the same thing," said Dean.

They bowed their heads, but Tess kept one eye open to watch Jonathan.

"Heavenly Father, we come to you in prayer as your children in need of guidance. We don't need to tell you why we're coming to you, but we do need your direction. Please give Tess and Jonathan the blessing of your love and forgiveness that you so willingly give to all your children. Help them find their way back to each other, without anger and finger-pointing. You know they both are new to your ways. Tess has grown so much in her understanding and acceptance of you and the love you have for her. Please help Jonathan to realize that you are real and that you want him, too, in the family of God."

Before Kevin could say amen, Tess said, "God, it's me, Tess. Sorry. I keep forgetting you already know who I am. Anyway, I know I've been a troublesome child of yours, and I'm really sorry about that. You know I want to change and be a better person, and that includes being a better mother to Jonathan. Please just let me keep my big mouth shut when it needs to be shut. My words cause a lot of pain sometimes, and I'm truly sorry for that. Please show me and Jonathan how this forgiveness thing works. I would appreciate all you can do to help us get on the right track. Thanks, God. Amen."

"Amen," Kevin said.

All eyes turned to Jonathan.

"I really don't want to go over the worst part of what I've done since my mother disappeared. It's sad and now humiliating. Let's just say I was consumed with greed and power and wanted my mother to suffer. It sounds horrible now that I say it aloud."

Tess looked at Jonathan with her newfound compassion.

She'd been on her own journey of mean-spirited emotions, so she understood his pain.

"Could I ask one thing before you go any further? Would you start calling me Mom instead of your mother? I'd like that. And I'll call you Jonny like I used to before you went and got so important in your job in New York City. I miss calling you Jonny."

Jonathan smiled. "I like that idea, Mom, and I miss being called Jonny."

After that, the mood lightened. The sunlight outside was fading, but the kitchen felt warm and bright, like the sun was still high in the sky.

Jonathan told his story from the time he had Thanksgiving with his friend Derek and Derek's family to the moment he felt a greater power overtaking his thoughts and actions. The clock ticked away, but no one noticed.

Tears were shed throughout the rest of the afternoon into the early evening. Finally, Jonathan stopped. His throat was dry from all the talking, but the anger and revenge toward his mother was gone.

The room was quiet. No one moved or said a word. Jonathan looked at his watch and was shocked to see it was going on five o'clock. He had been talking for more than three hours. During that time, the others had asked questions, but none were angry questions.

Jonathan looked around the table at the people he'd shared his most personal thoughts with. They were smiling at him. He didn't know what to do. *Where do I go from here?*

Kevin spoke to Jonathan in a gentle tone. "Jonathan, I don't know how the others feel, but I know God is working in your life! There's no other explanation. He's helping you find your way back to your mother!"

Tess stood up and moved toward her son—her Jonny. When she reached out to him, he stood and hugged her tightly. She started laughing, saying she couldn't breathe. He was overjoyed to hear his mom laugh.

"I've got to get back to my hotel and get some rest. I have the red-eye express to New York tomorrow morning."

Kevin, Sara, and Tess walked him and Dean to the door. Before leaving, Jonathan said he'd be in touch.

"I'm glad to know that, Jonny!" Tess said. "I don't have one of those cell phones, so you'll have to call me on the manse phone. Sara, did you give Jonny that number?" Tess was excited to know she would be talking to her son again soon.

When the two men got in the car, Dean assured Jonathan he'd make sure everything was cleared up about him and the law. Jonathan thanked him.

Dean dropped him off at his car, and Jonathan headed to Toledo, aware that he was bone-weary tired. The church service, the intense meeting with his mom and the others, and telling his story had left him drained.

"What's next, God?" he prayed. "Whatever it is, I hope I can do it. Right now, I'm not as confident with you as Mom is, so please keep that in mind. I have so much to learn. Please help me do this!"

Chapter 41

Jonathan's alarm went off at six o'clock Tuesday morning—too early, but he wanted to get to the gym before work. His workout routine had gone to pot the past few months. While he was shaving, he looked at his image in the mirror; it revealed a body that wasn't as fit as it used to be. *As long as I'm healthy, I can live with that*, he thought. *What I want and need to do is use my time and energy to make up for the lost time with Mom.* "Wow!" he said aloud. "That sounded strange, calling her mom!" He liked it.

He arrived at his office around eight, hoping to catch Doris at her desk before the other employees arrived. He wanted to give her an early Christmas gift. He found out she liked angel figurines and had purchased a crystal one for her.

Doris was putting on the coffee when he came through the door. She didn't see him, so he had time to go to his office first. After he hung up his coat, he removed the lavishly wrapped gift from the gift bag. He could hear Doris talking to Jeffery, who worked in the graphics department. When it was quiet again, he walked down the hall and stood in front of her desk. She didn't notice him until he cleared his throat.

When she looked up, he said, "Good morning, Doris. How was your weekend?"

"Jonathan, I didn't hear you. It was fine. Thanks for asking."

Jonathan was holding the beautifully wrapped gift behind his back. He brought it around, placed it on Doris's desk, and said, "Merry Christmas!"

Doris looked at Jonathan, then at the exquisitely wrapped gift. She was speechless.

"I wanted to give you your Christmas gift before things get hectic around here. I hope you like it. If not, I can get you something else. I'm new at giving instead of getting."

"I don't know what to say. It's so beautifully wrapped! Why, it's a gift within a gift!" Doris exclaimed.

"Go ahead and open it!" Jonathan urged.

After removing the sparkly bow, Doris gently peeled away the tape from each end of the small package. The paper had flecks of gold, glimmering like tiny lights. She smoothed out the paper to keep it, then saw the name on the box. Tiffany's. Her heart pounded as she opened the box, revealing the most stunning crystal angel figurine she'd ever seen.

"Well, what do you think?" Jonathan asked. "Do you like it? I found out you like angel figurines."

"Do I like it? Are you kidding? I love it! This is too expensive a gift, Jonathan! You didn't need to do this."

"I wanted to give you something special. You've put up with me and some of the other employees who walk by you every day and don't even say hello. I've been one of them, and I'm truly sorry for ignoring you all these years."

Doris got up from her desk, came around, and hugged Jonathan. She thanked him again and again, while he repeatedly said, "You're welcome." He asked about her Christmas plans, and she told him she was spending Christmas with her daughter and her family in upstate New York. She asked him about his plans, and he told her, at the moment, he wasn't sure where he would be.

Other employees started arriving, so Jonathan went back to his office and sat at his desk, wondering how he had changed so much in such a short time. His phone rang, startling him. It was Derek, wanting to know how his trip to Jonesboro went.

"I was just about to call you," Jonathan said. "You must have read my mind."

"So, how was your second Sunday in Jonesboro?" Derek asked.

"I can't talk right at the moment, but I could meet you for lunch if you're free."

"I am," Derek said. "Do you want to meet at Tony's Delicatessen around one?"

"That will work for me," Jonathan said. "So, lunch at Tony's Deli, one o'clock."

"OK, see you there," said Derek.

After talking to Derek, Jonathan turned his attention to tasks he needed to get done before leaving on Thursday for his third trip to Jonesboro. When he left his mom on Sunday, he said he'd stay in touch, and that's what he planned to do—stay in Jonesboro from Thursday until Sunday evening. He hadn't talked to them about it yet, but he felt sure they'd be open to the idea.

He dialed the manse, expecting Sara to answer. Instead, he heard his mother's voice.

"Hello. This is Tess."

"Mom, it's me, Jonathan."

"Why, hi, Jonny! I didn't think I'd hear from you this quick, but I'm glad."

"Is Sara or Kevin there? I want to ask them something."

"No, Sara went to the bank, and Kevin's at his office at the church. What's up? Can I answer your question?"

"Not all of it. I was thinking about coming to Jonesboro on Thursday and staying until after church on Sunday. Do you think Kevin and Sara would mind?"

"I'm sure they wouldn't mind," Tess replied. "You were going to ask me, too, weren't you?"

"Of course. Your answer's the important one. It's just that you're staying with them, and I wanted to get their approval first."

"I understand, dear. They'll be fine with it."

"Could you tell them I called and let them know what I'd like to do?"

"I sure will, Jonny."

They chatted a few minutes before hanging up.

At twelve forty-five, Jonathan left his office and walked the few blocks to Tony's Delicatessen. Derek arrived a few minutes later, and they got in line to order.

"So, tell me what happened."

"I don't know how to say this, but it was life changing. I mean all the scenarios running through my mind didn't match up to what happened. Let's just say I'm going back this Thursday and staying until Sunday."

"Wow! That's good, I guess." Derek didn't know what else to say.

While they waited for their food, they talked about the holidays and how excited Derek's kids were for Santa to come. Derek was always happy when he talked about his family.

As soon as their food arrived, Derek said, "OK, buddy, tell me what happened. Everything. I haven't seen you this happy—ever."

Jonathan started at the beginning, when he decided to go to Jonesboro for dinner and his mother recognized him. He shared it all—from Kevin calling the sheriff, going to the church to talk with Kevin and Dean, attending the Sunday-morning service, and finally, the joy of seeing his mom.

Derek sat quietly through Jonathan's story. Occasionally, he would ask a question, but most of the time, he just listened. When Jonathan told him his mother said she loved him, Derek was overcome with emotion, just listening to the happiness in Jonathan's voice. His story made him think about his own mother and how horrible it would be if he didn't have her in his life.

It was almost two thirty when Jonathan finished. When Derek asked what he thought changed him so drastically, he said, "Derek, you've known me for some time now, long enough to know I've never put much thought into religion. I've always seen it as silly. So, I've got to tell you there's something going on that's spiritual. I know, you can't believe I'm saying this, but it's amazing!"

Derek was a Christian, but he had never talked with Jonathan about his faith. A few times, he had mentioned that he and Nancy took the kids to church most Sundays, but he knew not to say much about it. This was a huge surprise.

"Well, you seem pretty sure about this."

"I am, and the most unbelievable thing is I like it!" Jonathan laughed.

Derek looked him square in the eyes and emphatically said, "I'm happy for you!"

The two left the restaurant and headed back to their offices. As soon as Jonathan sat down at his desk, the phone rang. It was Kevin.

"Hi, Kevin. How are things going?"

"Good, and yourself?"

"Actually, quite well."

"Hey, Tess said you called and wondered if we minded you coming to Jonesboro on Thursday. Of course we don't! That gives you and your mom more time to visit."

"I'm glad to hear that. I've missed out on so much of Mom's life. If I can spend time with her, it's a blessing."

"I'm glad to hear that. How about planning on having dinner Thursday evening with us? Would that work for you?"

"I'd like that, Kevin. Can I bring anything?" Before Kevin could answer, Jonathan said, "Wait! I know what I'll bring—chocolate cake!"

Kevin laughed. "Your mother sure loves her chocolate cake."

"There's a bakery not far from where I live that makes the best chocolate cake ever!"

"Sounds great. We'll see you around six o'clock Thursday evening."

"I'll see you then, Kevin."

❧

Jonathan arrived at the manse at six sharp, carrying a big pastry box with his mom's favorite dessert. He was almost prohibited from bringing it on the plane, but after he explained it was for his aged mother, they agreed, with the understanding that they'd have to put it in the serving area.

"Jonathan, come in! Here, let me take that box. How in the world did you get that on the plane?" Kevin asked, laughing.

Jonathan told him the story as they headed to the kitchen. Sara was at the stove, finishing up dinner, and Tess was sitting at the table. She looked up when he and Kevin walked in.

"Jonny!" Tess exclaimed, getting up and coming around to give her son a big hug.

"Hi, Mom," he said, hugging her back.

"What in the world do you have in that big box, Kevin?" Tess asked.

"Jonathan brought you a surprise from New York City."

Kevin gave the box to Tess. Her eyes widened, and her nostrils flared at the aroma of baked goods.

"Is this a cake? Maybe a chocolate cake?" Tess asked.

"Bingo!" Jonathan laughed. "You have an amazing sniffer there, Mom."

"I tell you, I can smell a cake a mile away. Don't you remember, Jonny, when you were a little boy, you always loved my birthdays for the dessert—chocolate cake of course!" Tess smiled at her son.

"Now that you mention it, I do, but that was a few years ago." Jonathan felt a sense of loneliness from the lost years with his mother.

Sara announced dinner was ready. The dining room table was nicely set, but it was missing one thing—the pot roast. Sara carried it into the dining room and placed it in the middle of the table. When she lifted the heavy lid from her mom's favorite Dutch oven, its fragrance filled the room.

Tess immediately raised herself up and sniffed its contents. "Boy oh boy, Sara, that sure smells good! I can't wait to dig in, but I know—prayer first."

Kevin offered a thoughtful prayer, including the pleasure of having Jonathan with them.

They spent the meal discussing everyday activities and how quickly Christmas was approaching. When it was time for dessert,

Tess went to help Sara. She reacted to the luscious cake, saying, "Holy moly! I can't wait to sink my teeth into that cake!"

Hearing her from the dining room, Jonathan and Kevin laughed.

Sara and Tess came back with the dessert and a pot of fresh coffee. While they ate the scrumptious cake, the conversation turned to Sunday and Tess's lighting of the last Advent candle.

"Kevin, I was wondering if it would be all right if Jonny helped me light that last candle. After all, he's family. That's if he wants to. Do you, Jonny?"

Kevin and Jonathan were surprised by her request.

"Well, how about it, Jonny? It would mean a lot to me to have a real family member helping me light that candle."

Kevin said it was fine with him and it was now up to Jonathan. Did he want to be in front of a room full of strangers, lighting a candle for the birth of a baby, when he was not sure he really existed? This was the time for making a decision about Jesus. Did he believe or not?

"I would be honored, Mom."

Tess leaned back in her chair and let out a whoop, clapping her hands and saying, "Thank you, Jesus!"

Jonathan responded, "Wow! I never thought I'd hear my mother say, 'Thank you, Jesus!'"

Kevin and Sara didn't know what to think. Kevin said, "Well, I think Sara and I have had another event to change our lives. I think this is wonderful!"

Around eight, Jonathan said he needed to get back to his hotel. He was very tired. They walked him to the door and shared hugs. He said he'd call in the morning about what he and his mom could do for the rest of his stay. Then he left for the short trip to Toledo. On the way, he turned on the radio. Christmas music filled the air. The song playing was "Silent Night." Its haunting melody was gentle and calm. Jonathan had heard that song every year, but now the words touched his heart.

Silent night, holy night
All is calm, all is bright
'Round yon virgin, Mother and Child
Holy infant so tender and mild
Sleep in heavenly peace
Sleep in heavenly peace.

Chapter 42

Finally, it was the week before Christmas. Everyone at the ad agency was scrambling to get their shopping done and preparations for Christmas Day taken care of. With Christmas falling on a Sunday, the agency was giving its employees Friday through Monday.

Jonathan planned to travel to Jonesboro for another long weekend. He was invited to spend it with Kevin, Sara, and his mom. At first, he declined, feeling uncomfortable, but Sara and Tess convinced him it was best for all of them. He accepted under the condition he would help with the last-minute Christmas preparations. He wanted to be a part of his first Christmas with his mother in many years.

He had just finished up finalizing an ad project with a major retailer when his phone rang. "Hello, this is Jonathan Farnsworth."

"How are things going?" Derek asked.

"Fine! It's good to hear from you."

"The reason I'm calling is I'm planning on taking the whole week before Christmas off. I promised Nancy I'd spend more time with her and the kids this year. I was wondering if you'd like to come for dinner tomorrow night. We can kick back with a glass of wine and catch up on you and your mom's visit this past weekend. What do you say?"

"Sounds like a great idea. I have so much to tell you and Nancy. You won't believe it."

"OK, buddy. We'll see you tomorrow night around six."

"Thanks. I'm looking forward to it," Jonathan replied.

The rest of the day flew by. Since he was taking extra days off, he had to stay late to get everything done so he could have dinner with Derek and his family tomorrow evening.

He was excited to take Derek's kids, Brian and Carrie, something for Christmas. He couldn't remember the last time he'd bought a child a gift. It must have been for someone at his office.

It was easy buying for Derek since they were friends but more difficult for Nancy. He ended up getting her a gift card to Bloomingdale's. *What woman doesn't like to shop?* he thought.

Jonathan arrived right on time.

"Come on in! Nancy and the kids are in the kitchen."

Jonathan followed Derek into the state-of-the-art kitchen. He and Nancy loved cooking, and their kitchen had all the top-notch appliances.

Nancy hugged him, and the kids, being kids, said hi and returned to what they were doing.

"I hope you don't mind, but we thought it would be more relaxing if we ate in the kitchen."

"Of course! I like that idea," Jonathan replied.

Their kitchen opened into a huge family room. Between the two rooms was a large table that could seat eight or more people. Nancy made it look intimate that evening by setting just one end with a festive tablecloth and a Christmas candle.

The dinner was homemade lasagna with salad and garlic bread, followed by Jonathan's favorite dessert, tiramisu.

After dinner, the kids went to watch TV, leaving the adults to talk.

"So, we can't wait to hear about your visit to Jonesboro. I filled Nancy in with the visit where you actually talked to your mother."

"I am so happy for you!" Nancy said. "I truly believe God had a hand in that."

"I think so too. If you knew my mother and the kind of person she was for years—well, the change in her says it all."

"Now," Derek said, "tell us everything."

He told them about Friday when he took Tess Christmas shopping in Toledo, then back to Jonesboro in time for another delicious meal with Kevin and Sara.

"Did your mom say anything about her time living homeless?" Derek asked.

"Yes. Let's just say it was painful for both of us."

"I guess it would be tough to talk about," Nancy said.

"It was. She talked a little about what happened but stopped, so we decided to let it go for a while."

Derek and Nancy saw the pain in Jonathan's eyes, knowing it must have been difficult for him too.

"So, how did Sunday go?" Derek asked, trying to get away from the talk about Tess's homeless situation.

Jonathan started to laugh, thinking about his mother and how the lighting of the last Advent candle went.

"Let's just say God was definitely guiding us. You see, it wasn't just one candle. It was four."

"Oh, that's right. There are four Sundays in Advent." Derek smiled. "I can't wait to meet your mom; she sounds like an interesting lady."

"She is definitely that," Jonathan agreed.

"Anyway, about the lighting, Kevin and Sara planned on lighting the candles with Tess, since the story goes that my mom is Sara's long-lost aunt. When I walked up with my mom and Sara to light the candles, the congregation looked confused. They didn't know who I was, which was very awkward."

Derek and Nancy laughed. Picturing Jonathan in church was hard enough, but lighting a very significant religious symbol with his mother had to be God directed.

"Before Mom lit the candles, I'd been asked to read the scripture. Me, Jonathan the skeptic, reading from a Bible! Anyway, before I read, Mom decided she wanted to tell everyone who I was."

"Awkward!" Derek laughed.

"You bet. She told them we'd had a falling out years ago, and God brought me back to her, saying it was the best Christmas present ever."

"Oh my!" Nancy exclaimed. "What happened next?"

"She started crying, I had tears in my eyes, and when I looked at the congregation, I could tell they were stunned!"

"I bet you wanted to hightail it out of there!" said Derek.

"Actually, for the first time in years, I felt at peace. I didn't want to fight for position, power, and money. I guess some would say I had a conversion. I don't know enough about that, but I do know I'm happy."

Derek and Nancy smiled at him. Being Christians, they'd had their own personal awakening to God in their lives.

"So, how did it end?" Derek asked. "I mean the lighting of the candles."

"I read the scripture, Mom lit the candles, then Sara, Mom, and I sat back down. Before the rest of the service started, Kevin said he was happy to be a part of our getting back together and asked the congregation to pray for us."

"Wow! That's an amazing event!" Derek exclaimed.

"The rest of the day was spent relaxing with Mom, Kevin, and Sara. Then I left for New York around four. That's it, the end of story for now."

"New beginnings, Jonathan." Derek smiled warmly at his friend.

"Now, let's get to the fun part of the evening," said Jonathan. "Gifts!"

At the mention of gifts, the kids came running.

∽

By Thursday, Jonathan was getting nervous about where he would spend Christmas. He hadn't heard from Kevin or Sara—or his mother.

Do they not want me there? Jonathan worried. He didn't know whether he should call and ask or wait a little longer. He decided he'd go ahead and get his car rental. Flying was out of the question for this trip for two reasons. First, he couldn't get a flight, and second, he had lots of gifts to take.

It was almost four in the afternoon when his cell phone rang. "Hello. This is Jonathan."

"Jonny, it's Mom. We are making sure you are coming tomorrow. We haven't heard from you, so Sara asked me to call."

"Hi, Mom. I never heard from anyone, so I wasn't sure if there was an invitation for me to spend the holiday with all of you."

"Oh, for Pete's sake, Jonny, of course you're invited for Christmas. Why would you think we wouldn't want you here? We're family, and that means we spend Christmas together. So, none of this thinking you're not welcome. You hear?"

His throat tightened.

"Are you still there, Jonny?" Tess asked.

"I'm still here, Mom. I'm just feeling happy."

"So, when are you coming?"

"I was planning on coming tomorrow afternoon if that works."

"Anytime is fine with them, sonny boy! They told me you're a sweet man."

"Do you think so, Mom?"

"Now you listen to me, Jonny. Things are different for both of us now. You're a part of me, and that means you have Hanes in your blood! They're fighters and don't give up for anything! So, let's not dwell on the past. Let's move to the future! You hear me?"

"I hear you, Mom."

"Now, go get yourself ready to get here tomorrow. What time's your flight from New York?"

"I'm coming with a car rental this time. I have lots of gifts, and anyway, I couldn't get a flight at the last minute."

"Oh goody! Gifts! I like to hear that!" His mom laughed. "Take care, son, and be careful. I'll see you soon."

"I will, Mom. I love you."

There was silence for just a brief moment, then a soft response, "I love you too, son."

After hanging up, Jonathan sat quietly in his office, not believing how quickly his life had changed. He thought about what he'd heard from Kevin's sermons: the strong message of love that came to us as a small baby born in, of all places, a barn.

He thought about how horrible he'd been in the past and where he was now at this very moment, going to share Christmas, the birth of Jesus, with his mother.

He closed his eyes and prayed his first true prayer: "I'm not sure how this works, but I want to thank you for helping me find my mother. I'm still embarrassed at how angry I was. But I'm saying this prayer also to thank you for loving me enough to give me a second chance to be a real son to my mom, Tess. I hope I can become a better person, too, so I thank you. Amen."

❦

Jonathan left New York City around six the next morning, hoping to make it to Jonesboro in time for dinner. He arrived at the manse around five. As he reached to ring the doorbell, the door flew open, and there was his mom, grinning from ear to ear.

"I saw you pull up in the driveway! Come on in. Can I help with anything?"

"No, I can get it."

"Jonathan! Come in!" Kevin called, walking out of the family room. "Here, let me take that suitcase for you. Do you have more to bring in?"

"Yes, quite a few things. I come bearing gifts, but I can get them."

"No, let me get my coat. I need the exercise anyway."

"Thanks. I appreciate that."

The two men went out to Jonathan's rental and retrieved the rest of the gifts and Jonathan's winter boots.

"I heard on the radio we're supposed to get a few inches of snow tonight," Jonathan said.

"I heard that too. It's been a long time since we've had a white Christmas, and Sara and your mom are excited about it. Me—I hate to shovel, but they're saying just a few inches."

After the gifts were put under the tree in the family room, Kevin asked Jonathan if he'd like a cup of coffee or hot tea. As a New Yorker, it had to be coffee.

Sara came home from delivering cookie trays to shut-ins. She gave Jonathan a big hug.

She is such a sweet and caring woman, Jonathan thought.

When Kevin brought the coffee, he included a plate of homemade Christmas cookies and fudge given to them by ladies from their church and Sara's own baking.

After visiting for a while, Sara and Tess went to the kitchen to finish up dinner, leaving the two men to talk.

"How was your trip?" Kevin asked.

"The traffic was bumper to bumper until I got away from the city. Then it thinned out. I don't travel much by car. I have the subway and taxis near my office and apartment."

"How long has it been since you lived in Ohio?"

"Let's see, I think it's been almost twenty-five years. When I first moved to New York, I worked for a couple of small advertising agencies. Then, fifteen years ago, I started with Conner-Williams."

"I guess it took a few years to get to the vice president position."

"Yeah, it did, but you know what?"

"What?"

"I'm tired of fighting to stay in the position. Some days I wonder if it's worth it, especially now."

"Why now?" Kevin asked, suspecting it had something to do with his mother.

"I think you know why, Kevin. It's because of Tess."

"I figured that," Kevin said softly.

Sara sent Tess to tell the men dinner was ready. They ate in the kitchen, where it was less formal. Jonathan liked eating there; it was warm and inviting.

"Tess, would you like to say grace for us?" Kevin asked.

"Sure, I'd liked that. Jonny, you've never heard me pray, have you?"

"No, Mom, I don't think I have."

"OK, let's pray."

"Hello, God, it's me, Tess. I'm really happy to have you taking care of us, especially now with your Son's birthday just days away. Thank you for giving him to us and for bringing my son back to me. Me and Jonathan are a little behind Kevin and Sara in getting to understand who you are and what you mean to people. OK, we're more than a little behind, but you know that, don't you? Sorry, didn't mean to get off track. That's just me. Thank you for this food and, as Kevin says when he prays, let it give us strength to do what is right for you. In your name, amen."

Everyone said amen. Jonathan looked at Kevin and Sara and saw them smile.

After dinner and the dishes were done, his mom asked, "So, what's the plan for this evening?"

"Well," said Sara, "we usually watch *It's a Wonderful Life* a few days before Christmas, so I thought tonight would be a good time. What do you think? I could pop some popcorn, and maybe Kevin could make a fire and we could do s'mores."

"I remember watching that movie years ago. It's sort of sad, isn't it?" Tess asked.

Sara was excited. "It starts out sad, but then the main character, George, who is going to kill himself by jumping off a bridge, unknowingly saves his guardian angel, who shows him what life would be like if he was not in it. It takes place at Christmas. The ending is awesome! George decides not to end his life and goes back to save his town from a mean old man who runs the place, and, oh for Pete's sake, let's just watch the movie!"

Tess, Kevin, and Jonathan laughed at her frustration.

"OK, sweetheart. We'll watch the movie," Kevin announced.

"Sounds like a great movie," Jonathan added. "I can't say I've ever watched it. How about you, Mom? Do you want to see it?"

"Sounds like a winner to me," Tess agreed, "but I bet it'll make you cry, won't it, Sara?"

Before Sara could answer, Kevin said, "Yes, it will. Lots of tears!"

Sara gave him hard look.

"I'm sorry, honey."

"Don't pay any attention to him, Sara. We'll enjoy it, tears and all."

They watched the movie, then went to bed around eleven, tired but happy.

✑

Snow arrived during the night, making Christmas Eve Day bright and white. Kevin got up early to prepare for the Christmas Eve service. He wanted to visit a few shut-ins before picking up the ham for Christmas dinner. Most of the time, he put the coffee on for breakfast, but this morning, Tess beat him to it.

"Good morning."

"Morning, Tess. You're up early. Did you see the snow outside?"

"I sure did! Maybe we can build a snowman later or make snow angels. I haven't done either of those things in years."

"I can't see you doing either of those at your age, Tess. I can barely do them, and I'm much younger than you."

"Don't remind me about my age, Kevin. It's hard enough for me to not think about it. Anyway, I'd do most of the directing for the snowman, and if I get down for the angel, you guys can help me up, right?"

Kevin laughed. Her enthusiasm helped him agree to give it a shot after lunch.

Sara met Jonathan at the bottom of the stairs as she was heading to the kitchen. "Good morning, Jonathan. Did you sleep well?"

"I sure did."

"I'm usually up earlier than this, but I was tired this morning. Not to talk badly about your mother, but she can be tiring to be around at times."

"I can see that from just being with her these past few weeks," he agreed with a chuckle.

They walked into the kitchen, where Tess and Kevin were eating their cereal.

"When did you all get up?" Sara asked.

"Tess got up before me and put the coffee on," Kevin said.

"I got up around six thirty. I couldn't sleep. Guess I'm excited about tomorrow," Tess told them.

"You know what, Mom? I'm excited too."

While the four of them ate, they talked about last night's snow and what needed to be done before the Christmas Eve service that evening, and if Jonathan wouldn't mind taking his mother shopping for a few things for Christmas dinner.

"No problem, Sara. I want to help out where I can."

Kevin and Sara left to go to his office to work on the Christmas Eve service, leaving Jonathan and Tess alone.

"Mom, I don't want to upset you, but why do you want to be called Tess instead of your real name?"

Tess didn't answer right away. Jonathan didn't know whether to ask again or just let it go.

"Jonny, we've talked about why I don't want to go over the way I lived for almost two years."

"I know, Mom. I just want to understand what it was like when you were homeless. I feel so bad about it. I know Dad and I contributed to your emotional pain for many years. I guess I'm wanting to be forgiven for all you've been through."

Tess patted his hand. "Hopefully we'll have plenty of time to mend all the fences and bridges we both have crossed, so let's wait until next year. It's only a week away."

Jonathan got up to leave before he said something to hurt his mother again. She could tell he was upset.

Tess said, almost in a whisper, "I didn't want anyone to find me. From the minute I left Central Foothills, I was determined that no one would!"

He came back, sat down across from her, and waited.

"I was scared to death those first few hours after I escaped. I never thought about my name until the first person I spoke to asked me who I was. That's when I said Tess—Tess is my name. From then on, I've been Tess."

"But Kevin and Sara and even Dean know your real name, and they still call you Tess. That's what's confusing me."

Tess went to Jonathan and kissed him on the head. "You're a good boy, Jonny. You just got involved with your father's idea of life—always money, power, and position. So now you know why I'm Tess. Let's go to the grocery for Sara and enjoy Christmas. What do you say?"

He agreed, and together they got ready for their first Christmas Eve in a long, long time.

∽

When Tess and Jonathan entered the sanctuary that evening, they were amazed to see all the decorations in their glory. The chandeliers were dimmed, and the lit candles in the windows gave off a soft glow. The Christmas tree in the corner seemed brighter.

Kevin and Sara came from the small room next to the pulpit area and went to the podium. The piano began to play, and Kevin and Sara began to sing the hymn "What Child Is This?"

Kevin and Sara's voices blended perfectly. Tess had goose bumps hearing the haunting words of the song. How precious they were as they sang about Mary and baby Jesus.

The service ended with the singing of "Silent Night" and the lighting of their own little candle. After the service, Kevin and Sara, along with Jonathan and Tess, talked to a few people. Most of them knew Tess, and now they were happy to meet Jonathan.

By the time they got back to the manse, it was going on nine o'clock. They were tired and decided to call it an evening. Jonathan and Tess climbed the stairs together. At the top, Tess kissed Jonathan on his cheek, telling him she'd see him in the morning. He hugged her, then retired to his own room, exhausted from the day's events. He smiled, wondering if Santa would show and surprise his mom! With that thought, he drifted off to sleep.

∽

Jonathan woke up to Christmas music. Groggy from sleep, he thought he was in his apartment in Manhattan. Then he heard his mom singing "Jingle Bells." Tess continued singing happily as she went down the stairs to the kitchen. Kevin and Sara were up, and Sara was already cooking eggs, bacon, and pancakes. She, too, was singing, but her song was "Joy to the World."

"Good morning, sweet pea," Tess greeted Sara. "Did you sleep well?"

"Did I? I was asleep the minute my head hit the pillow. I'm not usually that tired on Christmas Eve."

"I slept fantastic too," Tess told Sara. "Do you want me to get Jonny up? I don't want him to miss this special Christmas breakfast."

"You can. I'm almost finished."

Tess went up the stairs, humming yet another Christmas song. She knocked on Jonathan's door. "Rise and shine, sonny boy! Breakfast is just about ready."

"I'll be down in a minute, Mom."

"OK, dear."

When Jonathan walked into the kitchen, he was met with a variety of tantalizing smells. Sara had outdone herself. After breakfast, they went to get ready for church. Tess had a new red suit Sara had bought for her, and Jonathan made sure to bring his red tie to go with his gray suit. He was a handsome man, and many of the ladies of the church made it a point to smile or talk to him.

The church was packed. Tess figured it was hard for the kids to leave their new toys and electronics at home, but their parents wanted them to join in the celebration of the birth of Jesus.

The service overflowed with singing, kids to share the Christmas story with, and the sound of happiness coming from all the new people Tess had met over the past three months. What a joy it was!

After the service, most of the worshipers left quickly. When the four of them returned to the manse, they could smell the ham cooking in the oven.

Tess set the dining table for Christmas dinner, using Sara's china and crystal. The table was covered with a beautiful Christmas tablecloth. In the center of the table, Sara had placed her mother's silver candlesticks with red and white candles.

The men sat in the family room, relaxing from the hectic morning at church. Jonathan felt it was a good time to share his feelings with Kevin.

"I have to say your sermon touched me with the finished story of the birth of Jesus. In just a few Sundays, I've learned more about the Bible than I ever thought I would. I have to tell you, I'm interested in learning more."

"I'm glad to hear that. Would you like me to give you some scriptures that will help you get started reading the Bible?"

"That's a great idea! Thanks."

Tess announced that dinner was ready. After they were seated, Kevin offered a Christmas prayer: "Dear heavenly Father, we come to you this Christmas Day in celebration of the birth of your son—our Savior, Jesus. The miracle of his birth and the promise he brings to us is the best Christmas gift we could ever receive.

"Sara and I want to lift up our thanks for bringing Tess into our lives—and now Jonathan. These two are babes in the faith, but their hearts are ready to become a part of your family. Such a wonderful gift they are. Now, bless this food and bless Sara and Tess, who prepared it. In your name, amen."

When Kevin looked up, he saw tears in the eyes of Sara, Tess, and even Jonathan. "What? Did I say something wrong?"

"No, dear," Sara said. "You said exactly what needed to be said. Thank you, sweetheart."

Tess and Jonathan agreed, trying not to show how much it touched them.

After dinner, they continued to sit at the table. Kevin told Tess and Jonathan that he and Sara had something they wanted to tell them.

"Is it something bad?" Tess asked, concerned.

"No, Tess. It isn't anything bad, but Sara and I hope you'll be happy for us."

"Are you pregnant, Sara?" Tess asked hopefully.

Sara and Kevin laughed, and no, Sara wasn't pregnant.

"Then what is it? You're making me nervous."

"I've been offered a new position at a church in Wellington, located just outside of Dayton, and I've accepted it."

Tess didn't say a word. She just looked at Kevin and then at Sara.

"Tess?" Sara reached over and touched her hand.

"This will not affect you and us at all! In fact, we want you to come and live with us!"

Jonathan realized his mother was devastated by this news and decided to help Kevin and Sara out. "Mom, listen to me. You are not going to be alone again. You not only have Kevin and Sara in your life, but you have me too. I am going to be with you for a long, long time, so let's help Kevin and Sara celebrate this next step in their lives by being supportive, OK?"

Tess looked around the table at the people who now were her family: Kevin, the kind, gentle man who loved just about everyone, even nosey old Mrs. Applebee; Sara, who, if there ever was a sweeter person, she'd never met them; and Jonathan—her Jonny. Having him back in her life was the best thing ever.

"I guess I'm fine with it."

They all gave a sign of relief. This woman who called herself Tess had changed all of their lives forever.

"Now that I said I'm fine with it, let's go and have a real Christmas by opening all those gifts under the tree."

As they left the table and moved into the family room, Tess looked up and said a quick prayer. "God, thanks again. I owe you!"